T0375575

MAYPOLE

BLOSSOM RYECROFT

BALBOA.
PRESS

A DIVISION OF HAY HOUSE

Balboa Press books may be ordered through booksellers or by contacting:

Balboa Press
A Division of Hay House
1663 Liberty Drive
Bloomington, IN 47403
www.balboapress.com.au
1 (877) 407-4847

Print information available on the last page.

ISBN: 978-1-5043-0836-6 (sc)
ISBN: 978-1-5043-0837-3 (e)

Balboa Press rev. date: 05/26/2017

To my Mum and Dad,
Janet and Wilf.

CHAPTER ONE

BEING NINE WAS an important time for me; it was the year our Bertha's third baby, Eric, was born, and the year Mum's brother Charlie came to visit. I learned all the facts of life that year, in more ways than one.

Dear adorable bubbly Bertha, with her black hair and her beauty, full of laughter, full of plans for the baby, which she hoped would be a boy. Childbirth held no fears for her, she was a big woman: "the two girls had just slipped out, and what I'm really looking forward to is a week's good rest in bed."

On a damp Sunday morning in late July, Bertha's husband Alf cycled from their little terraced cottage in Silver Street, to tell Mum that Bertha had 'started'. Nurse Dinningsby had thrown him out of the house; she had a midwife's hearty dislike of husbands.

Bertha gave birth to a fine loud-voiced son at exactly midday.

This news was greeted in true Bigford fashion. Dad appeared to become rather hot, although the July day was cool, and he kept mopping his brow with a white-spotted, scarlet handkerchief. He seemed surprised by the birth, even though it had been almost the only topic of conversation in the cottage for the last six months. "My Bertha, she's far too young to have three children, whatever happened to my little girl." Bertha was a stately matron in her mid twenties.

Mum was overwhelmed; she had to sit down, her legs gave out beneath her. She cried a little, wiping her eyes on the hem of her apron. "Is my girl alright." She refused to be convinced that of course Bertha was fine.

Aunt Beat said she supposed everyone was expected to come up with a birthday present and bemoaned the lack of suitable gifts in the shops because of the war; and how could she afford anything anyway, as she got so little pension? Aunt Beat was an elderly, evil-tempered relative who Mum cared for. This was Aunt Beat's usual tirade upon receiving good news. No one took any notice.

Everyone offered profuse congratulations to Alf, "it takes a man to make a boy." Alf wore his usual stupid, bemused expression; he was very pleased with himself.

My sister Merle calmly covered the almost-prepared Sunday dinner, so that it could be eaten later, and made everyone a cup of tea.

CHAPTER TWO

RIC ALFRED WALTON was scarlet-faced, large, ugly, and very cross. "Oh Mum, he's the absolute image of Alf," announced Bertha, glowing with pride. I couldn't see it myself. Nurse Dinningsby announced he weighed nine pounds ten; and Alf snickered and said "yes, he must have cost quite that much". My Mum winced, and said quickly: "thank goodness none of mine were quite that heavy."

I performed the necessary adulation in the general direction of my new nephew, then I was thrown out of the tiny bedroom as my help was required to look after young Yvonne and Carol. The grown-ups had a great many other things to do and Bertha needed some sleep.

Downstairs in the miniature kitchen I felt superfluous. Minnie Weston, who always helped at confinements and deaths, had installed herself in the house for the day and was busy preparing some soup and a rice pudding on the tiny black-leaded range.

Minnie had never married. All her adult life she had worked at a local farmhouse. There had been some talk of her doing war work but her eyesight, even with the help of her thick-pebble glasses through which her tiny brown eyes peered desperately, had been deemed inadequate. Now, as well as the washing-up and dusting at the farm, she also hoed and pulled docks, and picked fruit and vegetables in season. Everybody had to do their bit in nineteen forty two.

Minnie had seen as many of the youngsters in the Silver Villages born as had Nurse Dinningsby. She was always on hand to cook a meal, or to lay out a corpse, to comfort bereaved children, or to wash blooded bed linen. Minnie had her worth in the Silver Villages.

We ate our lunch-time jam sandwiches at the kitchen table. Minnie did not bother to find the table cloth, but spread the plates on an old copy of the Daily Mirror. Mum would have been horrified.

After we had eaten I sat at the kitchen table and played old maid with Carol. Soon Carol's dark-lashed eyelids drooped and she fell into her regular post-prandial nap, her head resting on her podgy arms, little piglet snores issuing from her slightly-open rose-bud mouth. Yvonne was also asleep, tucked up safely on the couch in the tiny sitting room, covered by a colourful crocheted rug.

Because we had left home in such a hurry I had not brought myself a game or a book to read. I was bored. In common with all village children I was unaccustomed to being indoors for long periods during the summer. I tore into the garden when the sun came out briefly, with the brilliant intensity of the July midday sun shining between showers, but I had barely checked Bertha's Dutch doe rabbit and checked the ripeness of the raspberries when the rain pelted down again.

In the kitchen, Minnie appeared to be skimming fat

from the top of the soup pot, a perplexed frown on her face. I was aware she had not seen me.

I planned an amusing surprise for Minnie; I decided to hide away, and squeak like a mouse. Yes, that should amuse her!

I knew all objects in the tiny home intimately and I soon found a hiding place in the kitchen, in the cupboard where the food was stored. The bottom portion acted as a meat safe, and had a wire mesh door. I had noted that the meat safe portion of the cupboard was empty.

Soundlessly I opened the cupboard door, and with the stealth of a nine-year-old who has planned mischief, crept inside the meat safe. I fitted nicely, curled up in a little ball. I could see everything that was happening in the tiny kitchen through the mesh. I pulled the door closed behind me.

At every passing moment I expected the door to creak and alert Minnie to my whereabouts, but my movements were soundless. Safely installed in my hiding place, I patiently waited for Minnie to turn away from the range.

As she did so, and before I managed even the tiniest squeak, the garden door opened and Alf came in, shaking raindrops from his damp jacket.

Not a word was spoken; but a glance, potent with a power beyond my comprehension, passed between Alf and Minnie. I was frightened to breathe, frightened to move a muscle, frozen still in my hiding place. That glance propelled me to the world beyond childhood; a world I did not understand.

Minnie turned round to take a dish from the kitchen table. As she did so, Alf moved slowly behind her and put his arms round her, firmly grasping her tiny, almost non-existent breasts in each of his hands. Minnie spun round and kissed him firmly on the mouth, at the same time unbuttoning his fly and grasping his male organ so that it was fully exposed, in its ugly and engorged condition. Only one thought invaded my astounded mind. I knew they had done this before.

I knew the facts of life; babies were frequent newcomers in our family, and Ethel and Angie, my best friends from next door were always more than willing to share their encyclopaedic knowledge of human procreation with anyone who would listen.

The size of the organ did not horrify me; nor did the little squeaks emitting from Minnie as Alf slipped his hand up her skirt and appeared to be fiddling about somewhere inside her clothes. She threw back her head and her squeaks became loud regular groans.

Carol, her head still resting on her chubby arms, stirred in her sleep; but Alf and Minnie were oblivious to anything but each other.

Then Alf lifted Minnie's skirt and removed her knickers. They were long, pink, flannel, with elastic at the legs.

Minnie knelt on all fours on the rag rug in front of the range. Alf knelt behind her and entered her, like a dog to a bitch. When he had finished he stood up, adjusted his clothing, helped the half-naked Minnie to her feet, and left through the garden door.

Minnie stood quite still by the range for a moment. Then she pulled on the pink flannel knickers and adjusted her blouse. With the tiniest shrug of her shoulders she turned again to the soup pot and continued to skim fat from the soup.

Not a word had passed between the couple.

My horrified mind was turning somersaults. My greatest concern was discovery. I was frightened to breathe, frightened to move, my back and my head ached, and I had pins and needles in my arms and legs.

I felt soiled, guilty, as though I had been an effective participant in the act I had just witnessed. I felt revulsion towards my sisters, my Mum, to any woman who had ever consented to the entry of a male to the inviolate privacy of her body.

My eldest brother Len's wife was childless after a dozen years of marriage. That Iris must let our Len do that to her flashed at the speed of light through my mind; to be dismissed just as rapidly. That was why Iris had no babies. Posh and proper Iris, the headmistress of a school in a nearby village, would never permit that disgusting act!

The coarseness, the pure animality of what I had witnessed nauseated me so that bile rose and burned in my throat and I felt the skin on the back of my neck creep. How could Mum, my sisters, allow themselves to be used so abominably?

And yes, our Bertha! Bertha was lying in her bed at this moment, having given birth to Alf's son less than three hours ago. She was lying there, exhausted, bleeding, and proud of herself; confidant that Alf loved her and their bonnie children; oblivious of the fact that barely was her labour finished when Alf had been spreading the love she cherished as her own to anyone who would crouch down and take it. Our lovely Bertha, beautiful of face, lively of temperament, with her bouncing black curls above her laughing face.

I knew I would never tell anyone.

I lay in my tight little ball while Minnie completed the preparation of the soup. Little Carol awakened and stretched and asked for her Mum. Minnie grabbed both Carol and her own cardigan and walked up the stairs to visit the woman with whose husband she had just been fornicating. Only when I heard voices and laughter from the bedroom above could I release my stiff limbs from their prison and escape into the clean sunshine of July.

Before I had my tenth birthday Minnie Weston had astounded everyone by producing a baby son.

She had kept her pregnancy quiet and the birth came as a shock to most of the folk of the Silver Villages. Speculation regarding the paternity of Ernest Gordon Weston ran rife. "She hasn't been seeing anybody, not to our knowledge," "But it is disgusting, disgusting," was confirmed back and forth across many a village garden fence.

But there was a war on; there were a number of airfields nearby, and some respectable married women in the village were capable of throwing their hats over the windmill, or at least their bloomers, when faced with the throng of attractive and randy young servicemen that passed through the Silver Villages during the war years. Minnie was at least single, and she could not be blamed if she had been unable to resist temptation. The villagers had always seen Minnie as a lonely old maid. It took them a long time to forgive her; chiefly for the surprise she sneaked up on them.

Minnie asked no quarter, and got none; she never discussed the paternity of her son. She kept her business to herself, and raised her son independently and with very little support; not an easy task in an English village in the nineteen-forties.

CHAPTER THREE

MAUDIE WAS ANGIE and Ethel's Mum; they were my best friends, they lived next door. Sisters are rarely closer than the three of us were, chiefly because, although I had brothers and sisters a-plenty, I was something of an afterthought, and they were all adults before I was born.

Maudie was a fat, grubby, good natured trollop, who regarded sexual encounter as casually as most people regarded the good morning greeting, but with considerably more relish. It was Maudie's favourite activity and it left her without energy or inclination to do anything else. Any housekeeping was performed fitfully by Maudie's mother, Nellie. The grime of decades had settled like a velvet blanket over the interior of the cottage. Nellie, equally as fat, good-natured and grubby as her daughter, was well-past the distractions offered by her body or by anyone else's.

Maudie had lived in the cottage all her life. My parents had watched her grow up and had witnessed the arrival of Ethel when Maudie was just sixteen years of age, and then Angie. My Dad declared these were fortunate children, as they could choose their father, apparently from a very large field. The identity of some of the gentlemen who had come sniffing around in Maudie's past would astound you! Or so my Mum eloquently expressed it.

As Maudie seemed unconcerned by her children's questionable paternity, it was somewhat surprising that so many other people in our small community were seriously disturbed by it.

George Davenport was a commercial traveller; he sold seeds and feed to the farmers. His personal appearance was that of a hale and hearty man; and many would ask why, in nineteen forty-two, he wasn't doing his bit for king and country; but some of us have to keep the home fires burning!

Ethel and Angie left me in no doubt that their Mum was head-over-heels in love with George. Even at such a youthful age, those girls understood love. Well, Maudie always was, with her latest boyfriend, even if he was only around for a couple of nights; but to be fair, George stayed around for some months, loving Maudie on his twice-weekly visits on Tuesdays and Fridays.

Maudie thought he was the handsomest man she had ever seen; and she had seen lots of men.

The affair started with the spring, in May; fortunately we had a dry spring and summer that year. The May days were bright, the meadows green. Maudie took one look at George and there was one thought in her head. Not if, but when, and as quickly as possible, followed by as often as possible.

The twice-weekly coupling actually suited Maudie well. Although she claimed she was entirely faithful to George on the other five days of the week, she reasoned you never knew who may turn up. Maudie was always one to make the best of her opportunities. After all, who knew what George got up to on the other five days? Such a handsome man probably had a girl in every town. So, in spite of her often-voiced fidelity to George, the truth was somewhat different, especially after the mid-summer dance, or the visit of the West Kents in early August.

But, as previously stated, fortunately it was a dry spring and summer. After all, there were plenty enough village girls doing exactly the same thing; maybe not with the amazing frequency and variety of co-participants practised by Maudie; but it is a fact that a fine summer can provoke many hasty autumn weddings.

The real purpose of George's visit was to sell seed and feed, so the couplings were, of necessity, hasty events in themselves. The privacy of the nearest deserted lane or lonely meadow was sought. Once behind the hedgerow the loving tryst happened with amazing speed, but to the exhausted satisfaction of both parties.

Unfortunately, on more than one occasion the lovers were disturbed by thoughtless and inconsiderate tractor drivers preparing to mow hay, or school children walking home along the lanes. It became obvious that Maudie and George needed look-outs to warn them of possible intruders upon the privacy of their intimate and passionate moments.

So on Tuesdays and Fridays Ethel and Angie did not turn up at school. They had more important tasks to perform; a fact known to everyone in the village, including Aunt Beat who never stopped complaining that "it was disgusting and something should be done about that shameful girl." So it should have been; but the whole population of the Silver Villages had many a gossip and good laugh about it while it was happening. Life in the Silver Villages would have been so much duller without Maudie Pyle and her maternally-irresponsible habits

Every Wednesday as we strolled along the village street to school, and every Saturday while we played with our dolls in my garden, Ethel and Angie would regale me with the events of the previous afternoon's walk. "They had just started doing it, when who should turn up but the vicar with the infant class out for a nature ramble. Mum had to get her skirt down real quick, and George hid behind the may trees. His thing was sticking out like a doorknob, we were killing ourselves laughing. Our Mum smiled nicely and said hullo to the vicar."

I feared my Mum and Dad would overhear this edifying conversation and as a result I would be forbidden to spend time with such undesirable playmates as Ethel and Angie; and of course Aunt Beat would never have shut up about it.

It was late-August when Maudie dropped her bombshell, as she and George briefly lay in each other's arms in the warmth of a lengthening Friday afternoon sun, following a mutually successful union under the sycamore tree in Long Bottom Meadow. Maudie told him bluntly, straight out "I'm 'late'".

She only told him because she thought he should know. She had long ago formed the opinion he was married anyway; and that suited her fine. An offspring of handsome George, now that was something else! She hoped for a beautiful baby son.

13

George did not give her a moment to declare her lack of marital intention or otherwise. He jumped up, hastily adjusted his clothing and sprinted out of Long Bottom Meadow before Maudie got the chance to mention marriage, which she was not about to mention anyway. George had no intention of being hooked, like a trout on a fishing line. He jumped in his car; and before Maudie had finished dressing was already miles from the village of Great Silver, speeding over the Downs, never to return again.

September's feed and seed was sold to the farmers by a seventy-year-old who felt that he was doing his bit by holding down this position so that a younger man could go to war and defend King and Country.

Maudie did not miss George. She had something more important to fill her thoughts now. She had always enjoyed maternity, and her plans for her handsome son filled her days. She was not disappointed; Easter saw her delivered of a healthy baby boy who she named Peter. She claimed to all and sundry "ent he just the image of his father George." It was not obvious, or for that matter very likely. He had golden curls and eyes the colour pale blue china plates, and like his two sisters he bore a great resemblance to Maudie. Also, like his two sisters he could probably take a choice of father from a number of contenders.

CHAPTER FOUR

OON IT WAS September and time to gather hazel nuts and blackberries; time to return to school.

Returning home one afternoon, full of myself, bursting to tell Mum I had come first in the spelling test, I raced into the kitchen.

Sitting before the kitchen range were three visitors. Two of the visitors were Mum's sisters, Aunty Hilda Griffin and Aunty Mildred Plowcott; they both lived in cottages within the village of Great Silver. The third visitor was a stranger to me. He was tall and solidly built, with a mass of dark curly hair, tinged at the forehead with silver.

Something was wrong with my Mum! Mum had been crying; Mum was the happiest person alive, never miserable for a moment. It was unbelievable that mums could cry.

Aunt Beat was noticeable by her absence. For one wild moment I did consider that Aunt Beat had been taken ill; and perhaps that was not such a good thing after all.

I gawped at the assembled aunts. Aunty Mildred broke the silence at last: "Linda, this is your Uncle Charlie." He clasped my hand in his, a very clean hand, soft, with finely manicured nails; not like my Dad's, workman's hands with nicotine stains and calluses. "Hullo Linda, glad to make your acquaintance, how was school?" he asked.

He reminded me of Mum! The same fine skin, the same curly dark hair, the same handsomeness, and a generous build. Why hadn't I seen that straight away? But then I never knew Mum had a brother. She had a whole tribe of sisters, as well as Aunty Mildred and Aunty Hilda there was Aunty Elsie who had married a Canadian, Aunty Doris who lived in Salisbury, Aunty Gertie.... But a brother, I had never heard anyone mention a brother.

I looked from one face to another. My Aunties kept glancing sideways at Mum. Mum's face was turned away, in shadow. Whatever was happening here was entirely beyond my comprehension.

It was Aunty Hilda who spoke, disapproval sharpening her voice: "Where are you both staying, Charlie?"

"They can't stay here, I've no room, what with Aunt Beat and everything...," gabbled Mum; there was a sob in her voice. But this was not true! There was a spare bedroom, as Merle and I shared a room.

Mum would accommodate anyone. She would offer hospitality with graciousness and generosity and if necessary, kill the fatted calf and somehow put on an amazing spread out of her miniscule wartime rations.

Aunty Hilda and Aunty Mildred both nodded agreement that they had no spare room either. Aunty Hilda's residence was a huge house up on Silver Common. There was enough spare room in that house for a regiment to camp; in fact a regiment often did; Aunty Hilda was famous for her kindnesses to 'our boys'.

Aunty Mildred lived in a tiny cottage, not more than two rooms, behind the Great Silver post office; but Aunty Mildred was as famous as her other sisters for her unbridled hospitality; and she would provide anyone, even perfect strangers, with lodgings on her parlour floor. Okay, so Uncle Charlie was not welcome here!

"It's alright, Betty," Uncle Charlie gave Mum an amused, tolerant smile. "We're staying at the pub."

Who was 'we'? Was Uncle Charlie married; did I also have another aunty I had never heard about, or was he travelling with a friend, as the young soldiers who were so welcome in all the aunties' houses often did?

I was not about to discover that. Mum shooed me out to play in the garden, without even offering me a biscuit or a bun as my welcome-home-from-school nibble. Mum never even enquired about my day. And me with pictures to show and top marks for spelling!

Just as I was being shoved unceremoniously through the back door, Dennis appeared as if by magic on the doorstep, asking very politely if his Mum could borrow a quarter of tea until tomorrow morning.

My sister-in-law Florrie, Dennis's Mum, lived opposite the shop, but she inevitably ran out of money before payday and couldn't ask for 'tick'; or suddenly found she was out of the world's most necessary commodities five minutes after the shop closed. Mum was very fond of her eldest grandson and usually invited Dennis into the kitchen, to give him a freshly-baked bun, and have a quiet moan about lackadaisical Florrie's general ineptitude. Dennis would sit at the kitchen table, listening politely, and waiting to be handed the requested commodity. I never knew if Florrie paid Mum back the many loans. I doubt it.

But today the quarter of tea was virtually thrown at him without a word and Mum scuttled him out of the house without even placing a grandmotherly kiss on his forehead.

I dawdled in the garden, fascinated by the family get-together in the kitchen. I tried to sit on the patch of garden under the front window in order to hear what they said but nettles and ants stung my bum. Nothing said was worth hearing anyway. Mum and her sisters, usually so talkative, their cheerful conversations always interspersed with much ribaldry and intimate sisterly teasing, now spoke in monosyllables and hushed voices about the weather. No-one appeared to be speaking to Uncle Charlie.

Dad came home. He expressed surprise at finding me sitting forlornly in the garden. "You should be in laying the table, my girl."

Dad dropped his dirty boots outside the back door, and strode in hale and hearty as ever. I grasped his arm and was towed along by his momentum. I had begun to fear I would spend an abandoned evening in the garden.

Dad's face glowed with pleasure at the sight of the visitor. He clasped my uncle's hand in his big hoary one, clapped him firmly on the shoulder. "Charlie, how are you, man. Good to see you after all this time. How's Hughie?"

My uncle laughed and said Hughie was as well as could be expected under the circumstances. Both my Dad and my uncle seemed to think this was hilarious. My Mum glared at Dad as if she could kill him. Perhaps Hughie was my uncle's dog?

Dad and Uncle Charlie chatted for about an hour. Dad told Charlie all the village news; who married whom, which men were away fighting and where, all about the 'goings-on' next door. The last item caused Uncle Charlie to double up with laughter, and say "everyone to their own, but if you took on old Maudie, you wouldn't have to be too fussy, would you!" Dad shook his head in merry agreement, and Mum's face was a picture of shame and humiliation.

Dusk crept into the corners of the room until the oil lamp dispelled the haunting shadows. The aunties left; after all they had hungry husbands at home. They moved slowly and stealthily, hushed as in the presence of a corpse. Neither of them even looked at their brother.

After Uncle Charlie left Aunt Beat emerged from the sitting room which was her bedroom, with a face like thunder. There was no fire in her bedroom, and above all else she did like to be warm. I had never known her leave her favourite perch next to the range, in everyone's way, for more than a few minutes. She emerged blue with cold, but her face almost apoplectic, declaring loudly: "I am shocked and horrified, Betty, that you would allow that person to cross the threshold of this house! Have you so little concern for Linda's moral welfare? Personally I would refuse to spend time in the same room as that man! I just hope the vicar does not get to hear about it!"

Baffled, I looked to both my parents for an explanation. My Dad was attempting unsuccessfully to hide his chortles, trying to keep a straight face and failing miserably. Mum looked as if she could kill him, but she cringed under Aunt Beat's vituperative attack.

Tea was eaten in silence, without the usual cheerful banter and recounting of the events of everyone's day. After the meal Mum pleaded a headache and retired to bed early. Mum was always chipper and I had never known her to be poorly.

The next morning, rainy, damp late September with leaves and beech mast blocking the gutters, Ethel, Angie and I trooped along the village street in our navy gabardine macs. They were, of course, fully informed regarding Uncle Charlie's history.

"Your Uncle is queer," Ethel informed me, looking knowledgeable, as I stared flabbergasted. Queer! Aunt Beat sometimes said she felt a bit queer; especially if we had pork for Sunday dinner. It never agrees with me, she would say. This always caused my Dad to chortle behind his hand and Mum to glare him into silence.

So Uncle Charlie was ill. He certainly did not look it.

But Angie was bursting with more information. "That means he has do's with other men. Our Gran was talking about it last night."

"Oh yes," continued Ethel, and her eyes were huge in her beautiful face. "They puts their doodahs up each other's bums. My Mum said it must hurt a bit, but so what, if that suits your fancy. My Gran says they like that sort of thing and never do it with girls. Gran says they holds hands and kisses each other, just like courting couples do."

"Yes, an' everyone in the village is talking about your uncle – always," assured Angie. "Yes, always," echoed Ethel.

They must have been relieved the villagers occasionally talked about someone other than Maudie!

It's just that I wished they would get their facts straight occasionally. Not only had they been wrong about intimate relations between men and women, that they happened face to face, the man laying on top of the women; disproved by the sexual act I had witnessed between horrible Alf and Minnie Weston; but well, this latest little flight of fancy was too farfetched to be true. As if men would behave like that! Ethel and Angie always thought themselves so clever. Clearly they would believe anything.

CHAPTER FIVE

EFORE I STARTED school Ethel had left me in no doubt
that school was a never-ending party, happening every
day. You went there to make friends and have a good
time. "There is sausages and mashed potato for dinner, and
there is always pudding." Ethel was unaccustomed to such
a rich diet. There was no illness severe enough to prevent
her attending school. She was duly aware of her importance
as a veteran of a whole year's attendance at school before I
joined her. Little Angie would also join us, a year later. In
the nine years Ethel was a pupil at the village school, she
never missed a day's attendance.

Ethel's normal day-to-day school-attendance apparel
was a shabby faded cotton frock, not recently washed or
ironed. At the beginning of the autumn term the toes were
cut out of Ethel's old brown sandals, because during the
long summer holidays her feet had inconsiderately grown
rather more quickly than had her mother's store of spare
cash. The conveniently-aerated sandals would serve Ethel
for a few more weeks, until early October threatened
the first frost. Then a timely jumble sale in the church
hall or Potinger's second hand shop in the main street of

Middleford would – hopefully – provide a pair of winter shoes for Ethel, which would - hopefully – fit her.

Ethel adored bread'n dripping, which was the mainstay of the meals in the cottage next door. This was for her morning playtime. She wouldn't let it stand in the way of her enjoyment of her school dinner.

Ethel's enthusiastic promotion of village school days had not prepared me for Miss Landport, the little-ones' teacher; after just one look I was terrified of her. The terror never left me, even in future years when I flew up to the Big Ones, under the doubtful tutelage of Mister Taylor. Miss Landport's general unpleasantness, unhappiness, and serious desire to become a lady wife, were the source of conversations in many a cottage containing the little ones she regular beat up, for what appeared to be her own pleasure. A village girl herself, although she would never have admitted it unless she was forced, her history was known and understood by her small victims and their parents. In the Silver Villages, if you were an institution, which was a fair description of the aforementioned lady, every snippet of your personal life was ancient history known to anyone with time enough to concern themselves with knowing your business.

Now in her early thirties, Miss Landport had never received formal training as a teacher, but during her years as a pupil she had been the brightest child in the village school, and had been offered a job as a teacher's assistant at the age of fourteen, a position she had retained with admirable tenacity ever since.

She was aware the only way to retire gracefully from

such a vaunted position was as a decent and respectable wife. No-one had married her. It was no secret in the Silver Villages that she kept hoping.

On the whole, she thoroughly disliked her pupils, especially the boys. She made that very clear. The daughter of a farm labourer herself, she had no time for labourer's children. She considered them so grubby, and she deplored dirty fingernails. She liked prettily-dressed well-ironed little girls, with their nails trimmed of course.

The difficulty of maintaining the cleanliness of a five-year- old's fingernails whilst dealing with six other children in a leaky cottage with no indoor sanitation was not seen by Miss Landport as a reason for a drop in the maternal standards of village mothers.

Poor Miss Landport was exceptionally unlucky with her five-year-olds on my first day at school. One look at the new recruits told her she was in for a trying year. First was Walter Sikes, whose parents were gypsies and took off for Ireland, or Suffolk, or Westmoreland, at the drop of a hat, or the drop of a silver coin, which they much preferred. They regularly camped in a roughly-converted removal van on Silver Common, probably the only time during their ramblings that the six Sikes children attended school.

Then there was Billy Ticehurst, whose parents drank. Everyone knew Billy was a bit backward, was unable to talk properly, and was amazingly incontinent. Billy's Mum, coping poorly with that morning's hangover, had sent along a package containing three dry nappies and a dummy for him to suck if he cried. Miss Landport expected these disasters to happen at the beginning of each school year; sometimes she just did not know why she bothered.

And me, Linda Bigford! Miss Landport had taught Bigfords before; the Silver Villages were full of them. She had never enjoyed the task; difficult children, everyone one of them. She had rejoiced when she thought she had seen the last of them; thank you very much. She was not overjoyed to see another tall, skinny one in the line of new recruits at the beginning of another term.

Before morning-playtime Billy's chair was surrounded by a number of small pools of 'wee.' With the amazing cruelty of five-years-old, I thought that children as large as Billy must be a bit funny if they weed their pants. So I laughed. Miss did not find it amusing, and called me a nasty cruel child; and lost no time informing my Mum of my shocking behaviour when she came to collect me at half-past-three.

Only Miss Landport was entitled to hold adverse opinions regarding the children in her care.

From day one I had blotted my copybook with Miss Landport and at school. Neither of us got over it.

CHAPTER SIX

I MADE IT MY business to take Angie to school on her first morning. After all, I knew more about it than anyone else, with the possible exception of Ethel, who knew everything.

"Miss, this is my friend Angie Pyle, she's come to school, too"

Miss Landport glowered down from the great height of her wooden stool. If there was anything she could do without this term, it was another snivelling Pyle child. In two years of school, Ethel, now in the Big Ones, had learned very little; but there again, Ethel considered she had been born knowing everything, so fresh knowledge was entirely superfluous. Miss Landport considered Ethel Pyle to be unteachable.

Miss Landport surveyed Angie with disdain; she probably saw the child of an unmarried mother with doubtful public morals; a child not frequently washed, ill-clothed and ill-shod. She mentally steeled herself for what she knew would be a very trying year.

"Thank you Linda, please sit down. Angela, did your mother come with you today?"

"No miss, I came with Linda and our Ethel. Mum was tired and couldn't get up this morning. Our Gran made our breakfast."

At least the child had eaten. Be grateful for small mercies, she told herself. "Tell Ethel I shall need to talk to her before she goes home. I should not really allow you to stay without first seeing your birth certificate. I suppose it is most unlikely your mother even knows where that is." Miss Landport shrugged her shoulders and turned to the next child in the line of green recruits. Oh, how these troublesome children tried her patience!

Angie sat next to Billy Ticehurst. He would still be in the Little-One's class room when he was nine. The daily package of three clean nappies would be gone by then. The little pools of wee still appeared from time to time.

In spite of Miss Landport's worst efforts, Angie proved to be an apt pupil. She was the first to learn to read, the first to reach the end of the sum book. Not a good idea; this was the only junior sum book the school possessed, and so she had to start at the beginning again; with the firm proviso by Miss Landport that she must get every sum correct the first time. Oh, Miss Landport! Angie had already done just that.

Angie also won the religious-knowledge certificate awarded annually by the rural dean. This engendered enraged expressions of shocked horror from the mothers of daughters who had been overlooked. It was a crying shame that the coveted award had been won by a child from such an irreligious household.

Walter said: "I've got a pain in my bum."

A flush of anger suffused Miss Landport's face. Her bulging eyes were like gooseberries, the fat green gooseberries in my auntie's garden, which had little red veins all over them. Miss Landport was very angry indeed.

"Walter, we will have none of that language in this class!"

"I said I've got a pain in my bum." Walter wailed. He was only stating the obvious. His bum was part of his body, as were his arms, his legs, his chest, or even his willie. He was six years old; if it hurt, he said so. If he had stated he had a pain in his chest, Miss Landport would have demonstrated immediate professional concern. Instead, in a flash of violent anger she rushed to his desk and rapped him across the knuckles with her long ruler.

"Dirty, nasty boy," she squealed, lifting him bodily from the desk by the back collar of his shirt; and in the instant she did this, noticing how grimy it was. "Go and stand in the corner; you can stay there until it is time to go home. How dare you speak like that in my class?" She howled, pitching his small body against the corner of the room, so forcefully his head met the wall with a resounding thump.

Billy Ticehurst, comfortable in his recently changed nappy, snored gently into his dummy, whilst lying on a play mat at the back of the classroom.

"I have never known such disgusting language" she bawled to the uncomprehending, open-mouthed class of five, six and seven year olds, who were regarding her with mingled emotions of horror and fear. "Walter is a dirty, nasty child, and I am sure your Mummies and Daddies would never allow you to play with such a filthy little boy." Dirty, nasty, disgusting, filthy, were powerful adjectives to Miss Landport; words that described the world, especially that of little boys. 'Nice' was her very favourite word.

Her small charges gazed at her dumbfounded; Walter had a pain in his bum. Maybe he needed to go to the lavatory. To the village children the rear part of your anatomy, from which one conveniently defecated, was your bum. They had no idea what Miss Landport was talking about.

Walter grizzled into his grimy coat sleeve. The pain in his head from a large black bruise swelling along his swarthy hairline now hurt him far more than the original pain in his bottom.

Walter's parents could not read or write. They had never found it necessary. His diddiki father knew more about horseflesh than many vetenarians; this knowledge had been passed down through generations of dealers and traders, jockeys and breeders; by word of mouth; by practical application; by a silent watching and a quiet, not always lawful, doing. His knowledge was duly respected and often sought by the gentlemen of the aforesaid profession. The fact that he was unable to write it down was totally irrelevant to its scope and depth.

Walter quickly lost interest in school. By the time he was seven and ready to go into the Big Ones he could read, providing the words were not too long.

He became a master in the art of truancy. It would be fair to say he skulked a lot.

CHAPTER SEVEN

D AD WAS THE village carpenter, most of the cottages had
Dad's hand upon them somewhere, his restoration work
on the church rafters and the school roof was legendary.

When I was six, seven, eight years of age my very
favourite person was Ray's wife Florrie. Her son Dennis
was older than me, and whereas in our cottage you had to
behave yourself, be tidy, quiet and nice, in Florrie's cottage
these things did not matter. I played there often, usually in
mud, and a game that always involved my clothes becoming
wet, until Mum sternly called me home. I knew, even at the
age of six, that Mum disapproved of Florrie.

Mum had been horrified when Ray had made
seventeen-year-old Florrie Caundle pregnant. Mum always
said it happened one Saturday night when Ray was drunk; in
nineteen-thirty, if you made her pregnant you married her.
This was Mum's dismissive statement on Ray's marriage.
She never changed her viewpoint for the rest of her life.

The Caundles were the largest family in the village.
When they walked to school they filled the village street. If
they attended a church service, a previously almost-empty
Saint Edmunds appeared to bulge at the sides. Dad always

said that when it came to having babies, Mrs Caundle obviously had not realised what started it. For that reason she was powerless to stop it.

Miss Landport hated little Caundles. The Vicar's wife pitied little Caundles. Everyone for miles round knew a little Caundle or two. They were always slightly grimy and their clothes were threadbare. Mum said you could grow carrots in the soil under their fingernails. But more polite, well-mannered, happier children did not exist in the Silver Villages.

At seventeen, plump Florrie, the oldest Caundle, had shoulder length golden curls, eyes the colour of a summer sky, and a willing joyous nature coupled with an undefeatable optimism.

She had an enormous crush on our Ray. Mum was right; Ray did not stand a chance. Before you could say Jack Robinson, he found himself courted, bedded, wedded and a father. After that event, he was allowed a moment to catch his breath.

My two oldest sisters were Mary and Bertha, respectable matrons with small families.

Merle was the youngest of my three sisters; she was what the village chose to refer to as 'backward'. All families have their cross-to-bear, Merle was ours. Reading and writing defeated Merle. She could handle small amounts of money, run small errands, and collect basic groceries from the village shop. The village in general pitied the Bigford family, because Merle was - well, you know.........

Since she was sixteen silent Merle had 'given a hand' each day at the vicarage. Her duties had originally been to wash the dishes, to dust, and fill the coal scuttles. But over the years, the Vicar, Mr. Harwood, and his wife gradually came to consider life in the vicarage was intolerable without Merle's calm presence. She laid tables, arranged vases of flowers, although her favourites were never the exotic blooms from the vicarage garden but the wild plants of the meadows and hedgerows. She was a marvel at looking after small children; she had endless patience and never lost her temper. Dirty nappies did not bother her. Show Merle a colicky six-week-old, and she above all others was able to 'get the wind up'. The Vicar often said Merle was the village's most intelligent inhabitant. Merle rarely spoke at home in the cottage; answered questions only in monosyllables. Which was fine, the life of the vicarage and its visitors remained a closely guarded secret; and that was as it should be; Merle was not about to break her silence to anyone.

She was sixteen when I was born. The children at the village school pitied me, teased me because soppy moon-faced Merle was a bit barmy. I often tried to pretend that 'daft Merle' was not my sister. I always felt guilty afterwards; but I often wished Merle would go away or get lost. I blamed Merle for existing.

Aunt Beat lived with us. She was the bane of my life. I could never work out why we had to have her there; she made everyone's life a misery. The other kids at the village school did not have disagreeable old aunts making life hell in the cottage.

No-one was absolutely sure of her true relationship to the family. She had been left a widow at a fairly young age and after her husband Clarrie's death she was evicted from her tied cottage. Mum had invited her to stay for a few weeks until she could find somewhere else to live. Twenty years later she was still there. She informed all and sundry that she had been grateful to move in with the only family she had left in the world, my soft-hearted parents. My parents were too petrified of her prickly temper to ask her to enlarge on the details of the relationship; and anyway my gentle Mum felt sorry for her.

Relationships in the Springbourne and Bigford families, the largest families in the Silver Villages, were occasionally so convoluted. In years to come Bertha always said that Dad thought she must be a Springbourne cousin of Mum's and Mum thought she must be a Bigford cousin of Dad's. She had been with us for years before my birth. She had reconnoitred the sitting room of our cottage for her bedroom because she could not manage the stairs, and we conducted the entire day-to-day existence of a fairly large family from our tiny kitchen.

Everyone was terrified of Aunt Beat's vituperative tongue. She was not a loved family member, a dear old aunt who is the mainstay of her family. She was merely tolerated.

Tall and gaunt, she was impossible-to-please. Her disdainful tongue and sarcasm dominated family life in the cottage at Great Silver.

My Mum had been the village beauty in her youth; she was tall, raven-haired, and still handsome even in her fifties. Mum was patient & generous, gentle, quick-witted & funny. I adored her.

Mum had been a Miss Springbourne before she married

Dad and became Mrs Bigford. The Springbournes and the Bigfords were the two oldest families in the Silver Villages. There was a Charles Springbourne in the parish registers in the seventeenth century; and a Dick Bigford had fought with General Gordon at Khartoum. Mum used to hint, with a proud tilt of her head, that Springbournes had been gentleman farmers in Victorian times. Of all the Springbournes I knew, and in the Silver Villages and the other surrounding hamlets there were plenty of them, none of them would ever qualify for the title 'gentleman-farmer'. Dad used to laugh at Mum's pretensions and say he had a cousin who was a roadsweeper, and you would always need road sweepers.

I was related, one way or another, to most of the inhabitants of the Silver Villages.

CHAPTER EIGHT

THE EARLY DAYS of the war had little effect on the daily life of the infant's class of a Hampshire village school. Some of the dads went away to the war, but most of the menfolk of the villages were engaged in protected occupations and they continued to farm the land, or they were just too old to fight, like my Dad.

Our diet had always been plain and we ate mostly the produce of the cottage gardens, with meat once or twice a week, purchased from the butcher who travelled out each Saturday in his van, from Middleford, the nearest town. Bread was eaten at every meal; it was usually white bread purchased from the bakery, and not home-baked wholemeal. Eggs were a great standby; but occasionally a chicken grew too old to lay and was consigned to the pot. Chicken was a treat and eaten with relish, even if the fowl had been a family pet with her own name, petted and talked to, even cuddled, just a week before.

The boys went rabbiting; occasionally they were also lucky enough to catch a hare, a treat indeed. At harvest time rabbits were plentiful, as gifts from the labourers in the fields. Mum could cook rabbit more flavoursome than chicken, and we village children were not sentimental. After all, I had seen lovely little lambs in the spring, but I still loved a roast leg.

One of Maudie's dearest friends was a poacher and Angie and Ethel often had pheasant or partridge for their Sunday roast.

Although there was electricity in the village, such hideous and unnecessary monstrosities as street lights did not exist; and a good thing too, Mum would say, who would want them! Many of the houses did not have electricity, so the dark streets and blackout necessary for the war effort did not worry the inhabitants of the Silver Villages; our streets had always been that way.

Many of the village children had never possessed a new item of clothing in their entire lives, especially the younger family members, who just hoped their body shape resembled that of their older siblings, so the hand-me-downs would fit. The more fortunate wore clothes knitted and sewn by their mothers and grandmothers.

"What did you think jumble sales were for anyway?"

Mrs Harwood, the Vicar's wife and Lady Margaret Stockbridge-Howe up at the manor always gave generously to the jumble sales. Both ladies had children and grandchildren of school age. As the mothers said, you couldn't afford to buy that quality yourself and the knobs only wore them a few times before they gave them away. As a result, village children often wore clothes purchased in Bond Street; and many of the girl's summer dresses attended the village school for more years than did their original owners.

Early in the war the lack of new clothing in the shops

did not bother the villagers a whit. In common with most of the population of the country as a whole they thought the war would only last till Christmas, or it will be over by Easter; he'll be back before the next harvest.

CHAPTER NINE

ON A SAD, mild spring evening Mum took me with her to the peak of Barrow Hill, a high point in the North Downs, close to the Silver Villages. We cycled down the pitch-dark lanes under the tunnel of branches, like riding on the ghost train at the Michaelmas Fair. The only light permitted was a pinprick from our blacked-out dynamos.

We were not alone; on the hill there were some of the other boys from the Silver Villages, and adults I could barely recognise in the murk of night.

The splendid daytime view from Barrow Hill is of the whole county of Hampshire.

A luminous glow hovered towards the south, along the distant line of coastal hills. It flickered and glimmered on the horizon, lighting the night sky almost to the zenith above our heads; lifting and dipping, growing and changing, orange, yellow, amber and gold. Mum said we were watching Portsmouth burn. There was a sob in her voice.

The silence on the hilltop was deafening.

Portsmouth, where Aunt Beat said you could visit a historic ship called the Victory. I had been promised a trip when the war was over. Southsea, where my sisters had enjoyed many seaside outings in their courting days, now the scene of massive fires caused by enemy bombs; fires that could be seen from a hilltop forty miles away. Homes, factories, pubs and cinemas, all bombed, now burning; a port-city as old as England, now no more.

Mum, usually garrulous, especially about the war and what might happen to her precious boys, answered my questions in monosyllables as we cycled along the dark lanes to home. She was too busy with her memories of a Hampshire where the medieval towns had stood untouched by time.

When Mum broke the news at home, hard-hearted Aunt Beat wept. She had lived in Portsmouth when she was a child. She sobbed for the streets and buildings that now lived only in her memories of her glory days.

Whenever I climb the steep side of Barrow Hill and see the green vista of Hampshire spread below me: the little towns, the farms, the livestock, the crops, the deeper green of the river valleys, always in my mind's eye burning Portsmouth flickers on the horizon. Mum had wanted me to see history being made.

The war had a more urgent meaning for a young child now. There was no chocolate, or oranges. I could not recall the taste of bananas. The only men left in the village were the very old and the very young, and a few hopeless dodderers like my brother-in law Alf, who, as far as I could determine, suffered from nothing worse than flat feet and truly amazing halitosis. Mum and my sisters cried over the reports of London bombing on the wireless. Iris's nephew was dead, the vicar's sister had joined the ATS and was driving an ambulance, and Florrie's brother was a prisoner of war.

CHAPTER ELEVEN

AUDIE HELD HER curly golden head high. With a panache she considered befitted the lady of the manor she announced proudly that Angie was to have piano lessons. She asked Mum to 'put a good word in' with my brother Len's wife Iris. Iris played beautifully and Maudie hoped that Iris would teach Angie to play. Maudie said she would pay good money for this. The expression 'good money,' had Mum's immediate interest. Maudie rarely had any money, good or otherwise.

There were pianos in many Great Silver cottages, and usually these were strummed enthusiastically by people who played vigorously by ear; music lessons were a luxury that a farm worker's or tradesman's wage could rarely accommodate. No-one in our family, with the exception of Iris, had any musical ability whatsoever, so we did not have a piano; in fact music lessons were a novel idea Mum had never previously considered.

Aunt Beat, of course, claimed to have been a virtuoso at the piano in her youth before rheumatism and failing eyesight stole her touch. If someone else had planned to become an Olympic miler, Aunt Beat would have claimed youthful aptitude in long distance running. She was quite safe from having to prove her claims.

Maudie said she did not know how to go about purchasing a piano. She asked Mum to keep her eyes open for a bargain.

Maudie adopted what she considered to be a la-di-dah upper-class accent, somewhat difficult with her broad Hampshire vowels, but she considered a touch of class definitely befitted the mother of a potential prodigy. In fact Maudie's nose threatened to become poised permanently in the air. Angie had never been within thumping distance of a piano.

Maudie's Mother, Nellie claimed she was not surprised; it was bound to happen. "Angie inherited all this musical talent from my husband Henry," Nellie proclaimed proudly to any who would listen. "Henry used to play the piano in the Silver Bell every Saturday night and sang in Westminster Abbey when he was a boy soprano." Any connection between these two events was somewhat dubious, but as Henry had been dead for over thirty years, Nellie would never be asked to prove her claim. The possibility of a choir boy from a cottage in Great Silver singing in Westminster Abbey seemed somewhat unlikely; but who was to argue?

Also, it was most unlikely Henry's talents had been inherited by Maudie's children. Henry had died of drink and laziness a whole two years before Maudie was born. Now, in Great Silver there were a great many short pregnancies, some as little as five months; but these were mostly newly-weds. Nellie's pregnancy must have been the longest in village history. It must be taken as self-evident that Nellie's other four children may have inherited Henry's disputable talents but any abilities Maudie's offspring may possess originated from another source entirely. And Nellie had conveniently forgotten who that was.

Maudie purchased the piano from the one-bar-room country pub at Little Silver, where, for the last five years, it had been stowed away in a barn at the rear of the inn. It arrived at the cottage roped onto the back of a farm wagon hauled by Captain, Farmer Williams' bad tempered old warhorse, now relegated to ploughing and light haulage. All the children who lived in the main street, and a few inquisitive adults, watched in awe and disbelief as the piano was unloaded.

Maudie invited all and sundry into the cottage to admire her most precious possession, pointing out to everyone that it was German piano; oh, she knew they were the enemy, but when it came to pianos, you couldn't beat the Germans, could you? And could you please keep your fingers off it; she didn't want it fingermarked.

The timber was a showy walnut veneer, with pale green oiled silk, faded and torn, inset into the front panel. Two bent and blackened candlesticks also decorated the front panel. The left back leg was propped up by a book because it was about two inches shorter than the left front leg.

Angie gave a little tinkle on the keyboard. Most of the ivory keys were bent or discoloured, and many made no sound at all.

Iris was summoned to approve the marvellous instrument.

After Iris recovered her power of speech, she pointed out tactfully that lessons could not commence until the piano had been tuned. She could thoroughly recommend the man who tuned the piano at Silver Street School.

"No no, we want you to teach Angie, Mrs Bigford; we don't need no man. We want you to teach Angie where the tunes are, so she will know how to get them out." Maudie spoke slowly and emphasised each word; she had expected better from a school marm, but you just had to explain everything to this one, didn't you?

After Iris had again recovered her speech, she explained as gently as she could, that the piano had to be in tune before a tune could be played.

Maudie was amazed and also somewhat annoyed. She had spent a fortune on that darned piano and there was uppity Mrs Bigford saying it wasn't tuneful. What was 'in tune' anyway? Who did she think she was! She wasn't all that important; just a teacher at Silver Street School, but boy, did she have big ideas about herself. Maudie knew when she was being looked down on. All right, she would have it tuned, but it clearly wasn't necessary; all Mrs Uppity Bigford had to do was show Angie where the tunes were.

Angie had four lessons from Iris, all duly paid for on the spot with much show of pride by Maudie as she handed the coins over, always ensuring she had an audience before doing so.

Maudie was very disappointed in the result. After four lessons - four whole lessons - all Angie could do was thump out a couple of scales, and she had not even got round to trying simple tunes like The White Cliffs of Dover. It was obvious to Maudie that Mrs Big-Ideas Bigford was not all she was cracked up to be.

Angie was just too lively and giddy to sit still for a whole hour. Plans for Angie's glorious future as a gifted pianist were dropped by mutual consent of herself, Maudie and Iris.

But the piano had a lot of use over the succeeding years. Often in the afternoons we could hear Nellie crooning to herself, as she gently fingered her way through such tunes as "Two Little Girls in Blue" and "Just a Song at Twilight".

CHAPTER TWELVE

B Y CHRISTMAS EVE the whole of our Downland world was covered in a thick blanket of snow, which had frozen. All the village children adored snow, but not our parents. The farmers had their cattle safely in the cow sheds; the shepherds still had the sheep out in the meadows below the Downs. Sheep can tolerate the cold.

Just negotiating a trip to feed the hens in the chicken run at the bottom of the garden required the surefootedness of a skater; the path was like an ice rink.

The bus to Middleford had stopped running, the Downland roads were just too dangerous; hard luck to anyone who needed to last-minute shop. Not that village people shopped often in Middleford, except at the second-hand shop and the market. Middleford prices were too high, and the village shop stocked everything from paraffin heaters to boxes of dried dates.

Icicles hung from the thatch. In the cottages, the little ranges glowed red late into the night, only to be relit enthusiastically at five-thirty the next morning. Cottagers know it is easier to relight a warm range. Last week's washing hung frozen on the garden lines.

Who cared, that was grown-up stuff! A long line of village boys, and a few daring girls, took their turn to slide the length of the pond. There were whole families of snowmen in some village gardens. Teams of children pelted each other with snowballs in the village street. Homemade sledges, or at least Mum's old tin tray, served a purpose for a quick descent of Barrow Hill. A couple of wealthier families even had skis.

There was no water at the farm at Little Silver; the Williamses were melting snow for washing and cleaning; everything was frozen solid. The sheep stood like dirty grey statues against the endless white of the Downs.

Sir Francis and Lady Margaret, and the Vicar and his wife, as well as a couple of old stalwarts from the cottages, gave a demonstration of skating on the pond on Christmas Eve afternoon. They were much admired by the younger villagers; and it appeared only our grandparent's generation had acquired the elegance and skill required to skate.

CHAPTER THIRTEEN

I WAS THIRTEEN-AND-A-HALF THAT icebound January Saturday when Aunt Beat decided it was time I knew the truth. Mum had gone over to Silver Street to help Bertha with little Eric, who had croup; Dad was watching Dennis play football; Merle was at the vicarage, probably peeling Mrs Harwood's potatoes. I was left in the cottage, Mum had asked me to 'keep an eye on' Aunt Beat.

I was the plainest and tallest girl in the village school; I even towered over most of the boys. I longed for an ample cleavage which was very fashionable at that time, already possessed and exhibited with considerable pride by the two blonde beauties next door. They filled their brazieres, while my newly-acquired braziere hung like empty peg bags on my chest. My tiny bosoms resembled pimples.

Glowing scarlet acne lit my forehead and nose. My cheeks were the colour of raw pastry; my light brown hair was thick, and straight as a yard of pump water; beautiful I was not.

Ethel and Angie grew more beautiful, more sexy, by the month. It just was not fair! The perfect English rose complexions, huge blue eyes, and curly blonde hair only added to my anguish.

Dear Iris considered my cleverness to be a consolation; forget being clever, I wanted boys to like me, and Aunt Beat always said men could not stand clever women.

So misery-guts Linda was stuck in the cottage with only Aunt Beat and a reluctant cat for company. Now, happy people were bound to upset Aunt Beat. Placidity would offend Aunt Beat. Cheerfulness would set off an angry tirade which could last for hours. But most of all Aunt Beat disliked melancholy, even though she had personally cultivated misery to a fine art.

Aunt Beat snarled a continuous heckling reproach from her seat by the range. "Haven't you got something better to do with your time, than to walk around with a face that would set the milk sour?" "Isn't it time you did something useful, like ironing or cleaning the grate?" "Stop mooning around like a great ugly lummox and go and peel the potatoes!" Aunt Beat considered the peeling of potatoes to be the quintessential ambition of a woman's life.

Aunt Beat disliked everyone but sometimes I felt she really had it in for me.

She tolerated the other family members. My parents had lavished unstinting care and kindness on the miserable old harridan for almost two decades, and they had done so with no thought of reward. They deserved more than mere tolerance.

Mum had asked me to tidy up her needlework box. I had never been interested in needlework or remnants, or for that matter, thread bobbins. I would willingly do

Mum's bidding of course, she was Mum, but I knew I was a picture of misery. Aunt Beat was sitting watching me, a nasty expression on her face.

There was no escape from the inevitable tirade, Aunt Beat had found a victim; being vindictive to all and sundry was her favourite Saturday afternoon occupation.

She worked up to it gradually. A really nasty temperamental outburst is a work of art, after all, and Aunt Beat did not spare herself when it came to artistic effort. She emptied coals into the range, complaining about the poor-quality fuel and banging the scuttle. She threw the long-suffering cat out of the way, he who spent every cold afternoon in front of the range. Aunt Beat sat and ground her teeth, glaring at the untidy mess I was re-organising on the kitchen table.

The diatribe started. "You are a lazy bag of bones, my girl! Just like your stupid great lump of a Mother. What you need is a swift kick in the pants to wake you up a bit. Oh, Betty should have put you straight into a home when you were born. Your daft Mother was incapable of looking after you of course; and we've been stuck with you ever since."

Grinding her teeth like millwheels, she slammed the kettle on the hob. Although I was accustomed to Aunt Beat's frequent outbursts I had not expected this. I stared at her in flabbergasted silence.

She was sitting there saying my Mum was incapable of looking after me; that my Mum was useless and good for nothing; that Mum should have put me into a home at birth. What was she talking about? This was the Bigfords, family life meant everything; it simply was not what this family did.

Mum and Dad were not young when I was born. Let's face it, my brothers were married; Mum and Dad already had two grandsons. Surely my parents would have welcomed my birth even though my advent must have been a surprise because of their advancing age. I had always been secure in the knowledge of the love of my entire family; The thought of not being wanted was a novel idea and I found it terrifying.

I gazed at her, dumbfounded; but Aunt Beat had merely paused for breath.

"I told Betty at the time; its mother cannot look after it. Get rid of it, I said, but oh no, not Betty! After all the talk there was in the village, the people in this house could not walk along the street without being pointed at. Bertha and Mary had a dreadful time at work; even slovenly Mrs Caundle, with those slatternly girls no better than they should be, was looking down her nose at this family. You would have thought Betty would see sense, but oh no, not soft-headed Betty. I'll keep her and bring her up as mine, she said, and look what she got for her trouble. You! A useless great lummox! You do not belong in this house, my girl!" She hit the fire irons with her walking stick so that the kettle on the hob rattled and spilled its last drop of water, which evaporated into steam.

It was as though she had punched me in my head; the pain behind my eyes was agony. I reeled away from her tirade as though she had struck me physically. What did Aunt Beat mean? Betty was my Mum. My Mum was Betty.

But Aunt Beat said no. If Mum was not my Mother, then who was? This was not happening, not true. Mum was my Mother. Of course she was!

Aunt Beat rose from her spot by the range and tottered over to the kitchen table; she leaned over me menacingly and thrust her face close to mine. She was a tall woman. I could smell the stale old-woman odour of her clothes, and the bismuth tablets she chewed continuously were on her breath.

"Surely you knew you were not Betty's child," she snarled, her rancid breath inches from my face. "I'm sure the blabber mouths in this village somehow got round to mentioning it to you. And if you didn't know, then all I can say it is time you did!"

"No, you are gormless Merle's by-blow, my girl, and you are as big, stupid and useless as your Mother ever was. Sixteen she was, one afternoon, when she dropped you. No-one even knew the great fat bitch was pregnant. So barmy I doubt whether she knew herself! Then Betty says - I'll keep her, bring her up as mine! Couldn't bear to see her own flesh and blood in a home, she said. Ever since that day we have been stuck with you, the biggest nuisance that ever lived."

I no longer seemed to be sitting in the kitchen; I appeared to be teetering on the edge of a great, bottomless, pitch-black pit. Invisible arms were hauling me towards the pit and I feared I would topple in.

Aunt Beat had not finished. "Oh here we go! Don't act dumb; of course you knew! The blabbermouths in this godforsaken village would have made sure they told you. The brats at that school you are so fond of all know; their parents would have told them. That lot next door all know; not they have anything to brag about themselves. Don't you kid yourself; everyone knows you are daft Merle's daughter. And you think you are so clever, you with your would-be brains."

I finally toppled into the black pit.

My world crumpled. Not only was I not my lovely Mum's daughter, but big daft Merle was my Mother; Merle who was backward, not-all-there, the victim of cruel derision and pity. And everyone except me had always known: Angie and Ethel; Nellie and Maudie; Miss Landport, all the children at the school; the Vicar; all the Caundles. Then who was my Father? Aunt Beat had forgotten to harangue me with that snippet of information.

There was nowhere to hide. I wanted to die.

I tore up the stairs at the double and in to the tiny bedroom I shared with Merle. I threw myself on my bed; but there was no escape. Merle's bed was next to mine; Merle's bed with the stuffed golliwog Bertha had knitted for her, with her pillow, her nightie, her personal odour. I hated it; I hated anything to do with Merle; big daft Merle who was my Mother. I could no longer live in this cottage, sleep in this room, share life with Mum and Dad who had lied to me. I must leave Great Silver, where everyone knew me for what I was! I would never be Reg's and Betty's daughter again.

I grabbed my wellies and my navy blue mackintosh. I tore down the stairs and out the back door. I could not bear to spend another moment in that house. I had no idea where I was going.

CHAPTER FOURTEEN

THE GREY JANUARY afternoon was fading towards a moonless, starless darkness. Mist was softening the dark hollows in the Downs. The lanes shone black with frost. No wind blew, no rooks cawed, and no rain fell, just a blanket of fog that concealed all familiar sights and sounds.

I ran. I ran the steepness of the Down. A skew path slithers back and forth across the face of the Down, allowing you to climb the near vertical upsweep with comparative ease; but I ran straight up the side of the Down, not even realising I was doing this. I stopped for breath; my chest was heaving, my heart pounding in my body and I was sweating in spite of the insidious chill of the foggy evening. The exquisite view was hidden, grey and woolly, silent as a tomb. The beech hangers looming in the mist appeared like secret, crouching, dinosaurs; hovering, waiting for a careless moment to launch an attack; to strike, to kill. They could take me! I was not afraid of them.

Nothing was familiar. The summer Downs and the wildflowers I had known here belonged to Linda Bigford of Great Silver. I was not her.

I had never been atop the Down during a foggy,

freezing January dusk; but I had never been many other things either, alone and dispossessed. My breath sobbed. This place was alien to me. Linda Bigford, daughter of Reg and Betty, she walked here on fine midsummer evenings; but I was not her. I was a stranger in a strange land.

No birds called, no breeze blew. The church clock did not strike; no lights penetrated the swirling mist. I was alone in a frigid, silent wasteland. My feet propelled me forward, along the path atop the Downs. I walked for miles, towards darkness, towards a sightless void. I split the sole of my wellies; my bare knees were raked by extruding branches hidden in the murk. My mackintosh had become torn. Hunger and thirst assailed me, but I could not stop. I was walking towards oblivion; but away from Linda Bigford, daughter and sister, big, stupid, useless, and good-for-nothing.

I walked villages and counties. The termination of the Downland path pulled me up short. It ended abruptly on a high tundra of nothing; no trees, no buildings, never a trail; just lank grass, and pitch black night, as though someone had forgotten to add finishing touches. There was nothingness, just grey mists that swirled around my legs; no sound penetrated the encompassing blackness.

There was nowhere to run. I sank down on the rank dark turf of the Down. I wanted the Mum I did not have. I wanted to be in the cottage where I did not belong. I wanted to be Linda Bigford again, and to play and go to school, to be big and skinny and good at sums. First the tears came; then the sobbing; then the screaming; and finally when the impetus was spent and I had no voice left, came the silence.

As I clambered down the steep face of the Down I was aware of the first wintry dawn lightening in the Eastern sky. Before I reached the bottom I could see the dark bulk of farm buildings. No light showed anywhere.

I had no idea where I was, or how far I had walked or what the time was. My throat was parched and I was ravenously hungry. I imagined the people in the farmhouse lying asleep in their beds dreaming of family things, talk and laughter. I envied them. I would never talk again.

As I trudged along the path to the farmhouse door a couple of collies chained to the fence threatened to remove my lower limbs, and a large black tomcat hissed and spat. I hammered the door with my fists, and screamed for them to open up. After I had hammered and yelled for what seemed an eternity lights flared at the windows, like golden orbs in the frosty twilight. A man wearing striped flannel pyjamas, his hair mussed, his eyes sleepy behind his horn rimmed glasses, opened the door. Two pyjama-clad toddlers peeked round his legs to see what was causing the rumpus.

The warm air of the farmhouse kitchen hit my face like a mallet. I collapsed at his feet.

CHAPTER FIFTEEN

THEY TOOK ME back to the cottage at Great Silver. Farmer Williams came to collect me in his car; Mum sat beside him, her rosy complexion pale as paper. Dad sat behind; he was unable to look me in the face.

Liars!

I wanted to return to the cottage only because I could not imagine any other destination. I knew of no other place to go.

Doctor Webster from Great Silver sent a portable canvas stretcher along with Mister Williams. I was laid on it and carried ever-so-gently to the car while above my head the two-faced January sun threatened to melt the snow and reveal the hidden secret of snowdrops, before the next blizzard could hide them again.

With tender care they sat me behind Mum. Dad had his arms round me. At no point during the journey back to Great Silver did I acknowledge the presence of my parents. I could smell Dad's tobacco, also Mum's scented soap, and the fragrance was offensive to me. I could barely keep from retching.

If only the journey along the snowy lanes, through the

familiar villages, could have lasted forever. I did not belong in the cottage at Great Silver.

As I was lifted back on to the stretcher and carried to the front door, I wondered that the Great Silver Brass Band had not been called upon to play Colonel Bogey, there were so many villagers hanging around our front gate. Just at that moment folk who never shopped midweek somehow found it necessary to pass our cottage on the way to the shop, or strode out purposefully to post their pools coupon at the letter box.

Ethel and Angie, Maudie and Nellie were there of course; Maudie came over to the stretcher and popped a tiny bunch of snowdrops under my chin. I ignored her completely.

Inside the cottage, where I did not belong, nothing had changed. Aunt Beat was in her favourite perch by the range, glowering, I wondered if my parents knew of her part in the truth-telling. She would have made sure her story was good. She would have blamed me.

They carried me up the crooked curvy cottage stairs. My bed was now in the back room. I was no longer expected to share a room with Merle, my mother. She was nowhere in sight: probably down at the vicarage, peeling potatoes. I vaguely wondered if she even knew what had happened.

I was undressed and put to bed; Mum brought me a bun and a cup of tea. I ignored her. Dad gently ushered her out, and Dr Webster came in and looked at me; never examined or touched me, just looked and then he also left the room. I heard whispering on the landing and Mum sobbing.

Mary and Bertha came in the afternoon. Liars, both of them! I did not acknowledge their presence.

But the cat sat on the end of my bed and washed himself; the cockerel in the garden bragged to his hens; little Peter next door was playing tractors and making a racket about it; and somewhere far away in the afternoon, Nellie was playing Alice Blue Gown on the tinkling old piano. Bertha brought me a love-book, which she tucked under the covers and made me swear not to tell Mum, who would not approve. Mary cuddled me while good-natured Bertha twittered like a lively sparrow; Mum joined them; and then they were all laughing at one of Nellie's outrageous sayings.

Gradually, slowly, almost imperceptibly, I began to be Linda Bigford again.

CHAPTER SIXTEEN

MY DAMAGED HEALTH improved; the snow melted and February-fill-the-dyke found me sitting by the cottage range embroidering a doily as a birthday present for Mary. I gradually began to accept the status quo.

The nature of childhood is one-upmanship and extreme cruelty, if need be. In such a small community, Merle, with her limited mental capacity, became an obvious victim to the other pupils during her days at the school. Village memories were long, and though Merle had long since left school, as her sister, I also became a victim by family association; and from my earliest schooldays I was teased about daft Merle. The teasing caused heartache when I was in the Little Ones, and I would run home to Mum in tears; but as I flew up to the Big Ones and, being me, I grew taller by the day, I could probably have tolerated the teasing, but any visit I made to the shop, the village hall, or St Edmunds, I would see the village women glancing my way and at each other, with that knowing glance, that said.…..

In my heart I knew Merle to be a good-natured and simple soul; Merle would do anything for other folk, and her calm nature had diffused many a combustible Bigford family wrangle by the power of her self-possession and composure. My sister was a silent, gentle person but I had always accepted the definition of my schoolfellows and considered Merle to be barmy.

As I grew older I came to realise that she was not barmy. Perhaps Merle had always been treated as an idiot, therefore, even in her own eyes, she was one.

The circumstances of my birth were at first entirely beyond my youthful powers of understanding. That Merle had become a mother at sixteen, and no-one had been aware of her pregnancy until that incredible May afternoon when she began to experience labour pains, was an event beyond my powers of comprehension. Mum and Dad, with their familiar gentleness, acquainted me gradually over the next few weeks with the facts of my birth and my life. Those facts everyone else was already aware of. Just me that wasn't!

Merle was always plump; and her increasing roundness had been attributed to her age. She rarely left the safety of the cottage, and spent most of her time with Mum and her sisters. Afterwards it became obvious she was aware she was pregnant but had chosen not to acknowledge this fact, deciding to ignore it and hoping it would go away.

That's me all over; I did not just go away!

No-one had ever known Merle to have anything to do with boys. In spite of intense questioning by her parents and Doctor Webster, and the gentle intervention of her friend, the Vicar, she had never disclosed the identity of my father. She maintained her quiet repose, and refused to be drawn, in spite of threats and cajoling. My advent had been as if by a virgin birth. As I have already stated, Maud was not stupid and she would have known who was responsible, but she maintained her silence to the end of her days.

No-one was brought to blame. Apparently a young itinerate land worker on a neighbouring farm was considered to be possibly responsible. When the lad was confronted by Dad and Doctor Webster he had heatedly denied even speaking to 'big daft Merle', although he said he knew who she was; everyone in the village knew her!

Doctor Webster questioned Merle in great depth, though he did not force her to talk. She clammed up, and refused to answer questions regarding the father's identity, in spite of persistent interrogation from the family as well as Doctor Webster. Merle calmly ignored all questioning; but she managed to make it clear she knew what had happened to her; and that she had been a willing participant in the events that led to my conception.

It became generally accepted that my arrival was as the result of teenage experimentation. Life would never disclose to me the identity of my father.

My arrival had almost been a magical event; one day not there; the next day, very much alive and kicking. I would not go away. To say my birth wreaked havoc in the family is an understatement of gross proportions.

Merle became a cipher; accepting each day as it came, rarely speaking, being obedient and docile, and ignoring the child she had borne. She recovered from the birth quickly and continued her simple day-to-day existence as if nothing had happened.

I was taken to the cottage hospital at Middleford, to begin my days as one of life's little mistakes.

Doctor Webster counselled the distraught family and suggested the healthy and strong baby girl be taken into care and eventually relinquished for adoption. Mum and Dad were utterly thunder-struck and speechless, with shock, disbelief and horror clouding their judgement. At first they agreed that this must be the resolution.

Ray and Len, Mary and Bertha were called home from their places of work. They stood unblinking in the cottage kitchen, in their minds still listening to the mewling of a newborn babe who appeared from nowhere. All four agreed without reservation that the babe must be taken into care.

Merle was cosseted and comforted by her loving Mum and sisters; Dad received the manly approbation of patted shoulders from Ray and Len. The family would never recover from the shock but they would stick together to the last.

The news spread like wild-fire through the village; ammunition for the gossips, disgrace to be celebrated by the prudes. Mister Harwood, the Vicar, came to the cottage and with gentleness offered prayer to Merle and her bemused parents. Nellie and Maudie from next door brought round a cup of tea and some sandwiches; and gazed with a true understanding from a respectable distance.

Of course, Aunt Beat ranted and raved, blamed everyone in the family; raged and shouted, complained the family would never live it down and something should be done about that immoral Merle and shiftless parents like Betty and Reg. Everyone had only got what they deserved, she said.

It was a wonder she did not shout this from the rooftop.

Merle, tacitly accepting the loving care of her bewildered parents, asked no questions, and did not query the future plans for her child.

In the days following the birth Merle recovered quickly and soon she was going about her minor household duties as if nothing had happened. But no-one saw into the deep well of Merle's soul, did they! It was incredibly convenient for everyone if Merle just forgot about her child. Mum also began to recover gradually from her original shock and horror. She had always worried about Merle, who was her cross to bear in life, because Merle was 'backward'.

As Mum began to recover from the shock she began to worry about the baby who was, after all, her granddaughter. After a number of sleepless nights, when she lay awake imagining the pathetic little mite with no-one to love or cuddle her, she appeared at Doctor Webster's surgery and pleaded with him to let her see the baby. Doctor Webster assured her "The baby is strong and healthy and receiving superior care at Middleford Hospital, where she must stay until various authorities can decide upon her future. She will probably be offered for adoption."

"No Betty, I really advise you against seeing the child. Her welfare must be considered along with that of Merle and the rest of the family; and in the interests of that baby, it will not do for you to become too attached to her".

It struck Mum like a bolt of lightning that her granddaughter was to be given away. The family would never see the baby again. Mum burst into tears and soon began weeping hysterically. Doctor Webster applied his most professional caring attitude, tempered with outright friendship, as he had known Betty Bigford and her family for almost three decades, but he was greatly concerned. He feared that the bewildering events would be too much for even her robust physical and emotional health.

The weeping continued unabated; Betty's husband Reg was summoned to the surgery from his job of repairing the village hall roof; but Betty could not be pacified. Doctor Webster understood village-life well enough to be aware of the burden of prejudice and intolerance the family had been forced to endure publicly as a result of what was commonly viewed as a shocking scandal, as well as the personal grief they had experienced under their roof. Doctor Webster capitulated: "Betty, I will drive you and Reg to Middleford; just one small glimpse, it is all I can allow, but obviously you must see that the babe is fine and healthy. Honestly, she will be placed with a family who will love her dearly."

Mum lifted me from my crib and the case for adoption was lost, never to be raised again. "Ooh look, she is just like Ray and Len were when they were babies, a true Bigford, no matter who her father was!" Mum peered again into the tiny face. "Mind you, I can't see our Bertha in her, but Bertha always was like me. Oh, the dear little tat; just look at those blue eyes; and the dinkiest little nose. Have the nurses given her a pet name yet?" Mum peered through her misted-up spectacles at the indomitable figure of starched and formal Matron Bolton.

Matron informed Mum that this had not happened; she personally did not permit such unnecessary sentimentality; and the hospital staff commonly referred to the child as the Great Silver baby.

Mum could be heard shouting three blocks away. Her grandchild, referred to as the Great Silver baby! Call themselves nurses, why, if she was sick she wouldn't want any of them to touch her with a barge pole! Didn't any of them have a heart? She would have them know she would take the baby back to her home at Great Silver immediately; no, she would not leave the baby here. That baby needed the loving care and attention of a good grandmother.

Mum refused to leave without me.

Doctor Webster pleaded with her to go home; he promised he would bring her to visit the baby each week until the adoption arrangements had been made; but Mum was adamant. That was her grandchild, that baby without a name. And she would not leave the hospital without that baby.

Doctor Webster had practiced medicine in various North Hampshire villages for almost three decades. The events that lead to the birth were not a novelty to him, although Merle was a more youthful than most of the mothers in this situation; but then again, he could remember younger! The adoption of the child by the grandmother, who became nominally the child's actual mother; while the youthful propagator resumed her previous life almost unaffected by the untimely confinement, and became in effect the child's older sister, was a situation he was familiar with. He had noted its success in a number of cases. An exceptional mother like Betty Bigford would probably fulfil the post of surrogate with more aplomb than many of his more sleazy patients whose daughters were just following the maternal pattern of producing offspring of doubtful paternity.

They let Merle chose my name. She called me Linda Margaret. It was her only maternal act. She paid me the same amount of attention she also reserved for her other sisters and her brothers. She was gentle, deferential, silent and distant. To her, I was never a daughter. I was her younger sister. She never spoke to me as a daughter.

I became Linda Bigford, daughter of Betty and Reg. Until I was thirteen-and-a half years old, I had never been in any doubt.

On the first school day after Easter my feet dragged as I walked to school. I was tempted to run back to the cottage and hide my sobs in Mum's apron; but the time had come for a showdown between me and the cruel world.

I was terrified of the bullies and the little bitches; I expected no quarter to be given. I prepared myself, once again, for a fate worse than death.

I was met with a deafening silence when I walked into the Big Ones.

Mister Taylor, the headmaster, followed me into the class room, and gazed at the silent pupils in disbelief; he was accustomed to shouting to make himself heard above the commotion of early morning chatter. "Isn't it good to see Linda back amongst us? We should all wish her 'good morning".

"Good morning, Linda," repeated thirty little parrots. Then they burst into giggles at the ridiculousness of it all. This was the greeting reserved for the Vicar, or a school governor, or Lady Margaret from the manor. This was not the way to greet Linda Bigford! After they all had their little laugh, everything seemed alright. Gradually I came to accept my schoolmates again, for really they had already accepted me. I was unaware of it in my over-sensitised condition.

The nine years I had spent at the school had treated Miss Landport harshly. She had become obese, with rolls of fat bulging over the waist band of her skirt, and below the short sleeves of her spring blouse. Grey showed in her hair, and her facial features had become bloated, her eyes still protruding like red-veined green gooseberries in her pasty complexion. She still harassed and bullied her little charges on a daily basis. No man had married her.

CHAPTER SEVENTEEN

I WAS NEARLY FIFTEEN. The final three months of my school life passed swiftly. It seemed I had sat at the ink-spattered desk for an eternity doing long division, learning grammar, taking part in the annual Nativity play; or marching up and down the asphalt playground, as Mister Taylor considered 'drill' to be a necessary part of modern education.

Suddenly my schooldays were at an end. I had never really considered my future. It was nineteen-forty-eight; girls obeyed their parents; I had never been allowed to make my own decisions.

I was offered no alternative; Mum had decreed shop work; and Mum had spoken. The possibility of choosing my future had never occurred to me; to opt for working on one of the nearby farms, or being a nanny, or a librarian or an archaeologist. I had only ever considered my future employment in terms of earning money, and going on the bus to Middleford each day. The reality of spending all day in a shop selling shoes, or frocks, or sheets, or blancmange was completely beyond imagination.

From the safety of the Big Ones I regarded work as one

long future holiday; and the thought of arriving home in the dark of winter evenings filled me with an excited longing for midsummer to pass. I had rarely been in Middleford after dark, except for the occasional trip to the cinema, which always involved the whole family. Suddenly I would be alone in Middleford and it would be dark, the lighted shop windows reflecting invitingly on the wet pavements.

The fact that it would probably only be teatime did not deter me; I was captivated by the bright lights of Middleford, with its score of tiny shops. The last bus to Great Silver left Middleford at five-forty-five, except on Wednesday, which was market day, and daring as it may seem, the last Wednesday bus was seven-forty-five. On Saturday there was a ten o-clock bus, always packed with the youth of the village, returning from an evening's fun and games in Middleford, sitting on the upper deck, flirting, smoking, singing You Are My Sunshine. I figured working for my living would give me the right to Saturday nights out and returning home on the ten o'clock bus. I could not wait.

On the day I left Great Silver school, as I walked past Mister Taylor's desk for the last time he faced me squarely and said: "Linda Bigford, you should not be leaving school to work in a shop; you should be going on to college. You and Angela Pyle; you both should take your education further. This is a criminal waste of intellect and ability."

I was amazed; he had never appeared to take more than a passing interest in me before; well, he never appeared very interested in any of his pupils. He regarded teaching at Great Silver Village School as a job he was stuck with. I considered telling Mum what Mister Taylor said, but I did not do so. To Mum, attending college was something 'the knobs' did.

Mum had been a parlour maid, in service at Great Silver Manor. Parlour maids were the frontline of domestic service, the maids who attended to the top hats and mantles of the visitors, and the maids upon whom the manner and organisation of the establishment might be judged. Only handsome girls with a sense of style were chosen for this vaunted position, and when she was a young girl Mum had been lovely.

Mum had waited on the best in the land; and because of the long association the Springbourne family had with Great Silver Manor there were regular visitors who had always known her name, her beginnings, and her parents. The marquises and dukes had watched her grow up; and would enquire after her retired gardener-father with great interest. Mum had greeted Lloyd George. Mum had been a successful career woman and she had left school at twelve.

And I was a carpenter's daughter.

CHAPTER EIGHTEEN

M Y BRILLIANT CAREER as a shoe saleswoman commenced with Middleford Co-op in August nineteen forty-eight. I was just fifteen.

Mum became a Co-op member with great haste. The previous week, neither Mum nor I had known such things as a Co-op divvie card existed. From that day forward everything the family needed, apart from the most basic foodstuffs, was purchased at Middleford Co-op. The store sold everything, from ham to evening frocks.

Bertha, Mary and Florrie also quoted Mum's divvie number on any visits they made to store. None of them had ever entered Middleford Co-op prior to my employment there; suddenly the store was inundated with Bigfords on every possible occasion.

The manager of Middleford Co-operative (Variety) was Mister Jenkins. He was a small man; at fifteen years of age I towered above him. He always wore a black jacket, striped trousers, a high-collared snowy white shirt and a black tie. His black shoes and his neat black hair were both polished to a patent leather-like gleam. He was polite and deferential to Mum, distant and formal with me. He promised Mum I would be trained to sell shoes in a professional manner, but firstly I would be expected to watch and learn, run errands and undertake minor cleaning tasks. He promised Mum that I would always be treated decently and fairly.

Mum was overwhelmed by my good fortune in obtaining such a position. Mum had left her home at twelve years of age to live at Great Silver Manor. She was fortunate that she had obtained employment in her home village; her younger sisters had found employment in great houses miles away from Great Silver. At twelve years of age, a rookie little maid, Mum rose each morning at five-thirty and blacked the grates.

She was allowed to visit her home for a few hours after church each Sunday. From the age of fourteen she also had a day off each month. It was considered inadvisable to allow girls under the age of fourteen a day off. The general consensus was that it would make them lazy.

Every penny she earned was passed on to her mother, although my grandfather was in secure employment and the family was financially comfortable. It was considered to be unfair to accustom girls to having their own money. After all, they would have none when they married.

She shared a tiny attic room with three other maids. On midwinter mornings the water in their wash jug stood frozen.

Maisie was an accomplished thief and helped herself to anything that was not actually nailed down; Ruby was an inveterate bully, not above pinching, hitting and kicking to get her own way; and Millie, a maid of all work and probably of a low intelligence, never actually washed herself unless forced to; she did not appear to understand that cleanliness was a personal requirement. Her family never washed at home. She could not believe the amount of time her roommates devoted to this pointless exercise. After all, you only got dirty again.

But the years saw Mum rise above the attic room.

Mum may have been ecstatic about my job, but I was not. I could not imagine a duller occupation than selling shoes.

I would pay my own keep and my own bus fares to Middleford. After all my expenses were met I would be allowed to keep about a third of my wages, but Dad insisted I deposited a weekly amount into a post office savings account.

My plaits had gone. I had some sensible lisle stockings and a suspender belt to hold them up. I planned to buy some nylons as soon as I could afford them.

Linda Bigford, grown-up!

Ethel had left school the previous year, but she had not managed to find employment, but there again, she never applied much enthusiasm to searching. She stayed at home with her Mum; the two of them spent their days reclining on the sagging sofa in the tiny sitting room, giggling the hours away. Ethel had already started smoking; and she always had enough money to buy cigarettes, or miniature toys or chocolate bars for her tiny brother, Peter. As I look back it horrifies me to wonder where or how she acquired the money.

She had one decent dress, an absolute find from Potinger's second-hand store in Middleford, it suited her totally and she looked stunning in it. Winter or summer, Ethel's legs were bare. She saw no point in wearing stockings.

Ethel was happy with her life.

CHAPTER NINETEEN

I LOVED THE SMELL of leather that was the essence of my new employment. I became accustomed to the draughty store room, the naked strip lighting in the showroom, and the customer's smelly feet.

My mentor was Miss Prendergast, a stern grey-haired lady of fifty. At first I was terrified of her, but I gradually came to realise she was as shy of me as I was of her. After I recovered from her superior and indifferent manner and she recovered from my shyness we got on like a house on fire. She taught me the art of sympathetic salesmanship.

Miss Prendergast had been born and brought up in Middleford. She knew the life history of many of our customers and she was an inveterate gossip, so in no time at all I knew the details of the love lives and the financial woes of many of Middleford's most influential citizens: told tactfully sotto voce when no-one else was around, of course.

Conversely, Miss Prendergast taught me order and personal organisation, how to handle customers' money, and the importance of total honesty. She taught me the value of her unassailable integrity. She had worked for the Co-op for almost thirty years.

On wet winter Mondays when customers were few and far between, and we had finally tired of tidying the storeroom or rearranging the tiny display we had in the corner of the street window, she would tell me about her personal life, about the boyfriend who went away to the first war. Nothing as sad as an untimely death; he merely preferred to marry a French girl.

She talked about her own family; she was the youngest, with a squad of older brothers. Being boys, they had all made their own way, had careers. Miss Prendergast had merely sold shoes at the Co-op and cared for her elderly, arthritic and temperamental mother alone.

Each year she took her mother for a fortnight's holiday at Weymouth. She looked forward to that with an almost painful anticipation.

I knew Miss Prendergast's first name was Olive, but I would never have dared to address her with such familiarity. We were always Miss Prendergast and Miss Bigford.

Although there were a number of young people employed at the Co-op I found it difficult to make friends. I had known the young people of Great Silver all my life; and my tiny fund of self-confidence was soon dissipated when faced with a bunch of apparently sophisticated strangers. Even though Middleford was a tiny town of about four thousand people it represented a sizeable metropolis to me. My relationship with my colleagues really was a case of "the town mouse and the country mouse". My youthful workmates were familiar with the cinema and the town hall dances, spending money on clothes because you want to buy them and not just because you need them, flirting in the memorial park and courting by the river.

I felt that they were all aware that I had only one change of clothes; and they could not fail to notice my height and skinniness, and my big feet.

All my previous visits to Middleford had been in the company of my family - and a Bigford family jaunt was always undertaken in great style; Mum in her best floral dress and navy straw hat; Dad wearing his twenty-year-old best suit. Mum would never consider a visit to Middleford that did not include either Bertha or Mary, or Florrie, complete with her tribe of kids. Dad always came along to buy the ice creams and hire deck chairs by the river. Very often one of Mum's sisters and her family came along as well. I did not realise until I commenced work how noticeable we must have been, as we straddled across the street, or blocked the pavements for other walkers. Our clothes were never town-smart. We carried packets of sandwiches and bottles of cold tea in an old straw basket. We were just a great bunch of noisy country-bumpkins out for a day on the town.

Faced with the town mice, this country mouse was struck dumb; they must have thought I did not have a tongue, but I had no idea how to begin to talk to them. Worse still, if any of the young male employees spoke to me I blushed crimson.

CHAPTER TWENTY

RNIE BADGER WAS an apprentice butcher, about nineteen, short, plump, with already a hint of baldness; he was not the type to set a girl's heart on fire. He teased me unmercifully: "Hello, here comes the prettiest girl from the village." My face would be as scarlet as a poppy. "How are the young swains of Great Silver going to get through today without their lovely Linda!" My eyes could not be dragged away from the floor. "I bet you have a lovely time in all those barns and hayricks out there, don't you Linda? Show the young yokels I thing or two, I'll be bound!" I would bolt out of the room quicker than a racing greyhound; behind me I would hear the rich chortles from all the male butchery staff. I knew that behind my back Ernie called me the Great Silver Maypole, again an illusion to my height. It was all very harmless; but sometimes I had a little cry about it into my pillow, when I thought how dumb I must seem. I longed to indulge in witty repartee, but I was too shy to open my mouth to answer even the simplest questions.

Paul Townsend did not think me dumb. He was a trainee floorwalker; he was even taller than me and reed thin. He reminded me of a great black rook, so dark were his hair and eyes against his white complexion. He always wore formal black suits, which hung on his skinny frame like wings folded to his sides. His shirts were frighteningly bleach-white and he wore a dark tie. His permanently-formal attitude suggested he never relaxed for a moment. When he walked the shoe department I would catch him looking at me slyly under his eyelids; and he would blush and look away.

The girls in the cosmetic department, and also those in lady's modes, had noticed Paul's blushes and they teased me about him: "He fancies you, when's the big date," "You want to hang in there, girl, he's a trainee manager," "Ooh, I can hear wedding bells for our Linda, and she has only been working here five minutes!" "What will Miss Prendergast say, when yet another shoe girl gets married." In response, I would of course blush, grin, and look stupid.

After work, Paul Townsend would sometimes follow me to the bus station, at a respectable distance, but I knew he was there. He gave me the creeps, but he was the only person on the Co-op staff who ever showed more than a passing interest in me. As my sixteenth birthday approached I began to think of him as 'my boyfriend.'

Ethel and Angie, who always found the minor details of my working life as exciting as any radio serial, were always chivvying me with questions as to whether any of the Co-op boys fancied me, or if I was 'getting off' with any of them. Neither of those two young ladies had ever suffered a moment's shyness, and if they had been in my shoes, figuratively as well as literally, they would already have a number of devoted followers. During my first months at the Co-op I would just nod my head, lower my eyes and change the subject; but as time passed I would consciously drop the name Paul into the conversation.

Ethel and Angie were enchanted. "What does he look like?" "Well, he has dark hair and he is taller than me," at least that was a step in the right direction. "When are you going out with him?' "Oh, you know Mum would never let me." That was the truth. "Is he an apprentice?" "Well actually he is a trainee manager."

Ethel's and Angie's eyes bulged with amazement; they were spellbound. No radio serial was ever this exciting. Linda Bigford had succeeded in life! Both girls believed that a little romantic dalliance did no harm but one did not merely dally with a trainee manager. They considered it was my duty to marry him with undue haste.

"Your Mum will be ever so pleased, why don't you bring him home." "It'll be one in the eye for your Iris; she always thinks she is so much better than everyone else. When you marry a manager, that'll show Mrs High-and-Mighty."

"What does he kiss like?" As if I knew! I had never been kissed, and honestly I did not think I would like it very much. Ethel and Angie, needless to say were already pass masters in the art of kissing. They believed one should 'kiss and tell' as often as possible.

CHAPTER TWENTY ONE

RECEIVED THE BIGGEST surprise of my life on my sixteenth birthday, which was a Saturday. As I walked into the Co-op shoe department at eight-thirty on the dot, Miss Prendergast's plain good-natured face seemed to smirk. She was not by nature a smirker. I was too self-centred to be curious about other people but I did consider Miss Prendergast's smirk odd, and I wondered why.

She wished me a happy birthday and asked me to tidy the store room, all in one sentence. I sighed and mentally looked forward to a morning of intense boredom, but did as I was bid.

As I entered the storeroom the most unbelievable sight met my eyes. A large box, wrapped in scarlet crepe paper stood in the middle of the floor. Hanging across the shelves, pinned onto the neatly piled shoe-boxes was a large banner made from an old bedsheet; with HAPPY BIRTHDAY LINDA painted in scarlet paint. I could only stand and gape.

"Look in the box" insisted Miss Prendergast, her voice a frenzy of urgency.

I crept towards it as if it contained a fierce wild animal.

80

"Oh, go on, it won't bite you." The blush rose in my cheeks, Linda Bigford looking stupid again.

Miss Prendergast giggled, a flashback to the girl she had once been. The box was cram-packed full of the strangest bits and pieces imaginable.

On the top of the pile was a smart tan leather shoulder bag, with fond greetings to dear Linda (she used my first name!) from Olive Prendergast, on a neat card. I tried to thank her, between scarlet blushes and stammering; I was overwhelmed.

Sticking up in the middle of the box was a length of dowelling painted with gold and blue stripes, with multicoloured ribbons hanging from it. A maypole for the Great Silver Maypole! With 'big kisses and see you later behind the bicycle shed' from Ernie Badger. An ornamental gift bag contained all the old perfume tester bottles; pens and pencils from the girls in stationery; some white net gloves, that had become marked, and had been washed by Elise the Ladies Fashion buyer; some broken biscuits, my favourite, sugar coated Nice, from groceries; and a carefully copied out recipe for stewed pig's liver, suitable for a manager's wife, from the butchery department, as well as a voucher for six private typing lessons, from Grace, the formidable company secretary, who believed all women should learn to type; she always claimed it would be more beneficial than learning to cook.

Grace proved to be an expert teacher. After only six lessons I was a fairly proficient copy typist.

I was queen for a day. My morning tea was poured for me. An iced teacake with a candle on it awaited me at lunch in the tiny crowded attic which served as our refreshment room. Everyone, even Mister Jenkins, wished me a happy birthday.

I would always be shy, I would continue to be Ernie Badger's maypole, I did not know how to talk to my peers, and I still stuck out like an extremely long sore thumb; but for just one day, my sixteenth birthday, my workmates at the Co-op made me feel important.

Creepy Paul Townsend was following me as I walked the hundred yards or so to the bus station, but I chose to ignore him.

The May evening was warm and sunny; birthday tea would be served in the garden; with every Bigford or Springbourne for miles round present to eat Mum's jam sponge and pass on their greetings. I would have so much to tell them. Grown-up Linda Bigford, the village bastard, was beginning to cope with her unfortunate parental history.

CHAPTER TWENTY TWO

THEL BECAME HEAVILY involved in her first romance during the halcyon days of early summer. Bluebells in the woods and cowslips in the meadows always produced romantic yearnings in our next-door neighbours. Maudie usually developed a passionate sexual liaison during May; and usually, but not exclusively, with someone else's husband. Fifteen-year-old Angie was already exchanging long looks with the blacksmith's son. Before September yellowed the leaves of the lime trees they would have exchanged considerably more than long looks.

Seventeen-year-old Ethel trolloped among the May blossom and cowslips with an ease learned by imitating her mother. Ethel's modesty had never been her most obvious attribute, and innocence and chastity departed without notice when she clapped her eyes on David Miller, an itinerant farm worker in temporary employment with Farmer Williams at Little Silver.

When David turned up at the Village Hall Easter Saturday Dance, Ethel could not believe her luck. He was eighteen, tall, stripling slim, and darkly handsome. From that evening onward Ethel and David spent every free moment together; and, as Aunt Beat lost no time in pointing out, their intentions were never exactly innocent.

Ethel had a served a sexual apprenticeship in most of the barns and haylofts around the Silver Villages that had begun when she was eleven. By the time the long evenings of mid-May exposed their liaison to any villager, even the half-blind or wall-eyed, they had progressed to an almost marital state of let's-get-it-over-with-as-soon-as-possible. (And as often as possible, Ethel insisted on that.)

Each weekend we three girls still spent long hours chewing the fat on the rickety wooden bench outside their backdoor. Ethel's only subject of conversation was her gorgeous David. She left nothing to the imagination and it was obvious even to me that their relationship had a powerful sexual basis. I still worried our conversations would be overheard by Mum or Aunt Beat, resulting in parental termination of my friendship with Ethel, for my own good, of course!

Ethel was convinced their passion would be eternal. Occasionally, if I could slip a word in edgeways between Ethel's breaks for breath, (and that girl could talk without obviously breathing for hours on end), I would drop Paul's name into the conversation. "Bring him home, let us meet him," they would both chorus.

I would jokingly say "I wouldn't let any boyfriend of mine within an arm's length of you two; if I did I would never see him again."

They loved it. They agreed.

CHAPTER TWENTY THREE

P AUL TOWNSEND STILL followed me to the bus station after work most evenings. Now I had a good look at him, I disliked what I saw, but if he was the only boy that fancied me, so be it. He was tall and very thin; I could not hold that against him, let's face it, so was I.

Paul wore unbelievably white shirts and he always ponged of bleach. His hands were as white as his shirt; I was accustomed to men who earned their living by their manual exertions and Paul's hands seemed effeminate to me. His fingers were long, and his nails filbert. If he talked, he began and ended each conversation with a snort. He looked down his long nose at the other young male employees at the Co-op with an air of superiority. No laughter or smile ever broke the already severe lines of his young face; he was devoid of any humour. Young mothers with prams or toddlers at their side, admiring the bed linen display in the Co-op would rate an angry glare. Paul Townsend considered that he was God's gift, not just to Middleford Co-op, but to retailing in general.

I did not fancy Paul but I wanted a romance, to have someone in my life, someone I could claim with confidence as being my boyfriend. I was aware he was snobbish, arrogant and conceited, but he was also painfully bashful with girls, and because of that my heart ached for him. Although I was pathetically grateful for his interest I never encouraged him to follow me but I did not discourage him either. I spent long hours dreaming of the day when he would ask me to the pictures or out to tea; and, better still, when I could bring him home and show Mum my trainee-manager boyfriend. I pretended to myself I liked him, that we might fall in love. Deep in my heart I found him repellent.

He finally plucked up the courage to approach me on a hot July evening. Not only did he follow me to the bus station, but he jumped on his bicycle and followed the bus.

Paul's normally pale face was pink with exertion and he was perspiring, but he also looked scared stiff. His voice was pitched squeaky and shrill. "Linda, will you come out with me?"

Would I! I could hardly believe my ears. Yes, this was Linda Bigford being asked for a date by a trainee manager!

I asked him if he had eaten tea; he said he had not. I invited him to come and meet my Mum, but he nearly died of fright. I agreed to meet him at the post office at six thirty. He disappeared into the shop to buy a cold pork pie and a bottle of fizzy lemonade, made lukewarm by standing unrefrigerated in the hot weather.

Now, to deal with Mum and Dad! Fortunately when I entered our cottage kitchen neither Aunt Beat, Merle, or for that matter any of the rag, tag and bobtail of numerous other family members were there; just Mum and Dad, sitting each side of the range, listening to the radio news.

"Mum, I have got a date; can I go out at half-past six?" I knew the answer would be yes; but I would have to endure the inquisition first.

I think what must be referred to as a knowing look passed between Mum and Dad. "Didn't I tell you, Reg," expostulated Mum.

Dad feigned an attitude of mild disinterest, but none-the less asked: "And who's the lucky young man?"

"His name's Paul, he's from work."

"Didn't I tell you, Reg," when Mum became excited, her conversation apparently became stuck on one to-be-repeated sentence.

"And do we get to meet Paul?" This from Dad.

"I asked him in for tea. I think he was too shy to come." Might as well try the truth.

Mum and Dad looked at each other and giggled; they sounded like Maudie and one of her idiot boyfriends.

"What does he do at work?" Mum's question.

"He's a floor walker, a trainee manager. He's eighteen."

Mum glowed, she preened, she gloated. "You've got a date with a trainee manager! Did you hear that, Reg! Oh Linda, I am so glad you're meeting nice boys".

Just ever so slightly, somewhere at the back of my mind a nasty, sneaky thought intruded that being a trainee manager did not necessarily make Paul nice. I quashed the thought immediately.

What's he like? Where does he live? Do you have lunch together? What do his parents do? Did he go to the

Grammar School? I dodged the interrogation as well as I was able; all the while downing bread spread with golden syrup, and a large chunk of walnut cake. I promised I would ask him to tea again next week. I promised I would be back at half past nine. I promised to be 'a good girl.'

Paul was waiting for me, his bicycle leaning against the post office wall. Glancing back along the main street of Great Silver to our cottage, he asked, "Is that where you live?" There was a hint of distaste in the question. I knew nothing about him, where he lived, or about his family.

He wanted to know so much, so many questions. Do you have brothers and sisters? What does your Dad do? How long have you lived in Great Silver? Wouldn't you like to move somewhere nicer? Do you really mean you haven't got a bathroom? It was clearly the evening for interrogation, but at least it meant that making ordinary conversation was unnecessary. Just as well; I would not have been able to think of anything to say.

When we reached the summit of the Down we walked over to the top of the old disused chalkpit and sat with our feet dangling over the edge, exposed for all the world to see. No high jinks or shenanigans here.

The huge crimson ball of sun set behind the Downs; the priceless view began to fade into a muted lilac dusk. He talked about his plans to move to a bigger town, Reading, Southampton, and complete his training in a large store there; eventually he had his heart set on working in Bond Street. His Dad was a funeral director; his two older brothers would follow their father into the business. He had piano lessons, and was hoping to learn to play the saxophone. He was fond of chess and was a local champion.

After he had established the comparative lowliness of my origins he did not appear to be interested in anything about me; which was good, as I still could not think of anything to say.

I was home by nine o-clock. I had agreed to meet him on Saturday evening in Middleford. If the weather was fine we would walk by the river.

Ethel and Angie were enraptured. No romantic radio serial could ever compare with Linda's working days and great romance at the Co-op.

Mum continued to pump me for every detail of Paul's life; at least I was able to tell her his father was a funeral director. "Not Townsend's the funeral directors," she squeaked, "Did you hear that, Reg! Oh Linda, you hang on to him! You could end up owning your own house. You could have a car, go on holiday every year, even go abroad," She still had not 'run down' ten minutes later, and she was already saying that perhaps the village hall would not be quite good enough for a Townsend wedding reception!

Dad chortled with laughter every time Mum started on her usual theme. Dad said she was put on this earth to be a Mother-in-Law. Mum swiped his arm with the tea towel.

Paul and I were two people who had spent a couple of hours having a very one-sided conversation while our long legs dangled over the edge of the old chalkpit. I felt the prospective nuptials were slightly premature.

I tried to smother the feeling that I heartily disliked Paul, but it crept through at the most inconvenient moments.

CHAPTER TWENTY FOUR

W E HAD AGREED to keep our relationship a secret from our colleagues. I suspected Paul suggested that because he was ashamed of me.

Saturday evening was cool and cloudy, threatened rain, but never actually got round to it. We walked down by the river, below the willows, where the yellow irises and white milk maids glowed phosphorescent in the dismal evening light as we crossed the water meadows.

Paul talked about work, making snide remarks about Ernie Badger, "totally gormless; full of blab and bluster with no brain; it's a good thing he is an apprentice butcher; that's all he's fit for!" He looked down his long nose at the female staff from cosmetics, lingerie and ladies fashions; "Just stupid small-town tarts who have just one thought in their facile little minds, and that's marriage. Then there's that frustrated old battle-axe, Miss Prendergast, or whatever her flipping name is; she should have been pensioned off years ago."

I tried to defend my friends. He assured me that they had got me exactly where they wanted me. "Don't listen to them, Linda. Can't you see they are just using you? They call you a maypole behind your back."

Actually they called me a maypole to my face!

I gathered he did not like our colleagues, the people whose friendship I valued greatly. I should have told him there and then to clear off, but I could not face not having a boyfriend, being 'someone special' to a particular fellow. The trouble was, I felt he did not like me either. Goodness knows why he was dating me.

In the gathering dusk we sat on a fallen tree bole, bright with orange speckled fungi, at the end of a small coppice. The spot was hidden, darkly secret, made for lovers. He suddenly gathered me into his arms and kissed me. Well, this was it! His lips were dry and stiff, he forced his tongue into my mouth. I tasted sour breath. His skin smelt of coal tar soap; his black suit was old and musty, perhaps it was one of his father's ex-funeral suits. I smelt his personal odour; slightly sweaty, cheesy, stale like dead mice. The kiss seemed to last for an eternity. My only thought as we drew apart, what was all the fuss about? I knew I would rather not be kissed by Paul. I also knew there would be more kisses.

The rain was teeming down by the time the bus arrived at Great Silver post office. The potholes in the gravel of the village street were filled with muddy water; raindrops spattered from the branches of the elm tree outside the school door. I was grateful for the security of home; even Aunt Beat glowering as she listened to "Take it from Here" on the radio was a comfort in the face of my destroyed romantic dreams.

Mum's face was bright, expectant, awaiting her vicarious

enjoyment of the exciting details of a trip to the cinema, or tea in a café. I felt ashamed of a walk by the river. I knew that Paul was not about to spend any of his money on me, and I really did not see why he should. I earned so little that I did not have enough left over to pay for my own café delights.

"We, um, had tea at the Cadena," I volunteered.

Mum was duly impressed. "Did you hear that, Reg? The Cadena! Oh, I would love to have tea there. The white table cloths are always so nice when you look in the window. You are lucky, Linda, to get a young man with Paul's prospects; someone who can afford posh teas out. You wouldn't get that with a Great Silver boy; all you get then is a visit to his Ma on Sunday afternoon," Mum swiped Dad's arm with the ever present tea towel and Dad chortled into the Evening Standard.

"We, um, only had tea and cakes," I was hungry, and required a large helping of bread and golden syrup as a matter of urgency.

"Yes, Oohh Linda, now that is smart! Of course you would expect a young man of Paul's background to be a bit refined." Unfortunately too refined to eat proper meals! I headed for the larder and the breadboard.

But Mum was in full flow. What was his house like? (I did not even know where it was.) Did his Mum have a cleaning lady? (Not what teenagers spend Saturday evenings discussing.) Does he like dancing? You must invite him out to the August Bank Holiday Social. (Heaven forbid.) Can he ride, he surely had riding lessons? (All the better to look down on us lesser mortals.)

I volunteered he had piano lessons and was hoping to learn to play the saxophone. Mum immediately invented a marvellous musical talent to go with the enviable job prospects. Mum insisted I invited him to tea. I said he was too shy at this time; and that at least was true.

By bedtime Mum had got me into a detached house, with university educated children, my own car, and a maid. She was enjoying herself. I wasn't. I tore off to bed before she had me buying Great Silver Manor or had Paul knighted for services to retailing.

I crept into the safety of my bed, and cried a tear or two into my pillow because kissing was so horrible. I lay there listening to the hiss of the rain on the roof and tried to work out why I continued to date Paul. I needed to have my own fella, to be lovely enviable Linda whose boyfriend has prospects, even for a short while, even if it was just not true. I was unable to face telling him to clear off.

CHAPTER TWENTY FIVE

P AUL AND I agreed to meet and walk on the Downs on Wednesday evening. I was sweet sixteen and supposedly meeting my sweetheart. In my true heart I was dreading it. I was hoping it would rain and our meeting would be abandoned but Wednesday evening was fair, cloudless, with a light breeze and the peal of St Edmunds' bellringers practice in the pure Downland air, to be heard over all the Silver Villages.

I was aware that Paul was totally self-centred. So was I, if push came to shove, but I was too shy to talk about myself. Paul was describing in great detail his amazing ability to play tennis when we started to climb the skew path across the open face of the Down. He was undoubtedly a brilliant player; his long slim body was naturally athletic, his every movement perfectly co-ordinated; but he continually bragged about his various abilities, and I wished desperately that we could occasionally talk about something other than his self-sought brilliance. None-the-less, the somewhat one-sided conversation was pleasant enough. I was unable to think of a conversational gambit anyway. We did not hold hands, in the fashion of so many country sweethearts, but walked companionably side-by-side.

At the summit of the Down there was an area of rough sheep pasture, which in August was a riot of colourful wildflowers. It was too early for rosebay, with its daring, shocking pink blossoms; but the ultramarine and purple wild geraniums and white and yellow bedstraw bloomed in abundance beside the brilliant poppies. In the corner of the pasture there was small spinney of beech trees growing on a grassy indentation in the chalky ground.

We sat together, our backs against a sturdy beech, side-by-side; our legs straight out in front of us.

After a while we began to kiss, almost casually, lightly, his tongue staying coyly inside his own mouth. The truth was I found this almost pleasant. I gazed into his eyes, which I had always thought of as being dark brown, almost black; but they were actually the deepest blue, the colour of wet slate roofs in the gloom of a winter dusk.

I was aware of his erection, as he pressed his body hard against mine, but it did not trouble me; it was what I had expected. His hand gently clasped my breast; and I quickly pushed his hand away with a breathy 'no!' He returned to stroking my back between my shoulder blades; it felt tender and pleasant and I could have enjoyed that for a long time.

"Linda, you are so beautiful!" He said that! I wanted to protest, 'No! I am too tall, skinny and ugly,' but my delight in hearing this marvellous lie was so intense that all I could manage was another breathy sigh. All my life I had longed to be told I was beautiful.

Gradually his caresses became more intense. His

tongue intruded; his passionate kisses made demands my lips could not return. His fingers gently edged under my T-shirt, inside my bra; in spite of myself my nipples had hardened at his touch. Then he withdrew his hands from my clothing and clasped my face in his hands, gazing into my eyes. He was trembling and he had become extremely hot. "You are the most beautiful girl I have ever seen. Oh Linda I love you so much!"

My mind was not in my head, my body. My mind was somewhere on the perimeter, watching this scene and telling me that this was Paul Townsend who loved no-one but himself. I switched my mind off.

What I really wanted a nice canoodle while Paul told me again that I was beautiful and he loved me. Paul wanted something entirely different; and I needed so desperately to be loved that I was powerless to prevent him.

He removed my skirt and my knickers; I felt a moment's shamed embarrassment that they were white cotton with elastic legs, and not silk with gorgeous coffee lace trims. With immense care he removed his trousers and his underpants, folding them into a neat pile on the grassy turf, and stood in his shirttails. He looked totally ridiculous; and somewhere my mind tried to intrude on the scene and prompted me to laugh. I smothered that. Being loved was a serious business.

I do not know why I thought the sexual act would not hurt. Well, it did; it hurt like hell. My whole body felt as though it was being ripped apart. All I could see was Paul's head wagging up and down, his eyes closed and his teeth clenched as he furiously bounced on my protesting body. The stones of the hard ground felt as though they were breaking my back. As the pace of the bouncing increased he started to utter ugly, guttural, animal sounds, blending with my own shrieks of pain. The rhythmic bouncing and the groans grew in pace like a speeding express train, ever louder, ever more painful until I thought I would die; and after three massive shudders he suddenly stopped. Still inside me, he propped himself on his hands, and drew in great sobbing breaths. Tears, spittle and snot were on his face. His body smelled of dead mice. He withdrew from me and flopped down on top of me, his head buried in my breasts.

I hated him! With one almighty heave I shoved him off. He rolled onto the floor of the spinney, with a little grunt of surprise and pain.

I had to leave. If I had stayed with him one moment longer I would have died of humiliation, shame and embarrassment. Or I would have strangled him.

With speed borne of desperation I jumped up and grabbed my scattered skirt and knickers. I was badly bruised and blood was flowing freely down between my legs, my insides felt as though they had escaped. I would never be able to look him straight in the eyes again. Death still presented a welcome alternative; but I would not die here, not where he was.

I dried my tears on the hem of my bloodied skirt. I straightened my back and tried to adjust my expression to the bland pleasantness necessary before I entered the cottage and faced Mum and Dad. Paul was probably hiding himself, dealing with his own pain and humiliation.

I wanted to be in my bedroom, I wanted it to be dark. A flood of relief passed through me that I no longer shared a bedroom with Merle. I was desperate to be alone.

CHAPTER TWENTY SIX

I TORE THROUGH THE front door and bolted up the stairs three at a time. Mum and Dad gaped in amazement, which soon gave way to excited giggles as they clutched each other's arms.

"Their first lover's tiff!" This from Dad.

"I hope it's not all over," Mum, ruefully. She would wish that. "Kiss and make-up time, over sandwiches, lunchtime tomorrow in the park."

More giddy laughter from the pair of them. Aunt Beat snarled from her corner that I had no manners and I should be brought back downstairs to speak civilly to everyone. What the youth of today were allowed to get away with, etcetera, etcetera.

Merle regarded my fleeting intrusion with mild interest and returned to her crochet.

In the solitude of my bedroom I removed my bloodied underwear. Washing was done once a week in the cottage, usually on a Monday if the day was fine; and to wash knickers on a Wednesday evening would have caused much consternation and questioning. I stowed the bloodied garments away in the bottom of my drawer; I would wash them at the time of my period in a fortnight or so, and claim that my monthly flow was extra heavy. Experience had taught Mum to keep a very maternal eye on me, and she always knew when my 'curse' was due.

Spitefully, I wondered if Paul had got some of my blood on his underwear, and how he would explain that to his mother.

The gentle late spring dust crept around me as I lay on my bed with my handkerchief stuffed into my mouth. I refused to cry. Although I had never actively encouraged Paul I had been prepared to accept everything he did to me. If I did not like the outcome, I had only myself to blame.

CHAPTER TWENTY SEVEN

THE NEXT MORNING dawned cloudy and inclined to rain. I struggled downstairs to the breakfast table, but I could not face eating the fried eggs and bacon Merle had prepared for me. "Too high and mighty to eat decent food," snarled Aunt Beat, as the meal was fed to the dog. I managed only a cuppa and a slice of dry toast, much to Mum's consternation. Mum would insist that everyone ate a good breakfast if the Day of Judgement was about to start in five minutes.

"Fallen out with the high-class boyfriend, have we?" sneered Aunt Beat. I seriously wished her marmalade sandwich would choke her.

Merle regarded me with mild interest, and then she got on with the washing-up.

Miss Prendergast was her usual bossy, friendly self. I received my orders for the day; clean this, tidy that, do something about that display. Miss Prendergast had also heard a snippet of juicy gossip about the head master of the local grammar school, and was making much of totally disbelieving it.

I received my orders, and Miss Prendergast's shared

confidences, in stony silence. I avoided her eyes whenever she looked directly at me.

I was dreading the moment when Paul prowled by, doing his floor walking. He did not floor-walk near me for a whole fortnight; probably he felt as self-conscious as I did.

After a week of taciturnity on my part Miss Prendergast was showing an almost maternal concern. "Linda, if there is something we can talk over, or if it is something I have done to upset you, then please say so." Puzzlement and bewilderment showed on her homely face, as I re-organised yet another Clark's Shoe display in desultory silence. I shook my head, turned my face away.

After a fortnight of my grim-faced silence and Miss Prendergast's almost grandmotherly concern Mister Jenkins called me into his office. He was friendly, but formal. "Now Linda, if there is something wrong here in the Co-op you must tell me!" I shook my head, not lifting my eyes from their intense inspection of the office floor.

"No trouble with your colleagues? I always thought you were a bit of a favourite with the other salesgirls; you have developed some worthwhile friendships in the short period you have been with us."

Head-shaking on my part; regarding the office floor with renewed intensity.

"You do get on alright with Olive Prendergast, don't you? She speaks highly of you; claims you are the best young saleswoman she has trained in many a long year. Oh, I know Olive can be difficult, and she is a bit old-fashioned, but are you having trouble getting along with her?"

He established that I felt reasonably happy in my work,

that Miss Prendergast's friendship was valuable to me. He sighed, "So you have got trouble at home." He did not wait for an answer, knowing I would fervently deny everything. "Just remember I have a very sympathetic ear if you need someone to talk to. Don't just give us up as being an uncaring bunch. Linda, we are your friends and we are worried about you. Middleford Co-op is a family concern, and in your family there is always someone to turn to, so don't fight your demons on your own."

But oh! What demons! I could not bear another living person to know my family history and background or the details of my corrupted relationship with Paul Townsend. I felt like dying, but that clearly was not an option on a Thursday morning in the manager's office at Middleford Co-op.

CHAPTER TWENTY EIGHT

I DID HAVE ANOTHER problem; I could not recall having 'the curse'. My periods had never been tiresome, unlike some girls at school who had suffered terrible pains, in bed for a week, couldn't walk, that sort of thing - but mine had always been painless and regular; just a good bleed for about three days.

Mum always kept a weather eye on my 'monthlies'; I resolved to save her any undue worry. I managed to convince myself that I had bled, but I had just not noticed. Yes, that was definitely what had happened!

Menstruation was a private thing and not for the general round-table discussion which occurred in our household over almost any subject under the sun. Modesty ensured that we burned soiled sanitary towels in the kitchen range early in the morning when Dad was at work.

Consequently I made a big show of burning three completely-unused sanitary towels each day for three days, and I had the bloodied clothes I had hidden following the evening with Paul, which I needed to wash. The dried blood was impossible to remove and involved me in much scrubbing and bleaching of my knickers. Mum merely observed that my period had seemed heavier than usual: "Being a woman is never easy, Linda."

Yes, I had noticed!

CHAPTER TWENTY NINE

WAS AMAZED THAT life went on as usual. August became September, and the lime trees yellowed. Bertha's children and schoolmarm Iris returned to school, and housewives began to lay up stores of coal against the approaching frosty mornings.

Merle continued her silent occupation of the back bedroom, and arranged flowers and children at the vicarage. Mum took all her grandchildren blackberrying; this was regarded as a formal outing second in importance only to Bonfire Night, Christmas and Easter. A row of varied jars of preserves grew along the cottage window sills. Mum pickled eggs in huge earthenware crocks and onions in small glass jars and the aroma of spice infiltrated the house for days.

Aunt Beat developed a bout of bronchitis and was confined to bed for a week. Mum was almost run off her feet, fetching and carrying at the old harridan's command.

Six days a week the Great Silver bus trundled up hill and down dale, stopping at every hamlet, corner, row of cottages, and signpost on its way to Middleford, dispersing and loading passengers far and wide and carrying reluctant Linda Bigford to and from the Co-op.

In late September Ethel and David's romance was still going strong. Most evenings after ten minutes of polite conversation with the other occupants of the cottage Ethel and David rushed for Ethel's bedroom; as her Mum and her Gran said: stopping them now was like shutting the stable door after the horse has flown.

Not one snippet of this interesting information had escaped the sharp eyes of the villagers at large; because let's face it, the Pyles were not a family much given to keeping secrets.

The affair shocked the good women of the village for whole afternoons at a time. The Vicar knew, but he was understanding; Miss Landport knew, but as she said, what do you expect from such a low family. Lady Margaret at Great Silver Manor had heard the news from her lady's maid, and was duly shocked.

The fact that young Peter would be snoring away on his pallet in the corner of the bedroom while the young lovers swooned and grunted through their loving, (Maudie claiming that kid would sleep through an earthquake), was another facet that had not escaped the villager's notice; and as for Angie, she had been threatened with her life if she entered the shared-bedroom before David was dressed and downstairs. Too, too shocking and something should be done about that family! But nothing ever was.

CHAPTER THIRTY

MUM SAID: "SHE shouldn't be moping round the house like this. She never goes out, not even round next door. She needs to see a doctor."

Dad said: "What for, does he know how to cure a broken romance? She'll get over it in her own good time. Leave her alone, she'll come round."

Bertha said: "Aw snap out of it Linda, plenty more fish in the sea." If that is the case, dear sister, then why the heck did you marry Alf?

Mary said: "Happened to me when I was sixteen; I can't even remember what he looked like now!" Possible short and dour, nearly bald, like Don?

Aunt Beat said: "You great lummox, did you really suppose someone from a good family like the Townsends would fancy you? Never in a blue fit, my girl. Not a big haporth of misery like you!"

Merle just glanced at me with her usual mild curiosity and got on with her knitting. I wanted to scream at her, to holler at her, to clang saucepans before her placid, composed face, to yell at the very top of my lungs: "Look at me! I am your daughter for God's sake! Can't you see me! Am I invisible or something? Look at me!"

That is when I knew. Yes, I was invisible. Paul Townsend no longer looked at me when he passed me. Why would he? Not if I was invisible.

During my daily journey to work, people still spoke to me on the bus, or when I walked along Great Silver Village Street. The village people were so understanding about invisibility. Invisible people never speak; so basically, I stopped replying when spoken too.

I was almost invisible at work. Miss Prendergast saw me; her kindness was overwhelming. Ernie Badger saw me. He still teased me, and I still blushed; but sometimes I caught him watching me with a querulous, inquisitive look on his plain freckled face. When I returned his glance he would purposefully look away.

The other people at work did not see me. The girls from lingerie, the boys in butchery, the ladies in fashions, and the office staff never looked at me now. It was just as if I was not there. Well, I was of course, but this invisibility made it impossible for them to know that. An invisible person signed for my wages packet every week. As I was invisible there was no point in going to the tea room. I no longer had tea breaks, and I took my lunch in the park each day, sitting in my sopping mackintosh in the teeming autumn rain.

CHAPTER THIRTY ONE

SPENT ALL MY spare time in my bedroom, sitting on my bed and staring at the floor emerging only for meals which I barely ate. Mum became concerned when most of the food I was served remained on my plate. Prior to this my appetite had rivalled that of the proverbial horse.

Some mornings I just felt sick. I only had to place my feet to the floor for the room to spin and vomit rise in my throat. Vomit would be visible, even if I was not, so I swallowed the vile tasting mess and waited for the room to stop spinning and resume its normal position. Mum grew concerned as I arrived at breakfast later each morning, my face pale as paper, to be presented with a meal I did not eat.

Mum feared I would lose weight, and my long skinny frame would become emaciated, but this did not happen. I actually put on a little weight in September and October, Mum said thank God I was growing outwards at last; after all I had spent enough time growing upwards. I was amazed she could see me.

At work Miss Prendergast praised my newfound 'bonniness', saying that a little more flesh on my bones certainly suited me; and I was fast growing into a fine-looking young lady.

I would need to be very careful; I did not want to attract attention. I had no wish to become visible again. I wore loose clothing and clodhopper shoes, and paid very little attention to my appearance. I stopped wearing make-up, although six months earlier I had been thrilled to be able to wear lipstick and powder every day; and with joyful anticipation I had looked forward to the time Mum would allow me to wear eyeshadow and mascara.

November came and bonfire night. The rest of the family traipsed down to Ray and Florrie's to watch the three boys let six months' hard-earned pocket money go up in shocking pink and lime green smoke in less than two hours.

Mum and Dad pleaded with me to accompany them. I said no, I hate bonfire night; and what about Brutus? He hates bonfire night too. This was true; and the family was delighted with my sudden concern for the great, hairy, smelly animal; Mum and Dad both remarking to each other, have you noticed how fond Linda is of Brutus just lately. Aunt Beat did not go of course; and so determined was I not to leave my room I was quite prepared to offer to look after her also, if it was necessary to ensure I was left at home. In retrospect I do not think anyone would have believed me!

Ethel's belly had grown very large, obvious even through her shabby mac; but it did not stop her running around like a giddy little girl. I was not surprised. She was a healthy seventeen year old girl, and her relationship with David had also been very - well - healthy.

I had not heard Mum and Dad discussing it, and I

no longer cared nor listened to what Aunt Beat said, but I figured my family were still unaware of this fascinating snippet of local news. Now that I was invisible I never spent time with Ethel and Angie, so I no longer knew the local gossip, or carried the tales home.

David had left Little Silver a week or so ago, at the finish of harvest. Momentarily I wondered if he knew about Ethel's condition before he left. Probably not; Ethel would no longer consider his presence necessary. She would enjoy motherhood, the anticipation and the fact, the way her mother always had. The presence of the father would only confuse matters.

Ethel may have found something to do with her time!

CHAPTER THIRTY TWO

I WORE LOOSE CLOTHING, working in a blue rayon smock similar to those worn by the girls in grocery. If they could have seen me, my colleagues in fashions and lingerie would probably have thought this odd. I was invisible, so it was alright.

Even Miss Prendergast and Ernie Badger became dim figures flitting around in the perimeter of my vision, occasionally looming before me, ships on a misty sea, their voices booming like foghorns.

I was obedient, biddable, quiet, willing, and totally in another world. I tidied the counter and stacked the shelves, but I may as well have been stacking bombs as pairs of shoes, such was my lack of awareness of my surroundings. I served customers with a polite smile; I was oblivious to their faces. I never looked straight at them, why should I? After all I was invisible to them. I knew they could not see me.

At home I smiled a lot, picked at my meals; ignored Aunt Beat and Merle, gazed at Mum and Dad with a distant silly grin and took no part in family affairs or conversations.

Mum and Dad worried volubly to each other over the

meal table about my state of mind and what would cheer me up.

I could not remember having my period; well, I must have, and I just did not notice it. I reflected that Mum would be upset if the pile of sanitary towels did not decrease with each month; so for three days each month I burned three perfectly clean sanitary towels in the range before anyone else was up, ensuring Mum could see the charred remains when she stoked the fire.

The sickness stopped and physically I felt much better, less tired than I had been.

CHAPTER THIRTY THREE

FIVE YEARS OF peacetime was to be celebrated with a good, old-fashioned Christmas. A huge spruce decorated with shining garlands towered over the Middleford Saturday market stalls in the town square, each stall lit with a lantern from the mid afternoon to ward off the swiftly-growing winter dark.

The shops glowed in the rainy midwinter gloom, displaying feminine scents and talcs in ornamental baskets, bottles of men's colognes in masculine deep brown and rich royal blue glass glistening in the brilliant light. For the purely practical family there were supplications to surprise Mum with a vacuum cleaner on Christmas morning. The amazing array of toys was unbelievable to a girl who had lived through wartime-home-made.

The grocery department at the Co-op was a delight with the oriental scents of dried fruit; chocolate boxes with beribboned puppies or views of Castle Combe, ornamental boxes of dates and Christmas cakes ready to be iced and decorated with plastic fir trees and snowmen. The nation was united in an almighty effort to surpass the famous pre-war Christmases of fond reminiscence.

Mum started to give the huge kilner jars of salted runner beans at the back of the larder shelf the glad eye. "I do hope they are alright. Reg does so love green beans with his Christmas dinner." Aunt Beat was crocheting something nameless and indescribable. In the past we had all received nameless and indescribable gifts from Aunt Beat. Merle was knitting doll's clothes as a surprise for Bertha's daughter Carol.

Briefly, I became visible again.

I felt so well, on the top of the world. I even smiled at people, with my eyes and my consciousness this time, and not just with my lips because it was expected of me.

I actually enjoyed my lunch hours, which were spent searching for gifts for my huge list of recipients.

I gave up eating my lunch on a park bench in the persistent December rain and returned to the friendly warmth of the attic. My colleagues welcomed me back cautiously, eyeing me guardedly from the unbridgeable distance of opposite sides of the tearoom as I enjoyed a few minutes close to the glowing tortoise stove before returning to Miss Prendergast and the freezing air of the footwear department.

We worked late on Christmas Eve, making premature preparations for the January sales. It was bitterly cold and river-valley foggy when I left work, and I ran to catch the Great Silver bus. The Salvation Army brass band was playing 'Oh Come All Ye faithful' under the spruce tree in the market square. Apart from their brazen consonance, the town was quiet as a tomb; all Middleford was at home, busy with their preparations for the most exciting peacetime Christmas morning ever.

The scarlet and green of the festive lights shone on the denuded shops.

I passed a vagrant dressed in an old khaki greatcoat, leading a small terrier dog on a string, tramping the bitter, foggy streets of Middleford.

CHAPTER THIRTY FOUR

A S THE BUS climbed towards the Silver Villages and the pure Downland air, the murk and fog of Middleford was left behind in the river valley. Above in a moonless sky the stars glittered: the Milky Way, the Plough, and the North Star, the star of winter; shooting stars and Christmas stars; look for your own Star-of-Bethlehem. The solstice had passed and spring was on its way, although the hoar frost glittered on the Downland grasses and the puddles were solid beneath my feet.

I was glad to be at home in the cottage; to enjoy the warmth of the range, to take pleasure in normal things: Mum rolling out yet another batch of mince pies; Merle decorating the tree in her inimitable style; Aunt Beat moaning and groaning and getting in the way; carols on the radio. Beyond, the eternal Downs slumbered in the frosty air.

Safety and gentleness, family! Although it lasted only for Christmas Day and Boxing Day it was as though the sun shone in the middle of the long dark winter.

I awoke on Christmas morning to the sound of communion bells at St Edmunds. I was not a communicant;

Mum was waiting for the next visit by the bishop when she would order me to attend confirmation classes. All the young people of my age would attend the classes when that happened; regardless of their belief or otherwise. You did what was expected of you in the Silver Villages.

Mum went to early Holy Communion only on special days; Christmas and Mothering Sunday. She would have been up some hours, leaving the makings of bread sauce and sage-and-onion stuffing on the draining board for later; then she donned her best hat and coat and strode purposefully along the village street, her warm breath standing in a white fug in the frosty air of the midwinter's dawn.

I knew just how important this early rising on Christmas morning was to Mum; she had been doing it all her married life. Before her marriage, in her Great Silver manor days, she would have been too busy with her humble chores to attend the luxury of an early church service; Christmas Day belonged to her ladyship and the family at the 'big house'. Boxing Day afternoon was the time Mum was allowed a few hours off to visit her own mother. Mum never got over her feeling of independent magnificence she experienced from going to early Communion on a hoar-frosty Christmas morning. This was Mum's personal sacred celebration.

We opened presents when Mum returned with much ooh-ing and aah-ing by everyone except Aunt Beat, who merely nodded, sneered, and placed her gifts in a neat pile on the arm of her chair. 'Thank you' did not appear to be a word in her vocabulary.

Mum and Aunt Beat, Bertha's family's Christmas

presents, along with the jars of salted green beans and the other residue of Christmas, were being collected by Alf in the car.

Dad, Merle and I mounted our trusty bikes, and pedalled furiously against the gripping cold. Merle's and my legs were clad only in our flimsiest nylon stockings, because above all else you looked your very best for Christmas dinner; but fine stockings were insufficient protection against the Downland chill, and our legs were blue with cold when we were barely out of the house for two minutes. We both gritted our teeth and tried not to think of the return journey late in the freezing evening.

Mum and Merle busied themselves in the kitchen even though Bertha, an organised housewife with years of Christmas experience, had already peeled a mountain of potatoes, scraped a stack of carrots and parsnips and shredded a brilliant green cabbage long before we arrived.

Me, Dad, Alf, Alf's Dad, and all the kids left for the matins service at St Edmunds. Aunt Beat was installed before the sitting room fire, moaning quietly to herself about the children of today. Mum, Bertha and Merle said they were too busy to attend church, and would stay home and cook, even though by that time there was little to do other than sit and wait for the tom cocks to tenderise.

After our vigorous rendering of "Oh Come All Ye Faithful" and "See amid the Winter Snow" we returned to Bertha's cottage, to find Mum and Bertha merry, their faces flushed and their eyes sparkling, singing some highly suggestive words to some very traditional carols. Even Merle was pink in the face and smiling. An empty bottle of Stone's Green Ginger and a well-indulged flagon of Mum's best home-made plum wine stood in the middle of the kitchen table.

Aunt Beat was asleep by the fire. She was partial to plum wine, she believed that it prevented sore throats and colds and for that reason she considered her consumption to be For Medicinal Purposes Only.

Mum produced the family photo albums (brought over with the stuffing and the green beans in the car that morning,) which produced a barely-stifled groan from Bertha. Mum reiterated at great length, complete with illustrations, on every Christmas the Bigfords had ever spent. Aunt Beat woke from her nap with a loud snort and an aromatic fart, and accused Bertha of not having a piano to accompany carol singing just to annoy her personally.

After Christmas dinner Eric was sick.

Merle and I shooed our elders into the tiny sitting room and donned two of Bertha's crossover floral pinnies, and prepared ourselves for two solid hours of washing up. It came as a welcome relief from close family company and Christmas cheer. I took a moment to wonder why Christmas was such a popular idea. I concluded that it was probably lovely if you were not a Bigford.

Mum finally finished the Bigford's Christmas story from about the middle of the last century onwards, trying Bertha's large store of patience to its limits, - and my sister was the most patient of women. Merle and I had replaced each plate, saucepan, cup, colander, into its home on Bertha's shelves; and Dad had beat Carol and Yvonne three times at ludo, which let's face it, granddads are not supposed to do.

Alf announced that seeing as we were going to Mary's for Christmas tea; he thought he should drive Mum and Aunt Beat (the empty kilner jars and the exhausted family albums) over to Mary's house before he got any drunker.

Dad, Merle and I donned coats and scarves; thanked Bertha profusely for the most delicious Christmas dinner ever; and kissed the kids, who were getting just a little bit fed up with politely accepting endless family kisses. We mounted our bicycles and headed through the gathering December dusk to the distant warmth of Mary's cottage. Her turn next!

Everyone waved goodbye to Mum and Aunt Beat, viewed through the rear window of Alf's car as he drove in a zigzag route along the dead straight Winchester Road.

Iris and Len visited us on Boxing Day, bringing a small bottle of dry sherry, which Mum hated but she was too shy to say anything, for fear of offending Iris. She had ever regarded Iris's taste as the epitome of sophistication. Iris also brought along yet another plate of mince pies, only hers were absolutely delectable, and of course she made her own mince meat.

Iris and Len wished us the compliments of the season in their usual formal, stilted manner, and my mind allowed me a brief glimpse of them wishing each other 'the compliments of the season,' with a brief, never-touching peck in the general area of each other's cheek, as they sat next to each other in their bed beneath the beautiful crimson silk eiderdown that Iris had so patiently hand quilted.

Florrie, Ray, their children, and various accompanying Caundles had been in and out of our house ever since the

121

Christmas season commenced, trailing mud on the freshly polished floor, and the new puppy piddling everywhere, much to Aunt Beat's shocked annoyance. Florrie, with a grand sweeping gesture and a deep bow, presented Mum and Dad with a large box of gaudy purple crepe paper crackers. Her kids then proceeded to pull all the crackers and the puppy to eat the purple crepe paper and the enclosed paper hats until the dear little creature produced some amazing purple-and-metallic sick onto Mum's hand-pegged rug before the range. Robbie got his Mother's back-hander for swearing when his cracker contained a tiny plastic thimble.

Boxing Day evening, a three-act-play on the radio, the gifts, cake, crackers, and excitement finished for another year. Mum heaved an enormous sigh of relief, flopped into her comfy chair, and declared: "That is that for another year, thank goodness, I'll never be able to work out why I do it!"

She knew exactly why she did it.

CHAPTER THIRTY FIVE

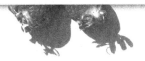

T HE NEW YEAR brought me no celebration; just more labour in the vineyard, or at least the freezing cold shoe department.

I could not remember when I had my period. I definitely had it; the decreasing contents of the box of sanitary towels in my wardrobe confirmed that. My waistline and bosoms increased in size; an increase so minimal it would not be noticeable to anyone else. I hid my true statistics, letting out the waistbands of my winter skirts by the light of my candle in the late evening, and attempting to stretch the unrelenting sides of my cotton bras. Miss Prendergast's pre-Christmas prediction of increased bonniness had never eventuated. I was still thinner than every other girl of my age that I knew.

Ethel's pregnancy, although little advanced, was exhibited with an ostentatious self-importance. She proudly flaunted pregnancy smocks in garish colours and patterns long before such disguise was necessary. She posted away requests for mail order catalogues which displayed an exciting range of baby clothes and furniture in pink, blue and fashionable lemon and dreamed herself a lengthy shopping list. When the time came she would manage with second-hand treats from Potingers; hand-outs from the Vicar's long-suffering fund for villagers in trouble; and the general good-nature of Great Silver people, who would knit and sew for her with willing hands and generous hearts.

The more self-righteous villagers sneered at 'that girl.' Ethel was totally unaware of the nastiest snubs. She would never snub anyone, and was too trusting and pleasant-natured to recognise such gross ill-manners in others. Hard-bitten old bags like Aunt Beat rarely made it into the village street anyway; and Ethel Pyle's impending happy event became just another occurrence in the day-to-day life of Great Silver. After all, the good women of the village had been expecting this pregnancy ever since she left school. Like mother, like daughter!

The girls at work were excitedly planning their outfits for Middleford's spectacular New Year ball to be held in the Town Hall. The conversation at tea-breaks and lunchtimes was all about full skirts and tight waists, broderie anglaise blouses, and shoes with heels like stilts, so they could jive with each other all night at the town hall, while the young men of the town propped up the bar and watched them.

I imagined myself in a full skirt, with my long skinny legs and my huge feet. My bony elbows were never meant for the delicacy of broderie anglaise. Enough! Invisibility suited me fine!

Mum and Dad could still see me. Merle had never been able to see me. Aunt Beat could not see me, and I could not hear her.

My sisters, Mary and Bertha, clearly could not see me;

they discussed me with Mum as though I was not present. "What's wrong with our Linda this time?" "A little Miss Misery-guts if you ask me; always sulking, always sour as lemons." "What she needs is to be taken out of herself!"

How did you do that? I was already as far out of myself as I could possibly be.

CHAPTER THIRTY SIX

J ANUARY BROUGHT SNOW. I remained invisible.

Angie cycled with a group of friends to the aircraft-part factory daily, rugged up in scarves and a scarlet tam o'shanter, wearing serviceable corduroy slacks and leather fur-lined boots. She always managed to look delectable, even with her nose scarlet and her cheeks purple from the bitter frost. The cyclists' giddy laughter at the simplest things warmed them as they furiously pedalled to escape the cold. They howled with laughter at tabby cats on gateposts, at men's long johns drying on cottage washing-lines; true laughter from their hearts.

I did not approve of laughing. It was months since I had laughed.

Mum and Dad were worried out of their minds over my silence. Mum announced she was taking me to Doctor Webster. Time to panic! I decided to have a day of normality and refused to go. You visited the doctor when you were sick; and there was nothing wrong with me, for goodness sake! No, they need not worry about me; I tried to assure them between false jollity and toothy smiles that I just hated the winter. I decided to buy a scarlet jumper; and demonstrated an almost scarlet enthusiasm regarding its purchase. I pranced around in it and preened before my bedroom mirror, showing it off to Mary and Bertha when they called round. Yes, I was very normal thank you. You just wait until summer; I promised I would positively bloom.

February came, and snowdrops, March and bitter wind and rain. My waist seemed larger still, but the front view of Linda was still a great, long, skinny yard of misery. My breasts developed a life of their own, and looked more like abscesses than pimples. I was not pleased; I had no wish to attract the attention of other people. I associated these unfortunate protuberances with the ability to attract men, which was so important to my nubile next-door neighbours.

Ethel, with genuine pride, paraded her enormous bosom before anyone who cared to look. The hand that rocks the cradle rules the world, Ethel knew that. In the meantime she thoroughly enjoyed her large breasts. Her interest in the opposite sex had not waned during the early months of her pregnancy; and although her belly expanded by the day it did not appear to have an inhibiting effect on the young men she met at the village dances. Poor David was almost forgotten; he had served his purpose.

Ethel was not averse to presents. She was particularly fond of chocolates, cigarettes and fruit. Ethel had quit wearing a brassiere; she bragged there were none big enough to fit her; and her large, hard nipples billowed beneath her cotton dress. She was delighted with herself, with life, and future motherhood.

I could not meet her brazen eyes. I avoided coming

face-to-face with her, and scurried off at the hint of her footfall.

The independence that working at the factory produced had a positive effect on Angie; she stood tall and elegant, curly hair gleaming like sunshine and a complexion like cream. Her taste in clothes, although flamboyant, suited her well and she never appeared common or gaudy. Men came running; but, unlike her sister and mother she was parsimonious with her favours; and consequently they became more desirable. Unlike her Gran and Mother, she did not swear, scream with giddy laughter, or scratch herself in the street. To the surprise of Great Silver as a whole, Angie Pyle seemed to be growing into a young lady.

She contributed readily to the family budget and was exceptionally generous to her little brother, Peter. She occasionally had great bursts of energy at the weekends; and had taken to washing the grimy floors and cleaning the cottage windows. She bought her Gran bottles of her favourite plonk; and was secreting away a store of little matinee jackets and bootees to surprise Ethel at the appropriate time.

I became more terrified of this paragon of virtue than I ever was of her virtue-less sister.

CHAPTER THIRTY SEVEN

STILL COULD NOT remember having my period, but I must have; and so I continued to burn three sanitary towels a morning, three days a month, in the kitchen range before anyone else was up and about.

Mum was serious in her intention to take me to Doctor Webster. I could not bear that, so like a programmed robot I produced smiles and cheerfulness at will; talking gaily with Mary and Bertha about nothing in particular; making an extravagant fuss of Brutus the dog; and even offering to wind wool for Merle. As soon as I considered my preposterous good-humour had been noticed by the family I lapsed back to taciturn, disgruntled, solitary, invisible Linda.

"That girl is the moodiest bitch I have ever met."

"Oh Bertha, show some understanding; you were like that when you were sixteen; it's her age, that's all!"

"Oh no I was not! Regular little ray of sunshine all my life; not all smiles and cheerfulness one minute, face as black as a coal bucket the next. What she needs is someone to give her a good shaking; tell her she could at least behave with politeness and good manners; and speak when spoken too."

"Oh, come on, she wound six ounces of wool for Merle on Tuesday evening."

"And that makes being a sour little sod, twenty four hours a day, seven days a week, okay, does it? The hell it does! She never does anything except mope around the place. And in case you haven't noticed, she has lost all her friends."

"Your Father and I are glad that she doesn't hang around with them next door now. Your Father and I are pleased Linda keeps herself to herself these days."

"The hell you are," growled Bertha. "You'd give anything to see her walking out with a nice boy, instead of making everyone's life a misery, moping around like a month of Sundays."

As I said, Bertha could not see me sitting opposite her at the kitchen table; me being invisible as I was. I am sure a month of Sundays cannot mope.

"Are you sure Linda is well, Mum? She always looks so pale and tired these days. I think you should take her to Doctor Webster, I really do. It's not right for a young girl to be as lackadaisical as Linda is. She never cares for her appearance now; never wears make-up or styles her hair. It wouldn't matter if she was real good-looking, like Bertha; but let's face it, Mum, she was behind the door when good-looks were given out. She needs all the help she can get."

As I said, Mary was also unable to see me. I was totally invisible.

"What's wrong with my big little girl? Not feeling the best?" A cuddle and a peck on the cheek from Dad. I was grateful he could see me; but I must be careful not to worry him. He might start asking questions. No, I could not risk that.

Time to have a short burst of ferocious good-humour and polite conversation, before I lapsed back to miserable, sad Linda again!

CHAPTER THIRTY EIGHT

APRIL BROUGHT EASTER celebrations; I sat at home in my bedroom, pretending to read the Women's Weekly.

Mum took Carol and Yvonne violeting; she remembered from her own long-ago childhood where the best blooms grew. Courting couples again walked the paths across the Downs. Daffodils and tulips bloomed in the cottage gardens; primroses and windflowers along the secret edges of the woodland walks. The sun probably shone; I do not remember it doing so: as I recall every day of that long-ago spring, I see each day as a miserable grey mist.

I was aware of my increasing size, and I had stopped eating. I did not want to grow any fatter because if I did, other people, Mum, Bertha, Mary, them next door, would only poke their noses in and talk about it. Invisibility served me very well, thank you! I intended to stay that way for ever, and that involved changing nothing of myself. I had even stopped feeling hungry. All I felt was a never-ending sadness.

I continued to work each weekday; a sad silent girl, smiling with my mouth at customers, never looking into their eyes; doing Miss Prendergast's bidding; being endlessly, mindlessly obedient.

I no longer noticed the other girls at work, or Ernie Badger; they may or may not have been working at the Co-op now, I was incapable of knowing or caring. I was terrified of Paul Townsend however. He never acknowledged my existence; he just gazed through me if we ever came face-to-face. I ran from him, I hid in cupboards, I slunk away behind doors, and I crouched down behind counters, rather than acknowledge his presence. I was totally unaware if any other living person noticed my extraordinary behaviour. Paul knew I existed, he noticed me; I knew he saw me, and hated me, and probably wished to kill me.

One Monday afternoon Mister Jenkins called me to his office. He was kind and sincere, and asked me if all was well with me. He told me I looked under the weather, and to go home if I wished. No-one expected me to work if I was ill.

Just imagine the fuss my early arrival home would cause! I had stopped using make-up weeks ago, but needs must; so I applied layers of rouge and red lipstick, plastered a supposedly pleasant smile on my face, and effected normality for a whole afternoon. I was extra pleasant to Miss Prendergast, who never criticised me for my churlishness, but suffered my sulky silences with gentle tolerance. Miss Prendergast fondly imagined I actually suffered from a broken heart; as she had done all those years ago when her soldier sweetheart had abandoned her for a French kiss. She had long ago given up praying she would meet a nice young man. Nowadays she just prayed that poor Linda Bigford would!

May would bring my seventeenth birthday and I was dreading it. I remembered with horror the simple celebrations organised by my colleagues when I had turned sixteen. I must have looked so public, so obvious and ugly.

My birthday in nineteen-fifty was to be on a Sunday; I was relieved it was not a working day. I was dreading being visible to my family; there would be the usual fuss that accompanied all Bigford celebrations, and any distant cousin for miles round would find it necessary visit the cottage, bring gifts and kiss me. I had decided I would be too ill to rise from my bed on that day. Yes, that was a good idea; I had decided that on my birthday I would burn the remains of the packet of sanitary towels, say my period was too heavy and I had cramp, and plead to spend the day alone in my bed.

CHAPTER THIRTY NINE

T HE DAY BEFORE my birthday was a Saturday. I awoke hollow-eyed from disturbed sleep. Dressing was uncomfortable because my enlarged breasts were straining every thread of my cotton bra and the waistband of my skirt seemed unbearably tight. The image in my bedroom mirror was still the same Linda; big and incredibly skinny, plain and pale as death.

As I descended the stairs Dad was almost ready to leave, dressed as ever in his navy serge overall over his second-best white shirt. Dad, in common with all other working men, always worked until midday on a Saturday.

Mum, in her floral cross-over pinny, was frying bread on the primus stove. Merle was dealing patiently with the strident demands of an extremely cross Aunt Beat, (she hated spring, but then again; she hated summer, winter and autumn too).

A soft breeze wafted the lace curtains which covered the lower half of the kitchen window, gently cooling the heat of the morning; the breeze distilled the Maytime scents from the creamy candles of the horse chestnut on the edge of the meadow and the lilac blooms over the fence from next door's garden, while red admiral butterflies caused a colour sensation on the buddleia by our back gate. Beyond the garden the green turf of the Downs gleamed in the morning light.

The breeze brought the sounds of the village getting down to a working Saturday; boys towing their trolleys along the street, dogs barking, cocks crowing, the gentle clucking of the wifely hens, a baby's cries heard through the open casements of a cottage further along the street. A shimmering haze already stood in the air; the day would be a stinker.

Mum plonked a plate of sausages, bacon and fried bread in front of my nose, with an imprecation to "Eat up, there's a good girl."

The pong of the lard she had used for frying made me vomit. And such vomit. I could not stop myself heaving long enough to leave the table; and I was vaguely aware of motherly concern, fatherly horror and sisterly amazement. I know Aunt Beat boomed in the background, but I could not hear her. Dad was supporting me under my arms while Mum wiped my face with the edge of her apron. Merle was trying to clear the mess. And still I threw up; it seemed everything I had eaten in a month came back at me. Revolting green and yellow mucous poured from my nose. I heaved and hacked and retched, and all the time the putrescent mess of half-digested food issued from my mouth. Vaguely I could hear expressions of parental concern; their muzzy voices floating in the heated air as though from a great distance.

"No work for you today, my girl!"

"The doctor for you on Monday, my girl! This has gone on long enough! And you are going back to bed."

"My monthly started this morning," I gasped between splutters. It did not; but as I said, needs must. "I think it's a bit heavy, that's all". In that instant I realised with horror I had not had the 'curse' for months.

"Bed and an aspro for you. Have you got bellyache? Backache? Do you need a hot water bottle?"

Not on the hottest day of the year.

I wanted to protest that I had to go to work; what would Miss Prendergast do? There might be a rush on sandals, what with the hot weather and everything; and what about lunchtime?

I could not rise from my chair. My knees sagged beneath me and I collapsed face-first into a congealing plateful of fried bread, bacon and sick. Dad's strong arms hauled me up, while Mum applied a cool flannel to the fragments of breakfast and vomit ossifying on my face. That was the last thing I remembered.

I awoke in a cold sweat. I was undressed and in my floral pyjamas. Well, I was sure Mum must have noticed that my period had not started. I had no idea of the time of day or how I got into my bed. I assumed poor Dad had carried great big Linda up the winding cottage staircase, my legs and arms flailing wildly.

Mum was all gentle concern. She said I did not eat enough; that I seemed so tired. I need not work at the Co-op ever again if I did not want to. She said I was definitely visiting the doctor on Monday. Bertha, who had recently learned to drive, would take us to the surgery first thing Monday morning. Until then I must stay in bed, and rest.

Dad had phoned the Co-op, and they were not expecting me back until I was truly well; and as Mum had already said, I did not have to go at all unless I really wanted to. She hinted that she thought this was all a recurrence of the breakdown I suffered when Aunt Beat so insensitively revealed the details of my parentage.

I could not think of a word to say. I thought perhaps if I just lay there, and did not speak or look at anybody, I may just die.

The scrambled egg Mum prepared sat on my plate untouched. I no longer had even enough energy for total self-absorption.

I slept fitfully for most of the day. Mum and Dad came to my room, together and separately, and expressed great concern, worry and love. Their gentle words and anxious looks washed over me like a fall of dew, forgotten in the heat of the next moment.

Bertha and Mary visited me; I ignored them. Merle did not visit my room.

I fell asleep before darkness fell. My last waking thought was that tomorrow I would be seventeen.

CHAPTER FORTY

WOKE IN THE moth-grey dawn of a hot May Sunday. Yes, it was my birthday. Mum and Dad were snoring at counterpoint with each other in the front bedroom. Mice families held Mayday races in the roof timbers above my head, a rooster crowed in next door's garden, and the birds in the sycamore tree were going berserk with their dawn chorus.

To my horror I realised my bed was soaked. A feeling of revulsion and shame enveloped me. I must have wet myself, how could I do such a thing? I struggled to a sleepy sitting position. Well, I must rise, wash and dress myself and change my sheets before anyone else awoke.

As I swung my legs to the edge of my bed, a searing wave of white heat possessed my body. The pain was excruciating, stealing the air from my lungs, hi-jacking my power to scream, just leaving enough breath to stay alive. After a moment the agony subsided, leaving me lying flat on my back, breathless, terrified and exhausted. I was ready for the next torture ten minutes later; a howl rose to my lips, but I gritted my teeth and swallowed my screams. I had no idea what was causing the pains but I knew I must ensure Mum and Dad did not hear my shrieks. What was happening to me? I knew only that I was on my own this time! I stuffed my mouth with my handkerchief and willed myself to silence.

The pangs ripped me apart again and again; each an excruciation, coming closer to its forbear; each more agonising, a wildfire serrating my body in two. The silent screams in my head were all I could hear. Dimly I was aware of urine and faeces as I writhed and contorted, and tried to escape from the engulfing fire. I forced myself not to howl or cry out. Something deep inside my being bade me to be silent.

Knives cut the inside of my body, tore my flesh apart. Red hot pokers burned inside me. Perhaps I did scream, I do not think so: the howling was bursting inside my head.

Then it was there, The Thing. It lay between my legs; bloody and messy, and alive! Where had it suddenly appeared from? Then I realised the source of all the excruciating agony. I had given birth to The Thing. I gazed flabbergasted at the babe on the bed; noting that it was a girl and it was breathing.

I did not want it to be alive; or for that matter I did not want it dead. But the Thing was here; and it was still joined to me by a bloody pulsating cord. A soft noise, like a chortle of laughter issued from the tiny mouth. The Thing was laughing at me.

With difficulty I reached for my manicure scissors and cut the cord. I stuffed The Thing's mouth with my handkerchief, as I knew it was about to issue the first cry.

Mum and Dad must not hear. Beneath my hand I was aware of the regular beat of its tiny heart.

I had to get rid of this Thing as soon as possible. It could not be mine; I did not know how I came to give birth to it. Life had gone seriously wrong somewhere and I could not even begin to work out why this babe was lying on my bed, while filth and putrescence gushed from my aching insides. This could not possibly be my baby. Neither Mum and Dad or anyone else, would want this aberration. I must abandon it as soon as possible, but how, where?

Even though the sun was brazen in the sky and the day was growing hot, Mum and Dad still snored noisily in the front bedroom. After all it was Sunday. My hearing had become ultra-sensitive; my ears detected the siff-siff of Merle breathing through her slightly-open mouth as she lay on her back in the middle bedroom. I could hear Peter Pyle grizzling quietly to himself in the cottage next door.

Another gripping pain deposited a bloody mess like raw liver in the middle of my sheets. What was it, why were my insides falling out? I looked round wildly for somewhere to hide the mess, but there was nowhere. Mum must not see that hideous bloody feculence, but how, where, could I dispose of it?

I threw on my dress, which was draped across the bed board. Quietly I opened the cupboard door, took the last of the sanitary towels, and thrust them between my legs in an attempt to stem the blood issuing forth from inside me. I found sandals for my feet, and wrapped the infant in an old cardigan.

She was still breathing. I raced down the stairs and

through the unlocked backdoor. It would never have occurred to Mum and Dad to lock the door, not in Great Silver. Thank God for the trust and the trustiness of country people. I thought I was making a fearful row and I dreaded discovery, but in my desperation I flew noiselessly.

Away from the cottages, I unblocked her mouth. She swallowed a great blob of air, and let out a pathetic mew like a kitten.

For the first time I looked into her face. How did she get here? I may have birthed her but she was not mine. She looked at me with the surprised, slate-coloured eyes of the newborn. Her hair, stuck to her tiny head with drying blood, was fine and very black. She started a pathetic wail; a plea for loving and tenderness, for gentle hands and full breasts. She got nothing.

I had been reared with a country child's respect for all life. This babe was a living thing and I did not want to kill her. All I wanted was for her to be somewhere else, someone else's.

If I left her in the shade of the beech spinney, a poor little babe in the woods, someone would find her. What else could I do? No-one would know I had given birth to her; after all, I had not been 'expecting', had I? I also knew I had to get back to my bedroom and to clear up the bloodied sheets and clothes before the family awoke.

I was aware that crimson globs of blood were dripping down my legs and onto the ground. My feet squelched on the blood in my sandals; and I was trailing a putrid stream behind me. I could not risk going into the street, as the child was howling now. With difficulty born of soreness and stiff limbs I climbed the back fence and picked my way along the old path that led to the Downs. The Thing was yelling enough to wake the dead. If only she would stop bawling, it would be much better for us both.

The path along the bottom of the Downs passed through the small beech spinney; welcome shade from the power-hungry sun. I needed to rest; my legs had turned to jelly, they would no longer obey my brain's commands to move forward. I was stiff and dizzy and every muscle in my body was screaming with pain.

I leaned my back against a stripling birch and unwrapped the child from my soiled cardigan. We regarded each other with mild curiosity; and then she continued to scream, her tiny face scarlet. If only she would shut up!

I inspected every inch of the minute body. My knowledge of babies was scanty, in spite of my plethora of nephews and nieces. Total detachment sharpened my perception. I saw a perfect baby girl, nothing more. I might have been glancing impersonally at a product in a shop which I had no wish to purchase.

My pains, soreness, aches overwhelmed me. The morning heat was unbearable. Blackness came. I remembered no more.

CHAPTER FORTY ONE

S LOWLY AWARENESS RETURNED. I was in an all-white place. Mum and Dad were beside me, but they were suspended in mid-air.

Gradually they came into to land, and I became aware that they were both crying.

I did not have a body. My head was lying on a large white pillow and below my head was a stiffly starched sheet. There was no body beneath it.

Mum spoke to me; her voice, fuzzy and blurred, echoed along a dark tunnel. "Linda, thank goodness you are awake! Oh my darling, it will all be alright. She's alive!"

I did not ask, as I was sure I should already know the answer; but who the hell was Mum talking about?

The voice down the tunnel again. "Your baby, she's fine. They found you both just in time. Oh Linda, why didn't you tell us? We've seen her, Linda, oh she is so beautiful. Your Dad and I can't wait to have you both home. Everything will work out, you'll see. Oh, why did you try to run away from us, my darling? You almost died."

Now she had completely landed it would have helped if I had just a tiny clue what she was carrying on about.

I did have hands! Dad found them under the white cover and clasped them firmly in his strong, horny, tobacco-stained mitt. His voice down the deep tunnel contained a sob and many unshed tears.

"You've caused everyone a whole lot of worry, my girl, but, good Lord, are we glad it's all over! Do you know you've been out of it for two whole days, and your little girl needing to have her feeds too?"

Here we go again. They've had two days to think this up. It's news to me.

"She is the image of you, Linda, just like you were on the day you were born; got your eyes, and she's got your long legs." Mum talked nineteen-to-the-dozen, her words tumbling over each other in her enthusiasm.

Time to ask. I tried to phrase my question but all that issued from my mouth was something between a snort and a squawk.

Mum clapped her hands, declared in enthusiastic anticipation: "Of course, you want to see your little girl! Don't worry, my darling, we'll always be there for both of you! I'll call the nurse, and get her to bring the baby in."

"Honestly Linda, you have given us a dreadful shock; but truly we are so proud of her. Oh my Love, why didn't you tell us? It's a terrible thing to go through alone, after you were deserted by the baby's father. You didn't have to do that, you know; we love you and we would have understood!"

Mum leaned on the alert buzzer with enough power to ring the bells in St Edmund's tower.

An apparition in a green striped dress, with a starched

white apron, a starched white headdress and a starched white face appeared on cue. Okay, so I was in a hospital as this was definitely a nurse. But why, what had happened to me? The nurse seemed flustered; Mum was making enough fuss to start a riot.

"Sister, can you bring in Linda's daughter? She is so worried about her baby and cannot wait to see the little dot is alright."

My daughter! Slowly memory began to creep back. Oh no! They were going to bring me The Thing!

Well, Mum and Dad have been through this once already, so they have had practice; but surely it is not the kind of thing you expect to occur twice in the same family. It was new territory to me, and I wanted no part of it.

I opened my mouth to scream a violent protest; but all that came out was the snort and squawk.

The sister had a soft Irish voice: "Perhaps I should ask Linda if she is ready yet. After all she has been through a lot and we don't want to wear her out."

Memory was flooding back. The pain, the fear, the mess, the blood, the Thing crying. No, the last thing I wanted was to see The Thing ever again. I remembered that she was not mine, not really.

I was extremely thirsty; and now that I had my body back my belly ached, I appeared to have lost my legs, and my breasts were in agony; and of course I was in my usual state of total self-absorption. I snorted and squawked. The sister took that as a 'no.'

"Come back tomorrow morning," said the kindly Irish woman, "and I will see to it that you all have a lovely, private family reunion. Until then I think Linda should get some rest. She has been through a lot; she'll feel better in the morning."

Mum and Dad took a slow parting, promising me prams, cots, babysitting, and toys; saying how wonderful it was, now they had become accustomed to the shock of it all, of course. They just could not wait to have us home. Dad was in raptures about the cradle he would make; and Mum had already got The Thing christened by the time they finally left me.

I had said not a word.

I did not know the time, but daylight flooded the room. I tried to hide my eyes under the bedclothes but I could not pull the covers up far enough. I wanted to be somewhere else; anywhere but here.

I screamed for the sister, she raced back into my room, and she held me while I howled. She spoke to me in her soft accent, calming and consoling, while I bawled and screeched, swore and sobbed. I yelled that I did not want to see the baby ever again. She pleaded gently that I give myself a little time to get used to the idea of motherhood. "I know it sounds trite, but you really will feel better after a few days rest, and you will be able to think more clearly. Most people have nine months to get used to the idea of motherhood. Poor you, to have it hit you out of the blue. You cannot make any decisions now; you are too tired and too sick."

She held my hand and bathed my forehead. The racking

pain was still in my belly; the sore breasts, and the terrible thirst that refused to go away. She gently swabbed my sore parts, all the while softly crooning, gently cajoling in her soft Irish voice. I finally fell into a troubled sleep to the tune of 'Galway Bay.'

CHAPTER FORTY TWO

I AWOKE THE NEXT morning to the noises of hospital life; a breakfast trolley; people doing unmentionable things with bedpans; babies crying; nurses calling one to the other.

I could not eat, I could not return to sleep. I tried to hide, but there was nowhere to hide or run to. I was a prisoner of my body in a side ward in a hospital in Winchester.

The thought of It, and the horror of It's birth would not leave me. I screamed and yelled; nurses flew to my side; they gave me medicine to calm me. I was not calmed. After aeons of screaming the medicine did take affect and I became drowsy.

Mum and Dad would be back soon. I was longing to see them; but I was also frightened of them and their expectations of me. Half of me hoped they would not come. Half of me would have been broken-hearted if they had not done so.

I was asked if I wanted to see my daughter. They gathered from my reaction that I did not!

Matron was very business-like. "I will ask Doctor Webster to discuss your options with you, Linda. Of course if you wish to give your daughter up for adoption then that decision must be yours and yours alone; but I do ask that you hold your daughter first before you attempt to make a decision. Just a little cuddle; either in the presence of Sister Connolly alone, or with Sister Connolly and also your parents. Holding your daughter will hasten your personal recovery from the birth, as it will stimulate beneficial hormones that assist your body to return to normal. However you will not be forced, or indeed even cajoled, into doing anything you do not wish to. If you do decide upon adoption, I am sure Doctor Webster will be willing to inform your parents for you."

"Fortunately she is a healthy child. I don't suppose anyone has told you yet, but she weighs six pounds. Mums always want to know how much their baby weighs. She is very small, but she is so beautiful; and, as I say, she is healthy."

"Your own recovery from the birth will be hampered by your over-excited state so we must ensure that you remain calm. Please trust us to have your best interests in mind, as well as those of your daughter. If you do not wish to have visitors, even your parents, well that is fine, we will talk to them for you."

Matron spoke as though she was addressing the parish council.

I pasted a smile onto my face, it hurt the corners of my mouth; nature no longer intended me to smile. "Please can I just see Mum and Dad? My sisters and that will want to come and see me but I can't face them at the moment. But please I never want to see the baby." As if I could be even slightly interested in how much the thing weighed!

Was that how easy it was? Normality just slipping off your tongue, just like that!

Matron left but Sister Connolly stayed for a few more minutes; she waxed lyrical about the beauty of the baby. She had a lifetime of experience with babies, she told me, and this was one of the loveliest little girls she had ever seen. All that lovely black hair, and such long limbs, surely meant to be a dancer.

Poor little brat!

CHAPTER FORTY THREE

MUM AND DAD were subdued; obviously Sister Connolly had apprised them of my reluctance to acknowledge the infant. Mum, previously bubbling with enthusiasm, was merely polite. "How do you feel, Linda, are you better today?" Dad sat with his trilby hat on his knees and looked faintly embarrassed. My heart cringed for them, these two people I loved best in the whole world. They could not understand my actions, or my reactions. They were horrified by my rejection of my child.

I wanted to throw myself into their arms and sob. I wanted the comfort that went with the childhood I had so recently abandoned.

They asked how the baby was. I said, Sister said she is fine. Enough about the baby. They provided small talk; Bertha and Alf had painted their kitchen; Iris was considering buying a car.

They asked me if I had seen Doctor Webster, I said no. Then we sat in silence, total silence, carefully avoiding each other's eyes. What was there left to say?

When they left, they both pecked my cheek. Mum, with

her concerned blue eyes, promised: "We will talk some more tomorrow."

As the door closed behind them I turned my head into my pillow and sobbed until my heart felt like it was breaking.

Sister Connolly returned; it seemed I had been crying for hours. She cuddled me to her ample bosom and said: "There, there, my girl, you'll find a good cry will help a lot. Now, I am sure you're feeling very scungy down below, why don't I ask one of the nurses to help you bathe?"

Upon the return to my bed, which had been tidied and the lilacs from the garden that Mum had brought were arranged in a metal jug on the bedside table, I even felt hungry, and ate some cold beef and salad for lunch.

An afternoon siesta was part of the hospital routine. When I awoke Doctor Webster was standing at my bedside.

"Linda, my dear girl, whatever happened to you? Now we have a lot to talk about, you and I, and if you wish, we can wait until your Mum and Dad are here, or even one of your sisters if you prefer. Or we can just have a cosy little chat now, just the two of us."

"But there are some questions I really do have to ask you. So, do you want to wait for Mum and Dad, or indeed, Mary or Bertha, or shall we go straight ahead and get all the unpleasantness finished with?"

I said, barely above a whisper, that I would talk now.

He asked me if I had been aware that I was pregnant; I said I had not been. He said did I realise when the pains started that I was about to give birth; I said I did not. He frowned and chewed his lip; he did not look surprised.

I could hear my own voice, and it sounded a load of codswallop; but it was the truth, as implausible and unreal as it now seemed. Surely anyone would recognise the symptoms of pregnancy. Well, I did not.

Doctor Webster obviously believed me, his tone and his questions were entirely non-judgmental.

He asked me if there had been a boyfriend, I hung my head and said yes, there had been. He asked me if the lad had forced himself upon me. I hung my head even lower and said, no, he had not.

He asked me if I now believed that I had given birth. I replied, oh yes, I believed that.

Did I want to keep the baby? No, I did not. Did I want to see my baby? No I did not!

He said he would ask me again in a few days. He encouraged me to see the child but I turned my head into the pillow and wept.

He offered to talk to Mum and Dad for me. Offer gratefully accepted.

CHAPTER FORTY FOUR

ETHEL'S SON WAS born on Whit Monday. She had caused a sensation at the Whitsun fete, having to leave in a hurry, dramatically clutching her belly, all squealing and fuss. The Vicar had brought Ethel and Maudie back to the cottage in his car.

Nurse Dinningsby paid Ethel a flying visit in the mid-afternoon, struggling up the hill on her trusty sit-up-in-bed bicycle. After a thorough examination of her patient, inside and out, she decided that her professional services would not be required for some hours yet.

Nurse Dinningsby disliked men. She had spent all her professional life cleaning up the results of their lack of consideration. Nurse Dinningsby had no difficulty getting through life without marriage, sex, or romantic love; and her patience snapped abruptly when faced with the situation next door. As far as she was concerned, women like Maudie and Ethel should be 'done', in the manner of a female cat. After all, she considered most female cats showed more discrimination in their choice of partners than did those two ladies. Nurse Dinningsby would be professional in her treatment of Ethel. Ethel could not expect additional kindness.

I lay on my bed glancing through the advertisements, 'When policemen ride on broomsticks, its kiss and never tell,' claimed an advertisement for Sans Egal lipstick. I had once considered that to be charming, incredibly romantic. Now I recognised it for what it was; just plain silly.

I read the agony aunt's column, 'I think I am in love with my sister's husband.' Clearly not written about Alf.

All the while the screams from next door continued at regular intervals. I had just one wish; to go to Ethel and tell her to get on with it and shut up.

Mum came home from the fete with a helium-filled balloon for Merle; Dad returned with a bottle of wine he had won in the raffle; we ate tea; we listened to the radio news; and all the while the screams from next door grew louder and closer together.

Ethel was screaming to annoy me. After all I had given birth myself and I never made a sound. My greatest wish was go round there and gag her.

As the late spring darkness tucked up the close-knit cottages in the village street there was no relief from the cacophony next door. We were to be denied even a wink of sleep until finally, deep in the night, the racket stopped. Mark Christopher Pyle had been born.

CHAPTER FORTY FIVE

A UNT BEAT DIED, just like that.

I would have expected her to die the way she had lived; with as much nastiness and obstreperousness, as much inconvenience to the rest of humanity as she could possibly muster. In my imagination everyone would be hurrying to and fro to address her slightest whim; Doctor Webster would be camped on the front lawn; poor long-suffering Mum and Dad would have been running hither and thither like scalded cats. All the while her voice would heckle, she would judge and censure, condemn and criticise. When the end finally came I would have thought that at least the bells of St Edmunds would be muffled and there would be a hearse drawn by black-plumed horses in the street. I would have expected her demise to be as unpleasant and inconvenient to everyone else as her life had been ever since anyone could remember.

But no; when Mum took her pills and her early morning cuppa on the day following Whit Monday, Aunt Beat was dead. No fanfare, no goodbye, just a spent and lifeless corpse.

Mum laid her out; Nurse Dinningsby was worn out

with birthing children. Mum made much of the fact that Mark's birth immediately preceded Aunt Beat's death; a birth and death on the same day had a great spiritual meaning for Mum.

And of course it was up to Mum and Dad to pay for her funeral, as Aunt Beat only had her small pension.

Surprisingly she did leave a will. Probably more surprisingly, she did have a few personal possessions to bequeath. Nothing for my long suffering Mum and Dad of course; they were never mentioned in the will.

There was a quantity of good silver in her closet and in her drawers: candlesticks, napkin rings, brushes and combs, a diamond brooch, an amber hair slide. Bertha appeared knowledgeable about these things and assured us they were valuable.

Mum expressed surprise that Aunt Beat owned such treasures. She wondered if Aunt Beat had pinched them when she was young and in good service. Mum said a lot of that went on in the old days; of course if you got caught you went to prison; but none-the-less the theft of small, valuable articles was commonplace and many regarded it as a form of insurance, putting things by for a rainy day. Mum said she would never have done such a thing, but she knew plenty who did. Aunt Beat did not have rainy days; she had my soft-hearted parents to keep her dry.

And Aunt Beat a common thief; it did not bear thinking about!

She left her treasures to her sister's boy. Aunt Beat had lived in my parent's house for over two decades, and yet neither of them even knew she had a nephew. He had never visited her in all that time; and Aunt Beat had not mentioned him. She probably never had time, what with her continual fault-finding about her host family.

He visited quickly enough when he learned it was to his advantage to do so. He attended the funeral, but did not question who was paying for it.

Arnold was in his early forties, tall and scrawny, with a receding hairline. He had small, white, cold hands. He was a civil servant, he informed us, which, he also informed us, was of course far superior to a carpenter. Arnold was the most uncivil man I ever met. He was a bachelor, and 'lived in' with friends. Bertha said in an aside to me that it must run in the family.

Arnold ate and drank a great deal at the funeral tea; perhaps his 'living in' did not include sustenance and he was eating for the future. He held forth on the current political situation in a loud voice, with an overbearing manner that defied disagreement. He curled his lip at the appearance of Nellie and Maudie, in grubby black, with saucy black lace hats. They assured him they were old friends of Beat's. Maudie was wearing a see-through blouse.

Arnold never mentioned his Aunt once. Even Aunt Beat did not deserve such an unpleasant nephew. He left as soon as the repast was finished; he was clutching his precious silver. He did not thank my parents and they never saw or heard of him again.

A week later, when Mum was finally clearing away Aunt Beat's possessions, she discovered Aunt Beat's marriage certificate, stuck to the back of one of her drawers.

We learned that Beatrice Alicia Maria Hodknott had

been twenty-nine years of age when she had married Clarence Aldwith Jenkins, who was twenty-one. Beatrice's father was an ostler and Clarence's a pigman. They were married in Portsmouth. I knew that way back in Aunt Beat's youth the most shameful thing that could happen to a woman was to be left on the shelf, and I wondered if Aunt Beat could see the shelf looming close and she had 'nabbed' youthful Clarence, rather than face the ignominy of spinsterhood, and probably before the poor youth had a chance to work out what was going on. Mum assured me they had loved each other dearly, had a deep and abiding affection.

Aunt Beat was seventy-eight when she died; she had been a widow for nearly thirty years.

I was astonished how sincerely both my parents mourned Aunt Beat. Mum would suddenly dab her eyes in the middle of serving breakfast, or ironing, or dusting, and say how much she missed the old lady. Dad would come home to lunch, look at the spot where the arm chair had stood for all those years, and say it wasn't the same somehow.

Mark Christopher Pyle continued to thrive. I heard every detail from Mum; what a perfect blonde baby he was, just like Ethel had been. I was not in the least bit interested in seeing the evidence for myself. I could hear him crying, that was enough.

One afternoon I was waiting for the Middleford bus outside Great Silver post office, when Ethel trundled along with Mark in the ancient dilapidated pram which someone had charitably donated to the Great Silver worthy cause. She insisted in showing me her son; and I must say he did seem a pleasant-looking child.

"Oh Linda," said Ethel, "it's a shame you gave your little girl away. She and Mark could have got married when they grow up."

Angie had her pretty hair permed, although with her natural curls it was quite unnecessary. She had taken to wearing shoes with three-inch heels, oodles of make-up and carmine nail varnish. She had planned a holiday at Butlins in Clacton during August, with her friends from the factory.

CHAPTER FORTY SIX

A FORTNIGHT LATER, ON Sunday morning, I was surprised to receive a visit from Olive Prendergast. She had persuaded an old friend to drive her out to visit me, she said, as she was concerned about my well-being, and wished to assure herself that I was recovering from my 'great unhappiness'.

Mum installed us in the sitting room; secretly hoping Miss Prendergast would notice the new mirror over the mantle, with swans etched into the glass; or the new plastic magazine rack. Mum provided tea in the best bone china teapot, the one that made the tea taste terrible but was always hauled out for important visitors. Mum fled.

Miss Prendergast and I sat, one on each side of the empty grate; two strangers who met briefly years ago and now had little in common. The stilted conversation proceeded from a few remarks about the July weather to comments on the Olympic Games in Helsinki. Miss Prendergast was not sure where Helsinki was; she thought it was either in Finland or Russia.

Miss Prendergast was anticipating her annual holiday with great pleasure. This year she had decided to have a change from Weymouth and would take her mother to Bournemouth for a fortnight. Miss Prendergast, who had visited Weymouth annually since about ten-sixty-six, saw this as a change of mammoth proportions.

Gradually the conversation crept round to the day-to-day goings on of the Co-op. Roland from menswear had been called-up; Doreen from accounts was engaged to a carpenter from Reading; she met him at a dance last year. Mister Jenkins was considering retirement 'for health reasons, you know.' Mister Jenkins had always appeared to be extremely healthy to me, but Miss Prendergast did not elaborate, and I did not ask.

Then she got round to the real purpose of her visit. I would be surprised to hear that Paul Townsend had left the Co-op. Apparently he had obtained a better position, in a large store in Bond Street.

Well, it is an ill wind that blows nobody any good, so they say! Paul had always been ambitious; he had his heart set on Bond Street.

CHAPTER FORTY SEVEN

"**Y**OU NEED SOMETHING to do," said Mary. She amazed me by buying me a second-hand typewriter; old-fashioned, battered, but in perfect working order. She bought me reams of quarto-sized paper, a couple of typing manuals, and a daunting tome on the procedures for writing business letters. Long ages ago I had received basic typing instruction from Grace, the Co-op company secretary, as one of my sixteenth birthday presents, and with a little practice I brought to mind all her instructions. I just had to remember the 'home keys' and in no time at all my fingers nimbled round the keyboard at surprising speed.

"There's smashing jobs in London these days, you could even earn up to ten pounds a week! No-one in this family has ever earned that much money, I'll tell you now."

Mary spent hours of her time checking my typing for errors, advising on the layout of letters, timing me for speed checks, and inventing invoices and sales dockets for me to copy-type.

Grace-the-company-secretary would have thoroughly approved of Mary's attitude.

I sincerely regretted all the grief I had caused Mum and

Dad; but I do not know to this day what I could have done differently. I honestly did not realise I was pregnant; and I certainly did not want the child I had given birth to. Mum and Dad had a lot to forgive; but bless their hearts, they had been into forgiveness all their lives. They did not, could not, understand my actions.

The village gave us all a hard time. Carol and Yvonne were teased about it Silver Street school. People would look away when Mum walked into the post office, but would talk nineteen-to-the-dozen when she left. That, or people would talk to her in hushed voices, about 'poor Linda, having to give her baby up like that,' all the while wearing their smug, 'we really know what happened' expressions.

CHAPTER FOURTY EIGHT

ALTHOUGH I HAD never actually resigned, or for that matter been sacked, from the Co-op, I dared not return; and no-one expected me to do so. I missed having ready money; and worse than that, my poor parents, along with all the other grief I had recently caused them, now received no keep money from me. As all Merle received in payment for her efforts at the vicarage amounted to pocket money, she made no financial contribution to the family coffers. My parents were now fully supporting two grown women. I realised the unfairness of this and resolved to find myself paid employment as soon as possible.

August is a delightful month in Hampshire. Agriculture is at its most productive and everyone in the village and on the surrounding farms were busy as bees. Tractors were gradually replacing the horse and cart on most of the farms, and the moan of their engines sounded continually from the surrounding meadows and Downland as the glorious harvest was gathered.

Mums were busy too, coping with long school holidays; and grandmothers were delighted at the opportunity to spend time and money on their grandchildren. The park and the paddling pool in the centre of Middleford were colourful sights on fine afternoons; bright with floral dresses, woollen bathing costumes, and beach balls. By September the Mums would be ready to throw their hands in the air, say Thank God, and return their little darlings to the doubtful care of Miss Landport and Mister Taylor.

Merle was busy as ever. Grand-babies visited the vicarage now; and she left early each morning to perform her magic on dirty bums and colicky tums. I noted she was very happy to do this; and I felt a rare moment of pity for the girl who had been my natural mother, but never had the chance to mother me. Also, if Merle were truly backward, as everyone made out, how come she was so good at caring for babies?

Mum had discovered that she enjoyed buying furniture and had promised herself a bedroom suite (a matching wardrobe and dressing table, with neat bedside tables) in cherry wood or Canadian pine veneer, as soon as she could afford it. She said she would gladly donate the elderly oak closet with the stained glass inserts and brass door handles to That Lot Next Door. She considered it old fashioned and so heavy, and after over forty years she was very tired of it.

The lounge suite in the sitting room was the first furniture she had bought since she and Dad had hastily put together the contents of our cottage when they married.

CHAPTER FORTY NINE

THE BAWLING BRAT was christened.

Young Mark appeared in his dilapidated pram, newly clad in a blue silk buster suit decorated with embroidered Donald Ducks. His quiff of blonde hair had been combed upwards and his perfect transparent complexion glowed with a glorious healthiness. He crowed with delight throughout the Christening service.

Mum and Dad were both godparents, which meant they felt obliged to provide most of the eatables. If Angie had chosen my parents as godparents I would have called it a wise move, and the provision of comestibles the desired outcome; but Ethel would never have considered such a fortunate result. She was genuinely, embarrassingly, overwhelmingly surprised and grateful for my parent's contribution.

It was fortunate Mum and Dad supplied the refreshments. None of the occupants of the cottage next door had given a passing thought to the provision of food and drink even though Ethel had invited most of the inhabitants of the Silver Villages to watch the naming of her son. Even Miss Landport had the nerve to turn up.

I did not. I stayed at home and watched the comings and goings from Mum's bedroom window.

A day or two after the Christening I wandered down to the post office to mail my latest batch of job applications. The Christening was still the main subject of conversation behind Great Silver hands, and this struck me as exceptionally ill-mannered, as on the day in question most of the gossipers had all partaken freely of my parent's hospitality.

'I am interested in the advertised position of Mother's Help. I gave my own kid away without even a second thought; but I am sure you will be happy to entrust me with the care of yours.' Seriously, this is what the letters should have stated, but of course, they didn't. I did not fancy my chances in the current job market.

A dark youth was standing at the bus stop outside the post office. I did not give him a second glance; I certainly did not recognise him. A deep male voice carolled: "Hi Linda, how nice to see ya!"

Okay, so I was not invisible today!

I turned in surprise, it was Walter Sikes! I had not seen hide nor hair of Walter since he disappeared from the village school at age thirteen; or for that matter I had never thought about him either.

I trotted over to the bus stop, with my best "Hullo, how are you?" voice. It sounded odd, out of practice. It was weeks since I had spoken to anyone outside my immediate family, and I had precious little to say to them.

"Good to see you, girl!" he said.

I stared at him amazement. He was seventeen, the same

age as me, but he looked much, much older. Although he was obviously freshly shaved his cheeks and upper lip had a faint blue tinge to them, which in a swarthy man meant he must shave frequently. Working at the Co-op had accustomed me to judging clothes and I was aware that his charcoal-grey suit was tailor-made. His shirt was dazzling white; his tie, pale silk, quiet. He grasped me in a quick hug; and I smelt bay rum.

We talked, it was probably for a brief five minutes; but I was so unaccustomed to human conversation it seemed an eternity.

He asked me where I worked. Best not to tell him of my immediate past! I just waved my batch of letters at him and muttered: "Job applications."

He asked after Mum and Dad, my sisters, my brothers and their wives, making a joke that he had always been really terrified of Mrs. Bigford, the teacher. He asked after Angie and Ethel.

I told him Ethel was the proud mother of Mark.

This was me, Linda Bigford, making conversation, taking an interest, however briefly, in someone other than myself. And the sky did not fall in!

I asked after his parents, secretly recalling them as scruffy diddikis travelling round in a battered removal van permanently set up with beds, a table and a primus stove. He apprised me of a different set of circumstances.

"Nah! Dad's retired. Mum's health is not good; had too many kids, I suppose. She always wanted a bungalow by the sea, so Dad relented, and they've settled down very nicely. They've bought a bungalow at Bosham, down on

Chichester Harbour. Mum loves displaying all her glass and china she has collected over the years, and using all her embroidered tablecloths; and Dad has taken up gardening. No kidding! Grows the best marrows in the street. Must be all the horse poo."

"You wouldn't get my Mum to travel again, no sir." Then with a little laugh, he said: "Well, except to America. My sister Anita married a yank from New Hampshire. Dad said he'll take Mum over there next year to see her grandson."

I gazed at him open-mouthed. So much for the superstition that diddikis were scruffy and careless, living only for the day and making no provision for the future. My parents had often spoken enviously about people who owned their own houses but it was a dream beyond their financial aspirations.

"I work in the racing industry," he continued. "Well, Dad has so many contacts; known the depth and breadth of the country, he is."

"I'm being trained to manage a stable, over Croxbourn way. Only just started, so I'll be training for years, but I've got a real feel for it, same as Dad."

"The boss, she's looking for a housekeeper. Well, and you're looking for a job!"

The bus was coming down the village street. Walter took a diary from his pocket and ripped a page out. It had a name and address on it. "Why don't you post one of your job applications off to her? She's looking for someone to live-in. She has a super house. Why not give it a try; it'd be a good job?"

He leapt onto the bus, and was gone from my sight.

I stared open-mouthed at the spot where he had stood. Images whirred before my eyes; a little gypsy boy who was Miss Landport's favourite victim; his parents driving the villages in the battered van; a handsome young man in a bespoke suit, with the world before him; my imagined view of a small, neat house on Chichester Harbour.

Then I saw myself, not in Great Silver, but out in another world, far away from the Silver Villages. Other people, another way of life was beckoning me.

I hurriedly posted my letters and then I raced home. I charged in the kitchen door and breathlessly flopped down at the kitchen table.

Mum gasped in amazement, and almost dropped her precious new electric iron. She was accustomed to me skulking around, never speaking a word.

The story came out in short, breathless sentences, the whole lot; the young man in the bespoke suit, his traineeship, the sister married to a yank, his father's retirement, the bungalow on Chichester Harbour, the proposed visit to America.

My diatribe ground to a sudden halt. No point in telling them about the possible job at the racing stables. Mum would not approve of my leaving home. And anyway, I probably would not get the job if I applied for it. It would probably be best if I forgot the whole darned thing.

Mum enjoyed gossip; village women believed they had a duty to keep up with everyone's news. Besides, you never knew when someone may need your help.

She oohed and aahed enviously about the bungalow at

Bosham. She remembered going to Chichester on the train when she and Dad were courting; it was a lovely spot.

Wasn't it a good thing that young Walter seemed to have a bright future? She wondered what the American from New Hampshire did for a living.

Mum was convinced that all English girls who married members of the American forces were leaving for a life of unadulterated luxury. Mum refused to countenance that Americans were ordinary working men with ordinary jobs; to Mum, to be American was to be wealthy.

Mum had always enjoyed her visits to the cinema.

CHAPTER FIFTY

E THEL, ANGIE AND I still sat on the bench outside their back door and gossiped away the long summer evenings.

I rarely thought about the baby at all, unless prompted by Ethel ranting on about the joys of motherhood, or by Mum having a little private 'wonder,' out loud of course, and always in my hearing, about what was happening to the baby now. I realised I would probably have to put up with Mum's wonderings for the rest of my life, and the prospect terrified me.

Fully recovered from the birth and with her hormones returned to normal, Ethel's interest had been titillated by a young farm worker who had appeared about a fortnight ago on Farmer Williams spread at Little Silver. He was not from 'round here'; he had a whining midland accent and his smart pub-going clothes were citified.

Village youths were being employed in the factories springing up in Middleford's outskirts; manufacturers which produced tyres, and Bakelite cases for radios. An extra, earlier bus from Great Silver to Middleford operated on week days, taking the growing workforce away from the village and into the town. Farmer Williams found it necessary to advertise the position of trainee herdsman in a number of far-flung local newspapers; he had previously always offered employment to a local lad who was able to persuade Mister Taylor at the school to give him a reference.

Ethel was fascinated by the young farm worker. She was convinced he felt forlorn and missed his family in his far-away hometown, and she planned to make his sojourn in the Silver Villages less lonely. Poor bloke, he did not stand a chance.

Angie had received a small promotion at the aircraft-parts factory and was now responsible for checking other people's work. She was duly proud of herself.

Angie had enjoyed her holiday at a Butlins holiday camp, and she and her colleagues were planning to return next year. She had met a nice young fellow, from Yorkshire, and she had an assignation to meet him, same time - same place - the following August. She relished the prospect; but in the meantime she was not about to let this proposed rendezvous spoil any amorous adventures which might eventuate during the intervening months.

Young Mark Pyle either slept peacefully or happily gurgled away to himself in his dilapidated conveyance under the shade of the crab-apple tree by the fence. Mark was a placid and pleasant baby.

Ethel and Angie usually managed to control their curiosity about my daughter; it must have been painful for them to forego such a juicy subject of conversation.

I had little else to add to the general banter during

our conflabs on the battered wooden bench; reports on Carol's and Yvonne's ability to do hemstitching paled in comparison to Ethel's exciting maternal life and Angie's career prospects, to say nothing of their romantic dreams.

I posted a job application to the address Walter had given me; a letter that probably would never be read, an application for a job that may not even exist. I considered it expedient not to inform the family of my actions; they would have thought I had gone completely mad.

I tried to forget about the letter, telling myself I could never obtain such a vaunted position. I dared not even consider the fool I may have made of myself.

CHAPTER FIFTY ONE

RECEIVED A POLITE reply from Miss Loretta Thackray, thanking me for my interest in the position of housekeeper and inviting me to attend an interview on Friday afternoon. Oh dear, time to inform Mum and Dad that I was considering leaving home.

Loretta and I took to each other immediately; and before the interview was concluded I even felt comfortable enough to advise her that I had recently given birth to a baby girl which I had placed for adoption. She looked stunned and slightly embarrassed, and I could see she had made a mental note of the information before she moved on to a million further questions. My dreaded secret was out in the open, as was entirely necessary, and the roof had not fallen on me.

We talked for hours. She enquired: "Do you know anything about the racing industry?" I did not.

"Tell me about yourself." I showed her school reports, certificates showing excellent maths and English work. Miss Prendergast had kindly provided a glowing reference citing my consideration for the needs of my customers, and my general efficiency in the day-to-day running of the footwear department, to say nothing of my total honesty and reliability in all things.

Why honesty is always cited so prominently in personal references? After all, no referee would ever state 'he - or she - is totally dishonest,' oh no; they would just leave the subject of honesty out of the reference altogether, which, when you think about it, says nothing.

Doctor Webster had also provided a personal reference, saying he had known me all my life; and I was honest, respectful and trustworthy.

We talked about cleaning, changing beds, typing, correspondence, and my dealings with customers at the Co-op. I was not beyond a little name-dropping; Loretta moved amongst Middleford's hierarchy too.

Loretta referred to her house as 'my cottage', even though it was large enough to engulf both the Bigford's humble abode and Pyle's cottage next door. The housekeeper's accommodation was in a small bed-sit in the rear of her huge house; I even had my own bathroom. This was opulence indeed to the long-time douser in the bungalow bath in the kitchen, with Dad's long-john underpants airing on the line above the range. There could surely be no greater luxury than a daily bath.

Loretta would provide breakfast and tea as part of my wages. I could visit my parents for a weekend every second fortnight.

My heart soared for the first time since I had met Paul Townsend.

These were other Downs, the Croxbourn Downs, and

miles away from home. It was the beginning of a great adventure.

As I waited at the bus stop outside Croxbourn post office to commence my journey back to Middleford and to Great Silver, I saw a gipsy on a pedigree racehorse, riding across those Croxbourn Downs as if he owned them. Which he did!

CHAPTER FIFTY TWO

UM AND DAD provided instant enthusiasm and approval; Mary, Bertha and my brothers were in total agreement with my plans; but brothers who had been to North Africa, even under the circumstances of war, did not consider a trip to Croxbourn to be an adventure. If Merle even knew what we were discussing she gave no indication.

The news of my employment was greeted by my next-door neighbours with unrestrained delight. To Ethel and Angie this was just another chapter in the saga of Linda's wonderful, dramatic and exciting life story, although their judgement was somewhat affected by stories in 'Secrets' and 'Red Letter' and by long-running radio serials. True, I had chosen to abandon my daughter, and this choice was totally beyond their comprehension; but with their never-failing optimism they fondly imagined that one day we would be reunited and would adore each other for the rest of our days.

Their best wishes for my future were that I should have a happy and successful love-life. What else was there?

I assured them the young men of the Croxbourn

Valley were quite safe from my ardent attentions. I jokingly admonished them that if this were their big adventure, the virtue of these hypothetical young men would be in the eminent danger of disruption.

They loved it. They agreed wholeheartedly.

CHAPTER FIFTY THREE

MISSED THE STRONG smell of Dad's tobacco and the warm musky body-smell of Mum, which had been my comfort all my life. To my amazement I missed Merle's quiet self-possession and her practical ways. Even Bruno the dog earned a brief tear. I missed the cuddled-up cottages in the main street of Great Silver, the warm untidy confusion of home, my brothers and sisters, all my aunts, and all the other villagers I had patently ignored during the past year.

Most of all I missed Angie and Ethel and their irrefutable, indefatigable optimism. I missed their giddy laughter and their half-baked ideas. More than anything I missed their unconditional friendship and support.

Loretta was the only other female in the stables complex at Croxbourn; I rarely met girls of my own age and I was thrown back on my own company, although the young stable lads who worked for Loretta provided me with the same teasing banter as Ernie Badger and the other young fellows at the Co-op had done.

I adored my working day. Loretta was charming and attentive, professional to the very end, and I grew to truly admire her. She showed every concern for my personal development.

The housework was simple; once Loretta discovered I had a head for figures and could type, my salary increased, and I undertook tiny bookkeeping tasks for her. Mary's manual-based tuition in book-keeping began to pay dividends; her basic coaching and my own common sense ensured I had few questions.

I began to type much of Loretta's personal correspondence; she preferred her letters to reflect her own personally casual style, almost a mirror of her spoken word, and she provided thorough tuition in order to obtain her desired outcome. The benefit of this as far as I was concerned was that I did not need to stick to the rules for the composition of business letters; which, let's face it, I did not know.

Loretta's new shiny green portable typewriter made typing a breeze; and my speed and accuracy increased amazingly. I allowed myself the odd few minute's pride in that. In just a few months I became Loretta's right hand man.

The racing industry is often referred to as a rich man's game. Each day there would be many visitors to the house and I became accustomed to smiling brightly at men dressed casually in corduroy slacks, tweed jackets and checked peak caps; clothes as smart and expensive as any I had seen. Their wives and girlfriends always wore cashmere sweaters, calf-length boots of the softest leather; and had long straight hair, perfectly styled and shining clean. Those haircuts, completely plain and without a hint of curl, had cost a fortune in Mayfair. I was aware that the plainest slacks and sweaters had cost a king's ransom at Harrods. Many professional men also visited, wearing faultlessly brushed and pressed dark suits, white shirts and pure silk ties.

Then I remembered Paul Townsend in his ex-funeral suits, with his personal scent of bleach and dead mice; and I remembered he had a pretty big opinion of himself. Really!

I dispensed cups of tea or coffee, glasses of sherry and tots of whiskey, relieved the visitors of their heavy coats and brollies, and patted the inevitable hound or beagle. The fact that I my knowledge of horses did not get beyond four legs and a head was totally irrelevant. Apart from casual comments about the weather and the traffic on the London-Road, the visitors did not require further conversation from me. I was a background figure, someone unnoticed. I had, in fact, almost become the parlour maid Mum had been half a century before.

After all, Mum-the-parlour-maid had welcomed Lloyd George; and she had known very little about the government of the day.

There were famous people; jockeys, rich owners who were financiers, authors, actors, politicians, many of them household names. We all shared about two minutes of such gripping conversational matters as ice and fog, the traffic in Maidenhead, and the price of petrol in the village. I am sure the face of Linda Bigford never registered in their awareness for more than a second. But then, I had been practicing invisibility all my life. Now I no longer wished to be invisible, I clearly was.

Loretta seemed to spend every spare moment with

a man friend. I had been formally introduced; his name was Ralph Barton. He appeared to be in his late forties, of heavy build, weighty rather than fat, and almost bald, with a heavy-jowled face. He made little impression on my consciousness; other than it struck me that Loretta, who was glamorous, beautiful and thirty-ish, could do better. He was just an overweight elderly man. I was seventeen; to me a fifty-year-old bloke seemed ancient.

I rarely saw Walter Sikes in those first few weeks at Croxbourn. He would occasionally appear at the front door; demand to see Loretta in a hurry as he was on his way to London, or Cheltenham, or Newmarket; and rush out after a hurried conversation. I was thrilled to see him, and sorry to see him leave so hastily. He appeared to own a number of expensive bespoke suits; and his choice of shirts, ties, shoes demonstrated a discriminating eye. He was incredibly handsome.

He assisted Loretta and her sizeable army of lads to school the horses. He had grown too tall and heavy to consider a career as a jockey, which apparently had been his first choice. Although he was stripling thin, he still would have been unable to maintain the miniscule weight scale which that profession demanded.

Walter had been such a tiny boy in the Little Ones all those years ago; but now we were of equal height; his body was athletic and well-muscled. During his periods in Croxbourn he spent his time in the stables or out schooling the strings on the Downs.

CHAPTER FIFTY FOUR

I LONGED FOR MY fortnightly visit home. Bertha or the dreaded Alf would pick me up after work on Friday evenings. If it was Alf he would gabble all the way home, usually about nothing. I only ever replied to him in monosyllables. I still hated him.

If Bertha collected me, often Mum or Merle would come along for the ride. Then I could talk nineteen-to-the-dozen, telling them the news of the last fortnight; the celebrities and the clothes, the winning horses and the losing horses, the stable lads, and glamorous Loretta whose life I envied so much.

Apart from lover boy, that is. I would certainly have found a nicer man than Ralph. But I don't think I ever mentioned lover boy in my verbal-assault on my family's poor long-suffering ears. He was not that important.

Dad was always thrilled to see me. "Hullo, how is my good girl!" Followed by a wet, soppy, tobacco-flavoured kiss. He would proudly play me his latest record of an operatic aria, or a movement from a concerto.

My sisters and their families would visit and we would catch up with all the sisterly gossip; I would hear every detail of Carol's and Yvonne's amazing progress in reading and sums and be expected to admire the latest school photos of Mary's two daughters, Thelma and Eileen.

I would stroll down to Florrie's untidy cottage to have a good laugh at their antics:

"Dennis cycled home from a party last Saturday night and he was a bit tipsy; couldn't remember where he was going. Well, he went round a corner he had already been round, and he ended up lost. Didn't make it home till Sunday dinnertime."

I sat with Florrie, her kids, her Mum's kids, any kids that happened to be passing; and I felt wanted, needed, a special person, in Florrie's giddy, happy family. Then I would cycle out to Silver Street to a formal welcome by Len and Iris. Schoolmarm Iris still daunted me.

A lengthy ride around the Silver Villages would take in all my various aunts and cousins; the panniers of my bike loaded with gifts of pickles and jams from Mum. Everyone would be avid for news of Linda's exciting life in the high-faluting world of racing.

Mum was even able to persuade me to place flowers on Aunt Beat's grave.

If, after this marathon of family devotion I had any energy left, then came the best part of my weekend at home, the most anticipated: spending time chewing the fat with Ethel and Angie. Angie was looking marvellous; she was always immaculately groomed even if all she intended to do was merely to walk down the street to the post a letter; her blonde curls were orderly and she always wore a touch of lipstick. Her clothes were spotless and in perfect repair.

Ethel had, quite frankly, become rather fat.

We would talk for hours; about their new romances, about the Jaeger sweaters I was saving for, about Angie's job at the factory, and the holiday at Butlins she was looking forward to so much. Mark was sitting up by this time; and he laughed and crowed from the depths of the dilapidated perambulator.

My parents had heard a rumour that Lady Margaret's youngest son, Adrian, a shy student from Cambridge University, had taken to visiting Maudie 'on the sly.' Ethel and Angie laughingly confirmed this. They regarded the whole thing as a May-December romance; and, of course, they always took romance seriously; but none the less screamed with laughter that their Mum may end up as lady of the manor. "That'd be one in the eye for 'er Ladyship, wouldn't it!" Apparently he was generous with his gifts of chocolate and flowers, "real ones, from the flower shop in Middleford!" and in return he received the kind of education universities do not provide.

Maudie's famous convoluted vowels, and the posh accent she had practiced during the period she was convinced Angie was a virtuoso of the piano returned with a vengeance. Her nose was stuck so high in the air I wondered she did not get a crick in the neck.

Mum shuddered to think what would happen if the next happy event in the cottage next door was the untimely arrival of Her Ladyship's grandchild.

With Maudie, anything was possible!

CHAPTER FIFTY FIVE

I RARELY GAVE A thought to child I had borne; she did not exist, had never existed. I had never made a conscious decision to put her out of my mind: she had never been there in the first place.

Work at Croxbourn continued steadily, even though winter had arrived and the Downs were permanently hidden in mist. My friendship with Loretta grew apace. We chattered happily during breakfasts and teas together at the cottage kitchen table. Her expensive prep school and Great Silver village school seemed little different during our reminiscences over Bovril toast.

She asked me how I knew Walter Sikes. I spared her the history of his family's meanderings in the converted removal van and explained he only attended Great Silver School for part of the year because his parents travelled. Loretta appeared to think they were international travellers on ocean liners, or something similar. I did not disabuse her.

Loretta was an only child, and she enjoyed my tales of my brothers and sisters, nieces and nephews, all the Springbournes and Bigfords, and was positively envious of my huge extended family. She only had one aunt, who was a mean old bag, thoroughly disliked by the rest of the family. I told her about Aunt Beat, and we both giggled over Weetabix and the common ground of elderly, unpleasant aunts.

She always looked marvellous, even at eight o'clock in the morning, as if someone had just passed a warm iron over her, and we spent many happy breakfasts discussing the endlessly girlish subjects of clothes and make-up. She did not discuss Ralph. My knowledge of him was based entirely on overheard snatches of their conversation and from the odd dropped comment. She never raised the subject of their relationship. I was aware that he was married with four children; and although he had vowed endless love for Loretta, he could not desert his family. According to Loretta he adored his kids and considered himself the consummate family man. Loretta knew their relationship was for the present; that it was without past or future. Unbelievable as it was, she appeared to adore Ralph.

Ralph spent three or four nights a week at the cottage, and they slept together openly. He was not separated from his wife but he did not conceal his affair with Loretta.

His wife must have been aware of his adultery. On the occasional night he spent at home I wondered what Ralph and his wife discussed at the breakfast table. How was Loretta on Sunday night? Was it possible they compared notes; did his wife know all the details of Loretta's glamorous coffee lace nightwear? His teenage children must have known about the affair; surely it soured their relationship with him. They must have hated him for his unfaithfulness to their Mother.

The stable lads were inveterate gossips and I was aware of the extravagant sexual claims some of them made concerning a number of the Croxbourn village girls. As far as I could tell, all the other lads appeared to believe these impossible tales word-for-word; even if they were most unlikely on the grounds of physical probability alone. The progenitor of the tales was generally admired by all. Is this what Ralph did? Did he brag to other disgusting, fat, bald, middle-aged men about his sex life with Loretta?

In Great Silver the open relationship would not have been tolerated; it would have been declared a public disgrace. I was aware though, from listening to my sisters' gossip, of the existence of certain immoral liaisons. These were always hidden under a cloak of absolute moral decency by the main participators. In Great Silver, everyone who was not deaf, blind, or wall-eyed knew every detail anyway; but custom demanded an attempt at secrecy, even if it was unsuccessful.

Ralph's and Loretta's total abandonment of convention was beyond my comprehension.

Ralph always departed the cottage before I arrived at the breakfast table. He probably took his previous day's dirty shirts back to the wife to wash, before he commenced his employment, selling expensive cars.

In his wake he left crumbs, crumpled napkins and the odour of cigars. Although I was accustomed to Dad smoking at every meal, including breakfast, the stench made me want to vomit.

Loretta would be glowing like a Belisha beacon. Ralph must have been very good at whatever it was he did for her.

CHAPTER FIFTY SIX

GLADLY ATTENDED THE Christmas social with Ethel and Angie, as I was now quite visible to all and sundry. I thought of very little else for the whole of my fortnight at Croxbourn. Loretta must have been heartily sick of me carrying on as to whether I would wear pink lipstick or cherry lipstick; my blue dress or my yellow one.

I could barely wait for Bertha and the car-load of kith and kin to collect me on Friday evening.

No-one in the family had commented on my outgoing disposition, the reverse of my taciturn and cantankerous temperament of the previous year, but the change must have been noticeable.

During the journey back to Great Silver I was apprised of all the family and village goings-on.

Mum had an interesting snippet of news about the butcher's van which still drove out from Middleford for the twice-weekly meat delivery. "Old Mister Timpson has retired now, over seventy he was, and as spry as a young chick. God knows how he'll get through the rest of his days, stuck at home with his mean witch of wife. Delivering meat was his whole life." I was amazed that any person would consider a lifetime of meat deliveries to outlying villages to be worth a lifetime's endeavour.

"Linda, you'll be interested to meet the new delivery man. It's young Ernie Badger, who worked with you at the Co-op. Always asks after you, he does; says he's dying to see you again."

Mum was obviously impressed with the new butcher. "Such a cheeky young monkey. He was surprised to hear Ray and Len were my sons. No, you're kidding me, Mrs. B, he says, you're their big sister really. You cannot be old enough to have such hulking great sons!"

CHAPTER FIFTY-EIGHT

I WAS UNABLE TO face the embarrassment of a face-to-face confrontation with Ernie Badger, as I knew Mum had some silly romantic notion that Ernie might be just the boy for me, even though he was so lacking in stature he barely reached my shoulder. I sneaked out to visit Florrie, hoping to avoid the butcher boy's call.

Well, I misjudged that one! Ernie delivered a joint of meat to Florrie, too. The thought that Florrie probably owed a fortune 'on tick' stole into my mind; but I dismissed it as unworthy of both of us. How did I know that Florrie did not pay her bills; and what business of mine was it anyway? We were laughing giddily at one of Florrie's outrageous stories about her huge family, when, after a sharp tap, the back door opened, and the familiar, homely freckled face of Ernie peeped round it. I was entirely unprepared for him. As he bounced and pirouetted before me, a wicker butcher's basket containing meat perched precariously in the crook of his arm.

I blushed scarlet; not just my face, but my neck and ears joined in the festive glow. The traces of remaining acne glowing here and there like unshaded electric bulbs did little to improve my complexion. I knew he would laugh; I knew he would tease.

"Lovely Linda, spare me your maidenly blushes! It is lovely to see you again! Why do you think I deliver meat at Great Silver, if it is not on the off chance of seeing you?

"The first thing I thought when I got this job - every Saturday I will see the loveliest lady in the Silver Villages and that will make my day. No, my week! My month! My life! Linda, life is nothing without you; please blush for me all the time! Be my silver maiden, Linda!"

Florrie was making a noisy job of giggling into her handkerchief. I cleared my throat and drew myself up to my full height. That should do it!   "How are you? It is great to see you again." This time it was me addressing the parish council. "How long is it since you left the Co-op?"

He wiped his hand across his forehead. He removed his cap, and clasped it before his chest in a sweeping bow. "Oh Linda, how could I stay there without you? You were my reason for going to work each day. How could I link sausages without your lovely smile to delight me over a tray of lamb chops? My heart was broken without you there! I had nothing to live for! I tried to mend my broken heart by working elsewhere! How could you desert me, Linda?

"A nice bit of brisket and a dressed neck of lamb for Monday. That'll be seven and a tanner, Mrs B. You just see that this lovely young lady gets her glad rags on, and comes down to the social at the hall tonight. All Great Silver will be there, just to admire this gorgeous girl. Tatty-bye for now!" He was away out the back door.

"You go, my girl, you go and have a good time. I would

have done at your age!" So said Florrie; well, at least that much was true!

"And don't you mind young Ernie. I believe he's courting a girl over Stamford way. He's all mouth and trousers, goes with the job."

Up to that moment I had been totally unaware that delivering meat necessarily involved a comedy act. I hoped desperately he would have his young lady with him at the social. I planned to avoid him like the plague.

Dad's eyes were wide with appreciation: "My good girl, you'll be the belle of the ball," he purred. Mum immediately went into paroxysms of excitement; "You look lovely, that colour suits you. Oh, Linda, I wish I was young again, and had the freedom you girls have these days."

"I would just love to be going out dancing, looking as marvellous as you do! At socials, they always have the old dances, the Gay Gordons and the Palais Glide; they were always my favourites."

"In my day we used to dance in sets, and even the waltz was considered - well, a bit daring. Now you all jitter around like bugs, with your skirts flying up your legs. We would never have dared; we were always so modest. Oh, you enjoy yourself, my girl! You look beautiful; you'll be able to take your choice of partners."

Most unlikely. When I stood up and showed my prospective partner just how tall I was, he tended to melt very quickly into the crowd.

I always wore flat-heeled pumps to any venue that may include dancing.

Mum kept giving Dad meaningful glances and little

jerks of her head in my direction. Dad never noticed Mum's apparently uncontrollable facial spasms, but I did. Mum had confided to Dad her hopes where Ernie Badger was concerned; but Dad had already forgotten what she had told him. Poor Mum, he just did not understand her obsession with the vaunted position of mother-in-law.

It's okay, Mum, I know Ernie will be there. No, Mum, I will not get myself 'promised' tonight. I am merely going along to view the local talent, not marry it.

Obviously Mum did not know Ernie was courting out Stamford way. Surely she must have noticed he was so vertically-challenged his head came approximately to my armpit.

I wallowed in my parent's approbation; it was necessary to bolster my confidence before I called next door and collected the two Great Silver beauties.

Old Nellie was sitting by the fire, smoking and crooning softly to herself. She had agreed to 'keep an ear open' for Mark, soundly sleeping in his cot in the tiny bedroom. Nellie was as deaf as a post and probably would not have heard an air raid siren, and her stiff old limbs prevented her climbing the stairs in under five minutes. Mark was renowned as a sound sleeper and probably would not waken, but it would be just too bad if he did; it was doubtful Nellie would be any the wiser.

As usual, Maudie's whereabouts were best not considered.

Ethel and Angie had each applied two hours of

necessary attention to their glowing good looks. Angie looked marvellous; every curl in place, faultless make-up, perfectly manicured nails with their deep carmine varnish.

Ethel's prominent cleavage was almost bursting through the pretty crimson silk she had bought at the church jumble sale. The dress had belonged to one of Lady Margaret's daughters and had cost a small fortune in Mayfair; but the young society lady grew tired of it when it was no longer absolutely the latest fashion.

Ethel did not care about fashion, she was well aware this dress displayed her charms to the utmost; which was more than it had done for the young society lady. It had cost a fair bit for a jumble-sale dress, as she lost no time in telling everyone; but then, you had to pay for class. She knew that! She pointed out it was hand-embroidered pure silk.

She looked fantastic, they both did. A pair of freshly-picked roses; in Ethel's case, definitely full-blown.

My tiny amount of carefully-garnered self-confidence fizzled away. It probably leaked out of the soles of my flat-heeled pumps.

CHAPTER FIFTY EIGHT

THE GOOD LADIES of the village had spared no effort in decorating the hall. Purple, turquoise, scarlet crepe paper streamers hung the length of the room; enough paper chains to hold us prisoner; huge earthenware jugs containing copper beech leaves, holly, ivy, and rowan. The tortoise stove at the back of the hall chattered merrily away under its breath.

The band, a family of brothers from Silver Street, were tuning up on stage, a saxophone, an accordion, a clarinet. Their sixty-year-old Mum strummed happily away on the ancient piano, positioned directly beneath, but to one side of the stage. Her music had been in the hit parade before the war, but everyone loved her anyway.

The brothers wore ancient pale blue suits with maroon velvet collars; the suits shiny from pressing with a damp cloth and much patience. Their Mum wore the black velvet and lace dress she had worn at every public appearance for the last twenty years. Her iron-grey perm appeared to have been screwed to her head.

On the left side of the hall stood trestle tables loaded with a plenitude of ham sandwiches, jam sponges and ginger kisses ready for the interval; courtesy of many a cottage kitchen. There was no bar; if you wanted alcoholic refreshment then you must nip down to the Silver Bell. The strongest beverage available here was weak Kia-Ora orange squash.

The youth of the village hung about the rear of the hall, waiting for the musical Mum to finish her opening repertoire. Then the fun began.

The entertainment commenced with games for the little-ones, blind man's buff and musical chairs.

Then the dancing started; first the Gay Gordons to get everyone on their feet, then the Dashing White Sergeant, the Veleta so the Mums and Grans can join in; and so on and so forth.

Miss Landport was there behind the trestle tables, lording it over the organising committee, and looking like a fat old hen; all the while she was planning to accept the praise for the toothsome spread, to which she had contributed nothing. She kept a weather eye on the door, just in case a good looking stranger of, say, forty-ish, should happen to pop in. He had never done so yet, and she had been watching the door at village socials for over twenty years. Hope dies hard.

Gradually all my friends were whisked away to leap around in the Gay-Gordons or glide gracefully by in the Veleta. I gratefully sank into a vacant chair and scrunched up my shoulders in an attempt to disguise my height. I was more likely to attract a partner if I was not actually towering above him at the time. I fixed on a pleasant smile and settled myself to endure a boring evening watching my friends dance.

Well, at least I had an excellent view of the entire proceedings. I would be able to relate the evening's gossip to Mum during Sunday breakfast.

Ernie Badger entered with the usual rowdy gang of youths from Stamford. I affected mild disinterest, even though I was keen to see his young lady. He was towing her along behind him like a reluctant puppy. She was small and pale, with stringy fair hair that stuck to her head; her dress was at least two sizes too large, and much too long, which gave her the appearance of a little child who has dressed up in her mother's clothes.

Ernie spotted me and whooped loudly: "Linda, Linda. Look at lovely Linda, the belle of Great Silver."

He had done it again. They could have switched the lights off in the hall. My blush was so vivid there would have been plenty of illumination.

I affected a cool exterior as he charged over and leapt about before me like a Jack-in-the-Box, dragging his reluctant partner behind him. I was sure he had her on a collar and lead. The unruly gang of Stamford lads followed too, guffawing loudly.

All eyes were on me; I was sure I would die of embarrassment. I wished Angie and Ethel were sitting with me, instead of off tango-ing their way around the floor. They would have considered this amount of attention to be their God-given right.

"This is Linda, the lovely one," Ernie announced to all

and sundry. (Yes, I have big ears, too; they were glowing red, like the rest of me!)

"Linda, meet my darling Elaine. Now she really is the most beautiful girl in the world. Sorry, Linda, I forgot to tell you - you're only second these days."

He glowed with pride. Well, she must have possessed some attraction that was not obvious at first glance. The unworthy thought entered my head that she must be good at sex. I suppressed the destructive idea as I clasped her proffered hand, tiny like a baby's, with little toy red varnished nails.

He then introduced every one of the Stamford boys: They seemed endless, Dave, Keith, Rick, so on and so forth, the names and faces flashed before me like a barely-remembered nightmare.

But Ernie was still in good voice: "Last but not least, and strictly because I belong to Elaine and I am no longer available to woo you myself, Linda, I want you to meet the new love of your life! Linda, this is my brother Ron!"

Ron's face was almost as scarlet as mine. One thing I noticed immediately was that at least his face was level with mine. Ernie's brother was obviously the tall member of the family.

"I've been keeping him for you, Linda. I knew he'd come in handy in the end!"

I did not know where to look; Ron did not know where to look. We studiously avoided each other's eyes.

Ernie was making a fuss about drawing the Stamford lads away from us: "Leave 'em to it, they've got to talk a bit; know what I mean?"

Ernie, Elaine, and the lads retreated to the back of the hall, to giggle, point and nudge. Ron's anguished eyes followed them, but the rest of his body could not; he appeared to be rooted to the spot, with no idea what he should do next. His face was more scarlet than the crepe paper Christmas bells hanging precariously on the centre light. The lads were fifteen feet away from him at the rear of the hall. They may as well have been in the next county.

Every eye in the hall was on us. Oh, God! You could be sure Mum and Dad would hear about this. Here we were, standing face-to-face, lively as a couple of stone statues, on the edge of the village hall dance floor, and it was the most entertaining spectacle the village had seen this year. The tittering, the gossip was already starting: "The butcher boy, you know, young Ernie, that comes round of a Saturday..................."

Even the band on the stage had noticed our discomfiture. They struck up an old-fashioned waltz, as the leader announced in his smoky voice through the megaphone: "for all lovers everywhere."

I thought, we cannot stand here like a pair of telegraph poles, do something Linda! I gently clasped Ron's hand, I whispered so I hoped no-one else heard "can you do this?"

A droop of his eyelids said, yes!

I straightened to my full height, and with what I hoped was amazing grace, I dragged reluctant Ron onto the dance floor.

We led the village in the old-fashioned waltz. After the third time round the floor I realised Ron was a born dancer.

I also realised something I had been totally unaware of before that moment. So was I!

We danced every dance that evening. We did not talk, laugh, kiss, cuddle, we just danced. But we looked terrific together, and we jolly well knew it.

We polka'd, fox-trotted, waltzed and quick-stepped. The other Stamford lads had got the little girls, of ten, eleven, twelve, on the floor and were leaping around like demented maniacs, much to the besotted amusement of their tiny partners. We let them. We were into serious dancing; what other people did was not our concern. There was still time for another tango.

During the interval we ate ham sandwiches and jam sponge together in an almost companionable silence. We were waiting to dance again.

CHAPTER FIFTY NINE

IT WAS ELEVEN o'clock before I noticed. I was prepared to leave Ron were he stood, even though I knew I would walk the length of the village street alone. Ethel and Angie would be busy snogging behind the village hall with tonight's conquests.

The lads from Stamford had other ideas. Jeff was Elaine's brother and was responsible for returning his sister back to the family home in Stamford, eight miles away, north of Middleford.

Ernie, Elaine and her brother descended on Ron and me as we stood at the edge of the swiftly-emptying dance floor, looking anywhere but at each other.

I was privy to whispered conversations: "You've got to see her home, for Gawd's sake. She only lives a step down the road. Blind me, you have been dancing with her all night!"

"Look mate,, we can sit and have a smoke and a bit of a talk. Take all the time you want, we're in no hurry! You need a good snog!"

"Ron, she's ever-so-nice. Make sure you ask her to the pictures or something."

At each predication, Ron blushed, stammered and expressed extreme reluctance.

Ernie went down on his knees before me, his hands clasped in front of his chest. "Lovely Linda, Ron wants to see you home. In fact, lovely Linda, Ron really wants to give you a big goodnight kiss. I implore you; please take pity on this poor swain!'

Enough! I grasped Ron's arm and galloped from the half-empty hall. I had enough embarrassment for one night. I could have quite gladly murdered Ernie.

We walked the length of Great Silver village street, to the cottage, in total silence. Although we were only an arm's length apart, it was as though whole continents separated us. I was not even dreading a snogging session at the cottage gate; fighting Ron off was going to be less of problem than racking my mind for something to say to him.

Our arrival at the gate would not have gone unnoticed; Mum and Dad had waited up. The glow of the table lamp shone through the sitting-room curtains and the record player was performing a concerto. Mum and Dad would be tightly cuddled up together on the settee like a couple of young lovers; and although Dad would be spellbound by the music, and Mum would be content just to be with him and see him happy, they would both have their ears open for my return. Family history had advised them of the necessity of this action.

My parents need not have been concerned for my damaged virtue on that particular night. I wonder Ron did not stand on the opposite side of the street he was so distant from me.

"Thank you for a lovely evening, Linda." ...... now Ron is thanking the parish council! "You really are a smashing dancer. I knew that when I entered the hall, before I even spoke to you."

It may have been a pitch black, moonless night, but he could see that I had not understood him.

"It was the shoes............... You were the only girl present who was wearing a pair of comfy shoes. All the others had gigantic high heels; so easy to trip over, or to lose your balance. If you really care about dancing, you'll ensure you're comfy."

I did not say: well, actually Ron, that is not why I was wearing flat-heeled pumps. Some things are better left unsaid.

He coughed and stammered, coughed again. If my parent's ears were tuned to this conversation, and they probably were, they could not be blamed for discerning that he probably required life support, he was puffing and hacking so much.

"You work at Croxbourn, don't you?"

In the dark, I nodded agreement.

"Do you know there is a Christmas Eve dance at Croxbourn?" I did know that, but had not spared the matter any thought. You cannot turn up at a village dance alone. Village dances were not exactly Loretta's and lover boy's thing, and who else was there?

"Ernie, Elaine and I are all going. I wondered if you would like to come, too. I expect you are coming home for Christmas, we could drop you off at Great Silver afterwards; it would save anyone driving to Croxbourn to collect you."

Well, yes, put like that! I was sure the only person free to collect me on Christmas Eve would be Alf; and the thought of his company made me cringe.

We said our good nights, from a great distance apart. The deal was made. He was picking me up at the stables, taking me to the Croxbourn Christmas Eve dance. This did not mean I was his girl, but I suppose it was a date.

It started to rain as he turned back towards the village hall and I walked up the path to the front door.

First there was the interrogation from my parents. Mum was impressed that my date was with Ernie's brother; that appeared to make it alright, to ease her concern regarding my virtue. When I remembered how mouthy Ernie was, and the things he said to his lady customers on the meat round, it seemed strange that so much saucy banter promoted inherent confidence in his actions. Mum would quite happily have trusted Ernie with my life.

Dad would always be anxious where my virtue was concerned. That is what Dads are for.

The next day, sitting on the sagging sofa in the cottage next door, Ethel and Angie pumped me and prodded me for every detail of the passionate snogging session they imagined had taken place on Bigford's front door step. My reluctance to even discuss the matter only confirmed what they already thought; that it had been a momentous event.

CHAPTER SIXTY

WHEN I RETURNED to Croxbourn on Sunday evening Loretta was noticeable by her absence; her car was garaged, and cups and saucers of recent usage were in the sink. I figured she was probably in bed with lover-boy.

My head in the clouds, I planned what I would wear to the Croxbourn Christmas dance as I took a long leisurely bath. I retired to bed early and was asleep as soon as my head touched the pillow.

During breakfast the next morning I regaled Loretta with the events of the weekend. As ever, she was immensely interested in my family life. She asked me what Ron looked like; and as I drew his face into my mind, I realised he was not bad looking. He was of solid build, like Ernie, but almost half as tall again; he moved with the nimble-ness of a cat. Like me he had more than his fair share of acne. As I cast my mind back to the dance I realised he had incredible eyes, dark brown and slightly slanted, with long curling fair lashes. A girl would be proud to walk beside him.

It seemed Loretta was more than happy to marry me off, as were my parents, my sisters, and even Angie and Ethel. In spite of being thirty-ish, independent, and saddled with Ralph, Loretta appeared to believe I was just waiting to fall in love.

The workaday life at the stables continued. More famous people: more of Linda fading into the background unnoticed; more beagles to be patted; more MGs parked in the drive.

Walter Sikes rarely came by the cottage. Loretta had him away in Newmarket, or Kempton Park, or wherever. One morning at breakfast Loretta told me Walter had begun dating the daughter of one of the wealthy owners and she was concerned that he was out of his depth. This young lady had just been 'finished off' at an expensive school in Switzerland; appropriate for the daughter of an earl. Loretta knew that any education Walter had received was at village schools throughout the South of England, although she was unaware of the details of his itinerant parents or the removal van.

Loretta voiced the hope that nothing would come of it; after all they were both of them barely eighteen. As a warm sexual being herself, Loretta was fully aware of Walter's undoubted charm and good looks. Apparently the young lady was fast growing into a society beauty. A frown creased Loretta's forehead; she worried that things had already passed the point of no return.

CHAPTER SIXTY ONE

S OMEONE ELSE HAD begun paying me almost daily visits, and had begun to bring me small gifts. Ralph dropped by most mornings; and the mere sight of his confident stride as he approached the cottage was enough to make my flesh creep. I prayed that the phone would ring, so he would be obliged to leave me alone; but, wily as he was, and accustomed to creeping behind the world's back to spend time with Loretta, he knew how to time his visits so that he demanded my full attention.

He leered. There was no other way to describe the way he looked at me. I told myself he leered at most women; but the thought afforded me scant comfort.

He would sit on the edge of the kitchen table and methodically undress me with his eyes. He would peer at my legs, almost as though he were counting the hairs on my calves; he would attempt to sneak a peek down my blouse or up my skirt. He tried to brush past me on any available occasion; always making sure his hand lightly brushed my breast. If he was telling me something he would find it necessary to put his arm round my shoulders; or clasp my hand in his large, red, sweaty mitt. I always edged away, putting a kitchen-length between us.

He brought me chocolate bars, which I politely refused. He picked me holly and mistletoe from the woods and hedges. He bought me a pottery elf in a gift shop, saying he couldn't resist it as it reminded him of me. You cannot refuse holly and mistletoe; and he appeared genuinely hurt when, again, I politely refused the elf, but refuse I did. He gave me the creeps. I found his attention disconcerting.

At breakfast Loretta said: "Ralph has taken a shine to you. He thinks you are quite a character. He only said to me yesterday: I would like to see the man that can take our Linda down; she's a very proud young lady."

No, Loretta, I have no doubt Ralph would actually like to be the man that would take Linda down!

But I said nothing! What could I say? It was hard to imagine that a sensible hard-headed Loretta could be head-over-heels in love with such a freak, but she was.

CHAPTER SIXTY TWO

A WEEK LATER I daydreamed my way though yet another workaday breakfast, my mind on the really important things in life, dancing shoes and nail varnish shades; while Loretta glanced through Horse and Hound. Outside the Aga-heated cottage lowering December skies threatened to engulf the Downs. Nothing moved in the grey landscape. Even the cawing rooks were silent.

Loretta spoke sharply, interrupting my reverie: "Linda, what do you think racing is?"

Her brown eyes observed me keenly, a look of puzzlement on her face. She inserted two more slices of bread into the electric toaster. "You have no idea what we are really doing here, have you Linda?"

The question had caught me unawares. I gazed at her, open-mouthed. My chin wagged up and down, but no sound came forth.

"Have you ever been to the races? Have you even ridden a horse, yourself?"

Discretion being the better part of valour, I thought it unwise to say that until that fateful day I bumped into

Walter Sikes outside Great Silver post office I did not even know that horse racing existed.

She spread best butter and home-made marmalade. "You never ask any questions! Would you have considered selling shoes without knowing at least a few details about the product? Do you know anything about horses? Even the smallest thing?"

"You are endlessly pleasant and polite, a brilliant asset in the house, and you obviously have a head for business. All my staff adore you."

Who, me, I do not think so!

"But you cannot spend the rest of your working days smiling nicely at strangers and talking about the weather. You should have at least some little clue about what really goes on here. Sooner or later a client will ask you a question; and you couldn't answer the simplest query, could you?"

"Have you ever backed a horse? Does your Dad ever back a horse? Could you differentiate between a bay and a roan horse?"

Again tact prevented me pointing out I would probably have difficulty between a black and a white horse.

The interrogation continued: "Do you know what I mean when I talk about 'the odds'? Do you know what flat racing is, or over-the-sticks?" She picked up her Irish linen napkin and wiped a trace of marmalade from her chin.

I had always known it couldn't last, my lovely job! I was out on-my-ear! I had been sprung! The sum total of my horse-knowledge was zero; I had always known that Loretta required so much more.

Mum and Dad would be disappointed; they had bragged in the village about my exciting new job. A tear escaped.

"Poor Linda, I did not intend to make you cry! It's just that things cannot go on as they are. I have found you very reliable, with oodles of initiative; but you really are rather short on knowledge of what we basically do here."

"In the New Year I intend to change that. It is my plan to put you on a sort of training course. I intend to teach you the racing industry from the bottom up. It is my promise to you that I will leave no stone unturned; and by this time next year you will be a very knowledgeable young lady."

I could barely stop myself from hugging her. This was more than I had ever hoped for! I would never be invisible again!

Loretta continued: "I cannot have you working here, and not knowing the front or back end of a horse. I will ask Walter if he will teach you to ride."

Oh, gorgeous, gorgeous, gorgeous! Oh, unbelievable! I had known for sometime that I was madly in love with handsome, charming Walter. This was better than my wildest daydreams.

"Oh, and another thing, Ralph has promised to teach you to drive. You can be immensely useful to me if you can pick up and deliver things in Croxbourn as well as going down to Middleford with errands to the vet's. Ralph has an old Volkswagen in his shed; he says it can be yours while you work for me. So there you are, Linda; you will be an independent young lady with your own car. Your friends at Great Silver will be green with envy."

I should have known it was all too good to be true.

The car, that would be wonderful; but being taught

to drive by Ralph, that was my worst nightmare realised. Trouble was, it was his car.

Well, my blush would have considerably brightened the grey morning!

Loretta regarded my quizzically. "Whatever's wrong now? Why the tears? This is my Christmas present to you; much better than gift-wrapped soap and talc, don't you think? I thought you would be pleased."

I stammered. I stuttered. "Oh, Loretta, yes! Oh I just can't believe it's all happening!"

More stuttering and playing for time. I knew I could not be in a car alone with Ralph.

"The trouble is, my sister Bertha has promised to teach me to drive. I don't want to offend her; you know, family and everything; it can get a bit tricky at times."

Bertha had promised no such thing. The family would be amazed that I would even consider such a daring act as learning to drive a car; but I could not think of anything else to say. Anyone but Ralph! That I could not do!

Fortunately Loretta started to giggle. "What a funny young thing you are. You would do absolutely anything not to hurt your family; and I must say I find your attitude thoroughly commendable. Never mind; you discuss it with Bertha at Christmas; and I'll ask Ralph what he thinks about it all. Trouble is, he really fancies himself as an expert driver."

That is not all he fancies himself as.

And sometimes Loretta sounded so old.

I should have anticipated the Christmas Eve dance with excitement. Ron, a nice young man, had asked me to be his partner; and this was me, Linda, from whom most nice young men would probably run for miles.

It would be wonderful to spend four days at home in the cottage with Mum, Dad and Merle; but all I could worry about was how I was going dodge Ralph's driving tuition without offending Loretta. Every time I thought about the possibility of being alone with Ralph - anywhere, and certainly not in a car - I wanted to vomit.

Ralph managed to drop into the cottage a number of times every day, but always when Loretta was absent.

This gave me plenty of time to get a good look at him; and what I saw appalled me. He was old, and incredibly heavy. His belly hung over the top of his trousers, which he had to keep hitching up as they slid down the mountain. He was losing his hair and his bald pate was crimson red. He had little ginger hairs sticking out the end of his nose, which was purple with the cold. Same with his ears!

I was, after all, only seventeen years old. To me he looked hideous. He was ancient, and repugnant.

CHAPTER SIXTY THREE

C HRISTMAS EVE BROUGHT howling wind and rain; no white Christmas this year.

Ernie, Elaine, Ron and Jeff, a reticent, polite and charming young man of nineteen, arrived at the stables in Jeff's ancient car to collect me for the Christmas Eve 'Do' at Croxbourn Memorial Hall.

I was dressed warmly in a red fluffy sweater and a soft, full mohair skirt in shades of grey and royal blue. The appalling weather ensured you dressed warmly; no flimsy party dresses for this event. I had applied my make-up carefully under Loretta's watchful gaze. Linda Bigford could not imitate perfection but at least she could be well-groomed and smartly turned out. Perhaps my acne would be hardly noticeable in the dusky light of the smoke-filled Memorial Hall.

The three-mile journey to the hall was not without event. Elaine chattered throughout the whole journey, mostly about nothing, in her high-pitched tone; all the while Ernie would throw in pithy comments on her topics of conversation, and Elaine would collapse into bouts of laughter which resembled a donkey heehawing. If everyone else did not join her mirth she would dig them in the ribs, trumpeting "Go on! Go on! Go on!" at the top of her tinny voice.

It got on your nerves after the first fifty yards. At least Ron and I were not required to add to the conversation. Which was just as well; neither of us could think of a thing to say.

The Memorial Hall was suitably decorated. Pleated crepe paper bells and balls, a mangy Christmas tree with scarred glass trinkets and moulting fuzzy garlands. Maybe the manger scene in the corner was a slight overstatement in a venue where fifty per cent of the guests would be rolling drunk by midnight.

It was also freezing cold. Dancing was very much the immediate order, to prevent limbs dropping off from frostbite. Couples were dancing the Veleta in overcoats.

Ron and I managed to have a great time. By interval, we had given up dancing at arm's length and were happily waltzing in each other's arms, both of us pink and glowing with exertion. He smelt of lifebuoy soap and toothpaste.

Ron and I danced every dance; that way conversation was rarely necessary. We waltzed, quickstepped, foxtrotted, jived. We looked good together, and we both knew it.

Ernie and Elaine were exceedingly merry by midnight; Elaine squealing with giddy laughter every five seconds; and Ernie clowning all over the floor. Jeff, who took his brotherly responsibilities very seriously, was drinking lemonade.

Ron and I had barely enough time for a cuppa at interval; we had been so busy on the floor. Some people have a relationship that is based purely on sex, others on intellectual compatibility. Ron's and mine was based on the Palais Glide and the Saint Bernard's Waltz. Conversation did not happen.

The hours of the clock seemed to fly round to midnight, when everybody kissed each other and wished each other the greetings of the season.

Ralph was temporarily forgotten.

We sang Christmas carols at the top of our voices during the car journey to Great Silver. We had all attended Church of England village schools, so we were word perfect, even if our tunelessness made the melodies unrecognisable. The deafening drumming of the rain on the car roof did little to improve our lack of harmony. Time flew by; in a trice we were at the cottage gate.

Even though it was almost one in the morning, the glow of the table lump shone dimly through the sitting room curtains. Ours was the only lighted window in the village; the possibility of children waking before dawn in a state of noisy excitement had sent the population of Great Silver to bed early. Mum and Dad had waited up for me even though Mum would be up before crack of dawn to prepare for early communion.

No embarrassing holding each other at arm's length, no goodnight pecks on the cheek; the teeming rain ensured that Ron helped me to the doorstep with my many bags and parcels, in great haste, and hollered: "I'll call you at the stables after Christmas, Linda," as he made a frantic dash back to the shelter of the car.

Dad opened the door. The warmth of the cottage, the peculiar ambiance of home engulfed me, wrapped round me like a pair of welcoming arms. Mum came to kiss me, wearing the quilted dressing gown with the warm tartan-lined hood she had owned all my life.

CHAPTER SIXTY FOUR

ERLE AND I visited next door with an opulence of presents for little Mark, who seemed to have received a gift from every person in the Silver Villages. He was an expert at sitting up, and his sharp eyes had already noticed the colourfully wrapped gifts underneath the tree. He was definitely planning to crawl towards it before New Year. Christmas had come as a surprise to him, but his excited crowing revealed his tremendous approval.

He was a large child, with skin the texture of rose petals and the silken golden curls. Mum had spent most of breakfast time carrying on in great detail about what a stunner that child was and how he would just slay the girls in years to come. How would they be able to resist those eyelashes, she gushed.

Glamorous grandmother Maudie was wearing a see-through frilly nylon blouse and a very tight skirt; to say nothing of queenly Aunt Angie, elegant as a mannequin about to be photographed. Even old Nellie, smoking quietly by the fire, and her milk stout dribbling onto her whiskery chin, looked cheerful.

Peter Pyle rushed here and there, getting under

everyone's feet; offering to make us a cuppa; showing off his numerous presents. His clothes had been dragged onto his small body in an urgent Christmas morning haste; the tail of his shirt hung over his flannel shorts and his unfastened laces tripped him at his every hasty turn.

Nothing in the cottage had changed. The clock on the mantelshelf had stopped working in nineteen-forty-eight, but made a convenient letter rack for a sheaf of unpaid bills. The dust on the mantelshelf predated the clock's demise. Nellie's cough mixture and its accompanying array of sticky teaspoons held pride of place on the piano top, along with odd socks, a brassiere, a spoutless teapot, and a very elderly cheese sandwich.

They were the Pyles. I loved every one of them.

CHAPTER SIXTY FIVE

O N NEW YEAR'S Eve Loretta threw a dinner party for a dozen or so of her most influential clients. She called upon me to assist her.

Actually Loretta had prepared most of the food herself; Loretta's skill and knowledge of culinary art amazed me and I came to the conclusion her expensive ladies' college education had taught her a great deal more than how to murder vowels with her plummy accent.

The dining table looked elegant and festive, decorated with greenery and berries, and Loretta's gleaming silver cutlery (I had spent all afternoon polishing it!) on the dazzling white damask cloth. She owned a complete set of royal Doulton old roses dinnerware, including sous dishes, meat dishes, and gravy boats. My Mum would have been green with envy. In my Mum's world you could be a cheat and a scoundrel, filthy and unwashed; but if you ate off royal Doulton and knew how to use the correct knives and forks, then you had passed the litmus test; you were obviously gentry.

Loretta was beautifully attired, attractively made-up, exquisitely coiffured, and of course totally poised and in control by the time the first guest arrived. Who would have guessed that an hour previously she had literally been sweating over a hot stove? My admiration for her increased hundredfold.

During our breakfast gossip Loretta had told me the parents of Jeanette, Walter's precious girlfriend, would be dining.

As the main course was served I took the opportunity to sneak a peek round the dining room door.

Lord Boswell and his wife, Lady Biddy would be sitting on Loretta's right hand of course.

I had expected a dashing hero of British industry; reality was an anti-climax. His Lordship was a tiny, thin man, who resembled an elderly wizened gnome. Lady Biddy would have been handsome if she had a scrap of dress sense and a good hairdresser; clearly she had neither. Her dowdy frock was a size too, and five years out-of-date. Her fuzzy brown hair was dragged back off her face by an arsenal of hair grips and I can never recall anyone wearing that shade of lipstick outside of a circus ring.

I very carefully fixed into my mind a picture of the Jeanette I had never met - the image I wanted to see was a tiny, skinny, fairy-like creature wearing jumble-sale clothes.

Jeanette was Walter's sweetheart; and I desperately needed her to be a freak. I was beginning to realise that I was besotted with Walter.

CHAPTER SIXTY SIX

THE WINTER OF nineteen-fifty-one had a snowless beginning, but February brought Downland blizzards that hid the lanes and levelled them with the hedge tops. My riding lessons were postponed until we could find the lanes again.

In the meantime Walter, on one of his rare visits, had taken me to the stables and introduced me to Marjorie, an elderly bay mare of gentle disposition.

Walter told me that it was official: Marjorie and Downland Monarch, alias King, Loretta's most prized jumper, were in a close personal relationship. They had loose-boxed next to each other for years, and if they were parted for any length of time both became morose and depressed. It was crucial to take Marjorie to the races, in her ancient horse box towed by Loretta's land rover, while King travelled in majestic style arranged by professional horse transporters. If King was to win, and he usually did, the presence of Marjorie within sight, sound and smell of him was a total necessity.

Marjorie enjoyed a good day out; Walter thought she

even had a stylish hat to wear in the ladies' enclosure, hidden somewhere in the depths of her horse box.

I had never been in such close proximity to a horse before, but we soon became firm friends. Loretta had ridden Marjorie when she was a child, so the mare was no longer young.

The thought of tall, slim, handsome Walter, Walter with his olive skin that never succumbed to the pasty common winter disguise of English people; Walter with his dark eyes, that I had thought were black, but like all gypsies, his eyes were the very deepest blue; his height and his athletic slimness - in my daydreams he helped me onto Marjorie's broad back, holding my arms, touching me, clasping me, cuddling me, kissing me; oh dear, these dreams filled my waking hours.

My night-time dreams were otherwise: after all I had lost my innocence a long time before. I would awaken to the chill of a February morning, but in my dream it had been May, and warm; on the Downs, by the river. Walter and I were naked - him, a perfect physical man; and somehow, naked as I was, I was also beautiful, sexy and self-assured.

I ached to return to Walter's arms in the warmth of the sun, but the interrupted dream could never be recaptured.

Modestly I tried to hide my infatuation with Walter. Walter was not mine, long for him as I may. Out there somewhere was Jeanette, the earl's daughter; and it was obvious from our conversations during our visits to Marjorie that he adored her. And yes, Loretta's fears were justified; they certainly did a great deal more than just hold hands.

Cool Linda, acting as though Walter was just someone I had sat next to in the Little Ones, all the while my emotions were once again in turmoil.

CHAPTER SIXTY SEVEN

WHEN I COMMENCED working for Loretta I thought she had employed me because she wished to train her own staff in her own way, to imprint her own high standards upon two young people. After a while I began to wonder if there were other reasons why she had offered me the job; I could hardly be considered a prize, not knowing the rear end of a horse from its head.

Loretta did not regard the gypsy and the earl's daughter as a classical romance. She considered it a dangerous liaison between two people who had nothing in common except youth, inexperience and physical attraction. Loretta was aware of Walter's sexual magnetism; she was even slightly affected by it herself. If Jeanette's parents disapproved of the budding romance, and it was fairly certain they would, Loretta may receive some blame for the assailment of Jeanette's virtue. After all, couldn't she keep her staff in better order, than have them out seducing the client's innocent, convent-educated daughter? Oh, yes, Loretta had her reputation and the viability of her business to consider. Word gets around, other clients had daughters.

Loretta had no wish to lose her trainee manager. Above

all else, Walter offered an innate understanding of horses that a business diploma or a private education could not replace.

The arrival of my letter of application and her subsequent conversation with Walter, which demonstrated a long-standing acquaintance, plus her discovery of my lack of romantic attachment must have given her food for thought. She was dealing with young people here, and the earl's daughter was absent most of the time. If enough temptation was placed before Walter, then hopefully he would succumb to that which was freely offered and at hand.

Loretta already knew I had a child so she did not imagine me to be a blushing virgin, needing a map of seduction to be drawn for me. She was aware of Walter's attraction herself, and she considered that if we were thrown together long enough a relationship between us was inevitable. The here-and-now and liberally-available would replace the earl's daughter, who, because of her parent's protectiveness, was not nearly so accessible.

All Loretta needed was the opportunity to throw us together; and the need for me to learn about horses had presented just that prospect.

Trouble was, I had little experience as a seductress.

Mind you, I couldn't wait to get started!

The weather continued seasonal, with black ice and Downland fog, even though the snow melted and we rediscovered the lanes between the hedges. The riding lessons were still postponed until icicles no longer hung by the wall.

When Walter made his rare appearances at the stables we would amble over to visit Marjorie in companionable silence. All the while my heart would be turning somersaults, my pulses racing. The entire purpose of my existence was to be in Walter's presence; to gaze at his handsome face, to touch his lean athletic limbs, and to smell the scent of bay rum that always hung about him.

Marjorie liked sugar knobs; liquorice allsorts were her absolute favourites. Walter would place his arm affectionately about her neck and murmur in her ear the sweet nothings that only those who value horses can whisper, and it was evident that Marjorie understood every word. Oh, how I longed for him to put his arm round me and whisper to me.

But if we spoke, it was usually about Jeanette, who was obviously perfect, or about Ron, who Walter imagined was my boyfriend.

Cool, cool Linda acted as though this was the status quo.

And all the while my heart was in turmoil.

CHAPTER SIXTY EIGHT

R ON WAS SHY, but pleasant company; a good friend, nothing more. He was gentle and well-mannered; and when he finally got round to talking to me he was an excellent conversationalist.

He had been considered backward at school because he was left-handed. The elderly narrow-minded village school teacher had tried to change him to a right-handed person in accordance with the mores and ideas of fifty years before. When he could not be changed, but still remained resolutely left-handed, in spite of canings and having his left hand tied behind his back, she basically gave up on him, and left him to his own devices. He told me that Sir Winston Churchill was left-handed, and no-one had ever called him backward. I have often wondered if that was true, and who told him anyway.

The long-term result was that although he was a voracious reader, Ron was unable to write anything down.

He worked on a farm because in that job it was unnecessary to handle a pen from one week to the next. He liked animals and the outdoor life anyway, and rain and snow did not deter him; but pen-pushing would have been beyond him. Not for him an apprenticeship in the building industry, because that involved days spent at the technical college; and driving a lorry or working in a shop would involve too much reading and writing. He said there was no future in farm work, but he was sure he would do it all his life.

Well, we had something in common: a total lack of self confidence.

We joined Ernie, Elaine and Jeff for a noisy singsong in Jeff's battered old car prior to spending most Saturday evenings dancing at a local village hall. We both adored dancing, and had finally learned to relax and enjoy each other's company. Ernie and the others, as well as many of the couples who visited the local hops, obviously regarded us as a courting couple.

We had exchanged a couple of clumsy kisses, but no lengthy snogging sessions, and for that I was grateful. If I was to be kissed, I prayed it would be by Walter. I never regarded my attitude as unfair to Ron. I valued his friendship greatly.

Elaine was already talking to anyone who would listen about getting engaged; all the while her hand placed proprietarily on Ernie's arm and a smug expression on her face. She knew the prices of rings with diamonds versus rubies, or sapphires versus emeralds. If you did not prevent her, she would hold forth on this subject for hours at a time. Ernie looked bored stiff; he was clearly not keen on the idea.

Upon our return to Great Silver or to Loretta's cottage at Croxbourn the others always left us alone on the doorstep.

Ernie and Elaine were busy in the back seat of the battered car and Jeff wandered off for a smoke.

The others would have been disappointed if they had known that Ron and I stood an arm-length apart and discussed each other's working week. A peck on his cheek as I left him was as romantic as it got. I was happy this way. It never occurred to me to even consider whether Ron was.

CHAPTER SIXTY NINE

I DAYDREAMED MY WAY into the kitchen for breakfast on a bone-numbing, bitter March morning, totally unaware that I glided about like zombie with a distant, unworldly expression on my face.

Loretta regarded me with tolerant affection: "I can see Ron treated you well on Saturday night. Had a nice kiss and a cuddle, did you?" She laughed knowingly.

I purred agreement. I had just got to my favourite bit of my Walter daydream, where he was nibbling the back of my neck as we both rode away on Marjorie's long-suffering back. Daydreams do not need to be probable, or even possible.

Loretta could think what she liked. My feelings for Walter were my secret. If she thought Ron could cause me to swoon with passion, that was fine by me.

She waved her hands before my face. "With us, are you?" she laughed. "I'll need to take a better look at your Ron. Whatever he's got, it's certainly not visible to the naked eye. Mind you, I always say it's the quiet ones that you need to watch."

Watch him all you like, Loretta. I shall be watching

someone else entirely, but that is my secret. I think you would be intrigued to know that secret, Loretta, but I will not tell you, or anyone.

Loretta finally claimed my attention for long enough to establish that I would like scrambled eggs. A plate appeared before me, complete with perfectly-browned and buttered toast.

"Now," she said, "to business. I did notice that Bertha does not appear to be providing the promised driving lessons, and I am anxious to have your services as a chauffeuse in the near future." She spread home-made raspberry jam onto wholemeal toast. "I really think it is in both our interests if Ralph starts teaching you this week. He has fixed the Vee Doubleyou. All I can say is Lucky You. Ralph is a trained driving instructor, you know." She poured me a cuppa from the bone china teapot. I suddenly thought longingly of the huge brown earthenware one on the kitchen table at Great Silver. "You really will learn more under his tutorage than you would if Bertha taught you; even though of course Bertha is one of the world's loveliest people, and you are incredibly fortunate to have such a gorgeous sister."

I gulped tea and scrambled egg, trying desperately to think of a reply. Ralph's leers had become more suggestive as the weeks passed. At first I had merely found him offensive; now I was genuinely scared of him. He always appeared when I was alone in the house, and inevitably he always managed to touch me, brush my breasts as he passed me by, or my bottom, or legs. He was so brazen; he no longer pretended this was accidental. I had slapped his hand sharply twice, and once I had stormed to my room in a white-hot fury. He roared with laughter.

He used the most unlikely pretexts as an excuse for his presence; borrowing a postage stamp, loose change to use the phone in the village. He seemed to treat it all as if it was 'our little joke' almost to the point of tapping his forefinger to the side of his nose as he left. I was not amused.

I continually promised myself I would tell Loretta that his behaviour distressed me.

I did not do so, of course. Like now! I just agreed that starting the driving lessons this week would be fine and she must let me know when Ralph could fit it in.

My mind was working overtime; whatever happened, I was not going to be alone in the car with Ralph. I would think of some means of avoidance. The thought of his short fat fingers touching me anywhere, even my hand, made my flesh creep.

But Loretta had more to say: "Now the biggest and best surprise of them all. My pals and I always have a super get-together in mid-March, usually about St Patrick's Day. A corker of a weekend in a luxury hotel in London: you know, go to the theatre, and have a decent meal somewhere. We always have a marvellous time, and this year, well, we would like you and Walter to join us. My treat, of course! What do you think?"

I was too flabbergasted to reply.

"Have you ever spent much time in London, Linda?"

Although Great Silver was only fifty miles from London I had never actually been there. Oh, all the rest of the family had; but the war had prevented my childhood visits to Madam Tussauds and the zoo; and then when I was grown and earning my own spending money I had mucked things up having by a huge bout of depression and a barely-remembered baby. Just staying alive in Great Silver and trying to establish myself in my job at Croxbourn had taken all my energy, to say nothing of my money.

I smiled politely and shook my head. A trip to London, staying at a real hotel, going to the theatre; never in my wildest dreams had I considered this possibility. And best of all, Walter would be my escort. I could not believe my luck.

All thoughts of Ralph and the dreaded driving lessons fled my conscious mind. I barely listened as Loretta told me little anecdotes about her pals: Sarah, who wanted to be a national hunt jockey; Caroline, who was studying to be a doctor; Anna, who ran a home for wealthy unmarried mothers. A superstition existed that privilege prevented unwanted pregnancy, and the pudding-club was merely the lot of working-class girls. Unfortunately, reality had established a different situation. Discretion demanded that Loretta treated these matters with the utmost delicacy.

I hope I giggled in all the right places. Loretta was an accomplished story teller; and if only I could have organised my scattered wits, I would certainly have been treated to a good laugh over my breakfast cuppa. As it was, my mind was racing; Walter at the theatre, Walter beside me in a posh restaurant, Walter in the same hotel. Oh, it was going to be my wildest dreams come true.

CHAPTER SEVENTY

I T WAS OFTEN necessary for me to pay tradesmen at the cottage door, plus there were other needs within the business for readily available small change. Loretta kept a cash box containing one hundred pounds hidden in the safe, to be used for such out-of-pocket expenses. Only Loretta and I had access to the locked cashbox. I enjoyed maintaining the petty cash journal and I had done so on the previous Friday afternoon and it had been correct.

Assorted banknotes of various denominations normally filled the box; about half were missing. I was puzzled, and I resolved to discuss this with Loretta at the earliest opportunity; it was unlike her to even open the box without informing me. A double-check of the journal revealed that it was out-of-balance by fifty-seven pounds. This was a small fortune; I had never owned that much money in my life.

I panicked. What could have happened to the money? Only Loretta and I knew the lock's combination. I concluded that Loretta must have taken the money before she left for her business appointment.

Then the phone started to ring; and Jim called in to check if Loretta had left him specific instructions for the day. The vet came, presenting a bill for his services. A dozen or so other interruptions and all thoughts of the missing petty cash flew from my mind.

Loretta returned to the cottage early the next morning. She bathed hurriedly and emerged half an hour later in a towelling robe, her hair dripping.

Obviously Ralph had accompanied her to Marlborough. Come to think of it, he had not made his presence felt on Monday; at least that was one day I did not spend avoiding his leers and his seeking fingers. I wondered if his wife was as glad to see the back of him as I was.

Loretta stood at the kitchen table while she swallowed tea and toast, making a list under her breath of things she must attend to that day. She asked where this thing was; had I seen so-and-so; had this letter arrived; was there a cheque for such-and-such? Passing me a hurried list of special instructions for Jim, she galloped off to the Newbury races with more speed than many of the horses taking part.

No chance to discuss the missing petty cash.

I finally spoke with Loretta late on Wednesday afternoon. The day at the races had been a financial and personal disaster. The horses she trained had not won; and she had actually backed them, which only made matters worse.

The head lad would cop an ear bashing as soon as

she caught up with him; not that any of this was his fault, Loretta was well aware of that. Frustration and temporary poverty had reduced her normally ebullient temperament to waspishness. I decided to avoid her company as much as possible until she regained her equilibrium.

None-the-less, I felt it prudent to apprise her of the missing petty cash. She looked stunned, and she required a moment to regain her composure. Then, a sharp edge to her voice, she suggested I handled other people's money with more responsibility. Balancing a mere petty cash journal could not be beyond me, surely! She stalked off in high dander to lick her wounds and probably call lover boy and cry down the phone line onto his waiting shoulder.

One thing was certain; Loretta had not taken the fifty-seven pounds with her to Marlborough.

I was convinced she would recover her usual good humour and by mid-morning her anger would have subsided; we would be able to discuss the missing cash.

Or would we? In her present frame of mind fifty-seven pounds probably represented a small fortune.

The dreaded driving lesson should have taken place on Thursday afternoon but Loretta was so busy she could not spare time to listen for the phone while I was 'out gallivanting with Ralph in the Vee Doubleyou:' those were her actual words. Obviously she had lost a large sum at Newbury on Tuesday. I was not sorry the lesson was cancelled; this gave me another week before I had to face up to touchy-feely Ralph. Yes, I could tell Loretta I just did not want to learn to drive, - but she would then ask me why, - I could not face telling her I feared her lover's wandering hands.

CHAPTER SEVENTY ONE

W E WERE LEAVING after lunch on Friday to attend the party that evening. On Saturday evening we were going to see the Cole Porter musical, Kiss Me Kate, at the London Coliseum. It had opened the previous week to ecstatic crowds and rave revues after its Broadway success. I could not fathom how Loretta managed to obtain tickets, they were like hen's teeth; and I realised her dalliance with the rich and famous had truly made her a women with influence.

The cost of my ticket to the theatre almost equalled my weekly wage, to say nothing of the hotel and the party. Mum and Dad were overjoyed for me when I told them of my good fortune. My sisters, and particularly Iris, who loved theatre, were green with envy.

And very best of all, Walter would be there! I had never mentioned Walter to my parents. They would only recall the inhabitants of the ancient removal van parked on Silver Common.

Ethel had said: "You are going to the theatre!" I might as well have been planning to attend a public beheading.

Angie had said: "Yeah, its Shakespeare, sort-of, to music!"

They nodded their heads sagely, and quickly changed the subject. They had attended pantomimes performed by the Silver Players in the village hall, and they had been bored stiff. So, what was I making such a fuss about?

I almost missed Aunt Beat. She would definitely have delivered a sufficiently spiteful remark in an attempt to spoil my enjoyment.

Ethel and Angie were more impressed with the London hotel. They imagined me having breakfast in bed, and pouring coffee, not tea, from a silver pot; and in the evening gliding down an ornamental staircase into the dining room to have dinner, not tea; and looking very glamorous, with everyone's eyes upon me.

Well, if it had been themselves, they would expect to attract a plenitude of male attention.

Mind you, Ethel and Angie were still awed by the idea of a bathroom and a flush toilet. I had become blasé about such things during my sojourn at Croxbourn.

The thoughts of the visit to London had turned my head. I would be dreaming of theatre, parties, restaurant meals, Walter, when I should have been cleaning the sink. The rich and famous visiting the cottage were copping a blank stare instead of the welcoming smile I had practiced so long.

I alternated between planning my appearance at dinner, breakfast, party, theatre. I would make a dramatic entry, looking stunning, wearing items from my limited wardrobe and cosmetics; to secretly bemoaning my countrified clothing and Woolworth's makeup, and dying a million deaths of shame that my meagre apparel screamed: half-witted seventeen-year-old with no money or fashion sense.

I longed for Angie's natural attributes. Life would be so much simpler if I had a scrap of her charm.

CHAPTER SEVENTY TWO

M Y LIST OF tasks for Friday morning was longer than for most full days; I forced myself to concentrate on work and not to think of the bay-rum scent of Walter, or of him holding me in his arms. This took an immense effort of will, as we were all travelling to London with Ralph in his Rover, which would surely mean Loretta sitting next to Ralph in the front seat, and myself and Walter in the back seat. The thought of Walter's intimate closeness for a whole hour and a half caused my senses to reel.

Various contingency plans were to be set in place as the cottage was to be left unattended, except for care-taker Jim, for a whole forty-eight hours.

Just before noon Loretta rushed into the kitchen, her perfectly made-up face a swamp of tears and soggy face powder.

"Oh, Linda, Linda, I don't know what to do!" More tears, hysterical crying. "My mother has just phoned me. Oh Linda, my dear old Dad has just had a heart-attack. They have got him to hospital in Cheltenham; but Mum fears he may not make it. Ooh! He cannot die, not my lovely Dad!"

She collapsed into a frenzied heap. Poised, capable

Loretta suddenly appeared so vulnerable, so defenceless. She wept like a small child; I wanted to hold her in my arms, as I recalled my sister Bertha would, but my innate coolness and detachment allowed me only to clasp her hand, gently stroking her wrist.

"It's happened before, a number of times" she sobbed. "He's always carted off to hospital, but after a few weeks he recovers, and everything goes back to normal. But it cannot keep happening; sooner or later it will be the last time. Then he will die! Ooh! It is so hard on my poor mother."

More hysterical sobbing; all the while I felt helpless. I tried to make sympathetic noises, but I had no experience of such a huge potential personal tragedy, and my attempts at compassion sounded trivial and juvenile.

"I was longing for this weekend so much; to see my friends; to see that marvellous show; and to be with Ralph! I'm incredibly disappointed; and I feel cheap and mean for admitting it when my poor Dad is so ill and Mum needs me so desperately."

I wanted to phone Ralph, but Loretta would not allow me: "He's at home, I never contact him there," she burbled. Gradually the frenzied sobbing became quieter, until finally she buried her head in her hands.

I cuddled her shoulders and stroked her brow, feeling totally inadequate. After a long moment of quietude, she gave her shoulders a gentle shake and sat straight in the chair.

"We must plan," she said.

She decided that Ralph, Walter and I must go without her. I was torn: I did not want to be any place within a hundred miles of Ralph, but I had eagerly anticipated being with Walter; and I knew I would feel cheated if the whole weekend was abandoned. I demurred, quite honestly, that it would be awful without her.

"Oh, Ralph won't mind," she said with strong confirmation. "He's crazy about you, and, well, Walter's himself; everyone likes him."

Especially me, Loretta!

It appeared that Ralph had told his wife he was attending a gentleman's convention at the hotel. Honestly, it was so tacky! I was certain that Ralph's wife was not deceived. It appalled me that she simmered at home, fully aware that Ralph was not convening with his gentlemen friends.

Loretta decided to leave for Cheltenham as soon as she had told Ralph her troubles. We sat the cottage kitchen table while Loretta phoned her Mum for the latest bulletin, and to say she would be in Cheltenham by teatime. I gathered my case and handbag from the bedroom, taking my time; I was trying to delay leaving, it would not be the same without Loretta.

So much for cool, calm and collected Linda, - not when faced with the possibility of Ralph's wandering hands!

I was idly rearranging my makeup when I heard Walter's voice, followed by Loretta speaking for a long time. I heard Ralph bumble through the front door. A rogue elephant on the rampage would have caused less mayhem.

Ralph treated Loretta with surprising gentleness, and he demonstrated considerable common sense in the arrangements he made. Loretta must leave before us; we had plenty of time anyway, and he wanted to ensure she got away safely. He checked the estate car's battery, tyres, petrol, water, oil. He made sure she had cash with her, and a large box of tissue handkerchiefs. He advised her to turn into a layby if she needed to cry, driving through tears was a bad idea. He was sure that her Dad's condition would improve once she was with him; and reminded her how important her presence was to her Mum.

He gave her a long, gentle cuddle, and we all waved the estate car out of the driveway, watching it until it turned the bend in the lane.

For a few minutes silence reigned. Then Ralph grabbed the Rover keys and turned to me: "If you don't mind, Linda, Walter and I are off down the pub for a few beers before we get underway. Everything's booked at the hotel, so we don't need to be there until after the party. This way we can go straight to the restaurant; it'll save a lot of messing about."

"So you pop upstairs and put on your best evening dress and your best evening face, so you are all ready for the party, and wait for us here. We will be back after we've downed a couple of bevies. Got to let the men get to the important things in life."

He leered at Walter, he did!

I did mind, I minded a great deal; but I suppose it was merely a rhetorical question.

Walter looked stunned, obviously the proposed 'bevies' were news to him; but he went gladly enough, off to the Friday lunchtime delights of the Croxbourn Arms.

I was faced with a couple of hours of my own company. Ralph had totally ignored the plans Loretta had entrusted to him. She had wanted us to be safely and securely installed in the hotel before the party, so we could luxuriate in hot baths and spend ages with the necessary dressing and makeup; and we were to travel to the restaurant by taxi, which would enable Ralph to drink freely, without fear of police intervention if his driving was less than perfect when we left the party in the early hours of the morning.

CHAPTER SEVENTY THREE

THE SUN WAS low in the western sky when Ralph and Walter returned. Walter appeared to have drunk very little; but Ralph was inebriated. His speech was slurred and his eyes glassy.

We all climbed into the Rover. Walter automatically sat in the front next to Ralph; and I crept into the rear seat, almost hoping no-one would notice me. They appeared not to; I might as well not have existed. The pub-talk of horse racing, cars and drinking continued, Ralph's conversation becoming more lewd and his language more vulgar, as the Rover ate the miles. Walter gave me the occasional worried frown over his shoulder, but he did not attempt to 'defend my honour.'

We tore through Croxbourn at an earth-shattering pace and hit the London Road with the power of a racing car at Silverstone. There were speed limits in all the villages and towns but obviously Ralph was not about to bother with rubbish like that. We blithely overtook everything on the road, Ralph weaving in and out of traffic like a maypole dancer skipping the grand chain. First in, then out, and in and out again.

I was unaccustomed to car travel, other than my

oft-repeated journey between Croxbourn and Great Silver in Bertha's car, and riding home from dances in Jeff's elderly banger, which often could not maintain the speed limit, let alone exceed it. Ralph's driving terrified me. My heart was pounding, my knuckles white, as I gripped the edge of the seat in fear. Once again I longed to be almost any place that Ralph was not.

The police stopped him at Maidenhead. Ralph had a deafening roadside quarrel with a very polite young traffic constable, Ralph using swear words which my innocent ears did not even recognise. We ended up in Maidenhead police station, where Ralph commenced another row with a more senior officer, who advised him in no certain tones to moderate his language or spend the night in the cells.

Walter and I sat in the waiting room for what seemed like an eternity, looking everywhere but at each other. Ralph finally emerged, yelling at the duty sergeant that HE had better mind his language; young Linda there was unaccustomed to such crudeness, she was a mere child and he would not have that little girl upset for all the tea in China. After all, she was like a daughter to him!

The 'little girl' followed Ralph and Walter out of the police station, making a mental note never to visit Maidenhead again. I was sure every policeman in town would remember me.

It gave a whole new meaning to the phrase 'known to the police.'

We resumed our journey, with Walter driving, while Ralph ranted and raved about a 'police state' and how he knew people, oh yes, you'd better believe it; he had influence and he'd see that sergeant suffer.

CHAPTER SEVENTY FOUR

I HATED THE PARTY. Jeanette was there. Loretta had not invited her, but she turned up anyway; and she and Walter sat holding hands and gazing into each other's eyes, or snogging in the corner, kisses that would wear your lips out. They were totally unaware that the rest of the party-goers existed.

Linda my girl, you'd be well advised to forget Walter right now! You cannot compete with those exquisite clothes, the perfect teeth, the straight, plainly cut hair that shouted 'style' from the very roots; plus Jeanette did just happen to be a graceful girl, tall and willowy, pretty rather than beautiful, with a country-fresh complexion and stunning hazel eyes.

I could have accepted Walter's passion if the earl's daughter had been a nasty bitch, but she was sweet and pleasant. I could have spent ages consoling myself that it was mere infatuation; he would probably get over it. As it was, I did not see why he should. He was obviously in love with Jeanette, and she with him.

Ralph flirted outrageously with Loretta's friends. A couple of times I caught a glance, one to the other, a raised eyebrow. They obviously thought he was a fool, but they parried his flirtatious overtures with style and panache; probably wondering all the while whatever their friend saw in such an ogre. He gradually became more inebriated as the evening progressed, until finally he ended up snoring loudly in a corner, to everyone's relief. At least they were no longer obliged to talk to him.

The food was two things – expensive and inedible. The poor quality of the dishes actually did not matter as little food was eaten. The purpose of the evening was to drink a great deal, and Loretta's friends certainly did that; no point in wasting time eating. The attractively-arranged hors douvres of grouse eggs and stuffed quail remained on the tables largely untouched until they were finally whisked away by the restaurant staff.

My cottage-trained sense of domestic economy was affronted at the incredible waste, of food and of money. I secretly hoped that leftovers were donated to a homeless shelter, or some other worthy good cause; the people who ate here were of the staunch English class that adored donating to good causes. I am sure the untouched food ended up in the dustbins.

The conversation, in their plummy voices and murdered vowels, was about women I did not know, called Harriet or Polly, Caroline or Cecilia, to whom the most devastating disasters happened. Each related tale of woe, or worse, was inevitably followed by chorus of loud hysterical laughter.

Then they started on their men. The bastards! Julian, or Sebastian were obviously the most horrific monsters who treated the poor little girlfriends so abominably; but sharing all the shocking little secrets helped, didn't it? When he got so terribly drunk and threw up in Daddy's Rolls, before he sneaked that appalling secretary into the cottage, he really could not help himself, could he, as he was obviously a raving idiot with miniscule intelligence and absolutely no manners? But so adorable, of course! And always so sorry afterwards!

They would forgive anything if the reprobate turned up with flowers or perfume the next day. They giggled hysterically over every appalling misdemeanour, every strange bra found in the bed, every drunken collapse.

I just wanted to go home.

Eternity will be shorter than that evening; but finally, when they had drunk enough, and everyone ran out of secretarial and alcoholically-stimulated vomit stories, they stopped giggling, woke up Ralph, disengaged Walter and Jeanette from each other's lips, kissed everybody a dozen times, and headed for the MGs in the car park.

I had been introduced to everyone when I arrived at the party as "Dear Linda, Loretta's right-hand woman." No-one spoke to me from that moment on. Fortunately I was practised in the art of invisibility.

CHAPTER SEVENTY FIVE

WALTER TOSSED THE keys to a commissionaire with a request to park the car. We all traipsed arm-in-arm into the Tropical Palms Hotel. The night porter bowed and scraped to Ralph, with a great deal of "Yes Mister Smith, no Mister Smith." ('Kiss your arse, Mister Smith,' Florrie would have added sotto voce.) Honestly, it got tackier by the minute. Did Ralph and Loretta really book into hotels as 'Mister and Mrs Smith' for their dirty weekends? It might have been funny, but it was merely pathetic.

We took the lift to the second floor, then Walter suddenly remembered he had left something in the car, which he needed urgently. Ralph handed him the key to his room, which was next door to Linda's, said Ralph; and Walter re-entered the lift.

We stopped outside room sixty nine. Ralph unlocked the door, switched on the lights and ushered me inside.

I do not know what I was expecting, but it was not this! The room was huge; masses of gold trim, fresh daffodils in a crystal vase on the dressing table, deep cream carpet almost to your ankles. The enormous bed, covered with a deep red silk damask cover, could have accommodated a small nation. I had seriously expected a tiny single bed, if it came to that, in a tiny single room, not this positively palatial royal court. I crept forward to place my suitcase beside the bed, not daring to blink in case it all disappeared.

"What do you think?" Ralph was beside me.

I was speechless.

"Not bad, is it? You can always rely on the Tropical Palms for a bit of comfort," Ralph hoisted his tooled leather case onto the bed, along with his camera and binoculars.

Now I understood. This was Ralph's room, the one he would have shared with Loretta.

"It's pretty impressive," I agreed. "Am I next door?"

"No, Walter-the-Gypsy is next door. Don't worry; he didn't forget anything. He has just nipped off to pick up his little totty from the restaurant, where he left her. Got to pretend he isn't screwing the earl's daughter. Got to protect the lady's reputation, y'know."

Where was my room? In that instant I knew exactly where it was!

Tears of fear and shame pricked my eyelids. Ralph was hideous, drunk, common, vulgar, bald, and old; and he thought I was going to sleep in this mausoleum with him. Not likely!

I made a lunge for my suitcase, but he grabbed my arm. I tried to push him away but he had a grip like a vice.

"Hey, c'mon girlie, let's have a bit of fun. Life doesn't have to be all serious, y'know." He tried to kiss my mouth but I turned my head. He bit my ear lobe.

"Where is my room?" I hoped my voice sounded authoritative.

He made a purring sound like a cat. Alcohol still slurred his consonants. "This is the only room, girlie. I cancelled the other booking. After all, we won't be needing it, will we?"

He nuzzled my neck; he made a frantic grab at my breast. His breath was heavy in my face, whisky, with traces of cigar smoke. His hand slid down my belly in the general direction of my crotch. I tried to pull away from him, but he had me in a vice-like cuddle.

"Hey don't be frightened, little one, I've done this before. I'll be gentle, trust me. You'll love it!" He tried to unzip my skirt.

Long years ago, Dad taught me this one; I never seriously thought I would need to use it. I lifted my foot and stamped my high heel firmly down on his instep.

Ralph yelped like a kicked dog; he sprang back, holding his injured foot. I made a quick grab for my suitcase and headed for the door.

He had locked it.

"Oh come on, Linda. It's not as if it is the first time. You've had a kid, after all!"

Well, thank you Loretta. Thank you for telling this freak that I was 'totty,' in fact – anybody's.

Not likely, Ralph; not with you, not like this.

My mind was working overtime. A change of tactics was necessary, so I forced back the tears and pretended I found him attractive. Swallowing my gorge, I sauntered towards him, smiling, hoping I looked suggestive and eager. I would get those keys somehow!

"I see you know all about me," I purred. I pressed my body against his, I kissed his cheek. Vomit rose in my throat, but I could hold on!

I unbuttoned his fly and exposed his penis. I gave it a few quick pumps and was reminded of Minnie Weston in Bertha's kitchen all those years ago. I had died, I knew that now. I was in hell.

I unfastened his belt and pulled his trousers down to his ankles. Another little kiss, I licked his ear. His face wore an expression of absolute bliss; he was going to lie back and enjoy this. Trying to hold my puke, I applied a couple more pumps to the offending organ.

I caught him completely off guard when I socked him in his face. I grabbed the keys from his trousers pocket, grabbed my suitcase and ran like mad. He sat on the edge of the bed swearing, trying to untangle his feet from his trousers and underpants, and looking totally ridiculous.

My fingers and thumbs appeared to be at war with each other, but finally I managed to escape, safely locking the door from the other side.

CHAPTER SEVENTY SIX

T HE REALITY OF the moment was me standing in the corridor of a London hotel at two o'clock in the morning, dishevelled and unbuttoned. I had no idea what to do next.

Walter! I needed him more than I had ever needed anyone in my life! I hurled myself at the door of his room, shouting and banging. It was a wonder I did not wake everyone in London.

The door was opened by Jeanette. I did not care. I needed Walter and that was all that mattered. I pushed past her into Walter's room.

Now this really was a single room, with a tiny bed just big enough for one person. One person was sitting in it, Walter. He was naked above the waist, and I suspected, below the waist also. His muscular olive-skinned body, with the black kiss curls on his chest, would have taken my breath away – if I had any left to take. Jeanette hovered in the background, wearing a long blue silk robe, the kind I had always longed for. I suspected she was also naked beneath it. Maybe it was only a single-person bed, but two people would sleep in it tonight. Loretta, who was paying for this room, would be horrified.

Walter's face registered amazement, followed by true concern. I realised I looked a sight. My clothes were hanging off my body, exposing my underwear for the world to see; my perm was standing on end and my lipstick smudged my cheeks.

As I flopped down on the bedside chair I noticed semen smudges on my blouse. That was the last straw; I collapsed into a sobbing, incoherent heap.

I recounted the events of the last fifteen minutes. Walter said: "The randy old bastard."

Jeanette said: "But he is so hideously coarse and ugly." Jeanette, it wouldn't have mattered if he had been Cary Grant. Ralph was a cheap, dirty trickster who filled me with repellent disgust.

By the time I finished the saga of Ralph's clumsy attempt at seduction they were sitting side by side in the bed.

Okay, so I had lost everything! I had lost Walter too, except that he was never mine to lose.

My tears and mascara were dried on my cheeks. I would never cry again.

I spread my arms wide in a gesture of hopelessness. "So, what do I do now?"

Walter and Jeanette exchanged thoughtful glances. They were like an old married couple who knew each other's thoughts without a word being spoken.

Walter chewed his lip. Jeanette was more alert. "It's okay, Linda, Walter and I will come down to reception with you and explain it was a mistake that your original booking was cancelled. The hotel will be obliged to provide you with another room. They may ask you to pay, though, as I do not know what arrangements Loretta made regarding that." Leaning back against the bedboard, she gazed into Walter's eyes.

Loretta made arrangements that definitely did not include you, Jeanette. I smothered the unworthy thought; after all, she was my salvation.

"We can lend you any money you need, can't we Walter?" Again she looked deep into his eyes. He nodded approval.

I knew at once I could not spend a night in this hotel. The nightmares were already haunting me, and I was not yet lying alone in a strange bed while the long night ticked slowly by, each minute seeming a lifetime.

I pronounced each word very carefully: "Could you call me a taxi. I need to go home. I'll catch a train from Paddington."

"You don't need a taxi. I've still got the keys to Ralph's Rover."

This from Walter.

Jeanette said: "Oh please, stay the night here, and then you can go home in the morning if you still wish. Honestly, Linda, I'm sure we can get you a room. Sleep on it, and then think again tomorrow, that's my advice. Hey, you may see things differently in the morning, and then perhaps we can all go sightseeing. Have you ever seen the Changing of the Guard?"

"Also, there aren't any trains in the absolute middle of the night. You'll have a long wait at Paddington." Jeanette was a truly practical soul, wasn't she?

I could not spend the day with those two, gazing into each other's eyes, thinking the same thoughts, ending each other's sentences. And what happens after the sightseeing? Do I still go to the theatre and sit next to Ralph? Paddington it was, I needed my Mum.

Jeanette spirited me off to the bathroom to repair my disfigured appearance, while Walter dressed. After Jeanette gently applied my makeup and carefully brushed my electrified perm we sponged the semen stains off my blouse, while she clucked in revulsion and disgust.

Then she grabbed her outdoor clothes and in a twinkling she looked like an advertisement for Tatler. I still looked like a tired seventeen-year-old country girl who needed a cuddle from her Mum.

They dropped me at Paddington, with concerned enquiries that I had sufficient cash for a ticket, to get some breakfast and to be sure to have a taxi from Middleford to home.

Jeanette gave me a little cuddle, and said she hoped I would soon forget horrible old Ralph. I knew I never would.

Walter said he would tell Loretta exactly what had happened; would make sure she understood what a randy old goat Ralph was. Walter said he would see me soon. I knew he would do none of those things.

It was three-thirty in the morning.

As dawn broke, the first train to Middleford left Paddington. It seemed to stop at every station, siding, level crossing, signal box, oak tree between London and home.

Paddington in the grey dawn light quickly slid into

West London in the grey dawn light. The London I saw was gasometers, endless railway sidings, sooty advertising hoardings, and factory chimneys. Whatever had happened to the London of my dreams of less than twenty-four hours ago?

For me there would be no waking up in the posh hotel room, sauntering down to drink coffee in the dining room. No luxuriating in a bubbly bath, followed by getting dressed to kill; no going off with all the smart, beautiful people to the West End theatre.

No Kiss me Kate, no Kiss me Walter.

The dawn came up regardless. I wished it would never be daylight again.

After an eternity of village stations, with porters shouting, bales of newspapers being thrown around and milk churns clanking; and after contingents of bright-eyed passengers had boarded, already loaded with handbags, baskets and eager, restless children off for a morning's shopping, we finally reached our destination. It was the first time I had arrived at Middleford by train.

CHAPTER SEVENTY SEVEN

MY PARENTS LISTENED in dismay as I related the events of the previous evening. I left nothing out, including Ralph's behaviour, and how I had finally acquired the bedroom door key, but I never mentioned Walter in my monologue, no point in reminding them, yet again, of the didicoy family.

Dad tut-tutted in horror, shocked that his little Linda had been treated so abominably. Mum wiped my fresh tears and provided the required cuddle. Merle produced bacon, eggs, toast and tea, as if by magic. I suddenly realised I was starving hungry.

Mum and Dad behaved predictably; they immediately summoned an extended family conference. I received sympathy and advice from a seemingly-endless stream of Springbournes and Bigfords: brothers and sisters, sisters-in-law and brothers-in-law, aunts, uncles, cousins, nieces and nephews. I wondered Mum and Dad did not charge admission fees. They saved me the discomfiture of retelling the story a number of times, by doing so themselves. Each repetition contained every minute detail of the events I was longing desperately to forget; I was sure I would die of shame and embarrassment.

The Springbournes and Bigfords agreed unanimously that facing Loretta would be difficult. The family was divided as to whether she deserved any sympathy, however. One faction said: "Poor woman, how could the man she loves treat her so shabbily? She will be broken-hearted". The opposing morally-inclined faction declared: "It is no more than she deserves. That's what you get for playing fast and loose with someone else's husband. If he'll mess around with her, he'll mess around with anybody."

It was generally agreed that an escort of family members must accompany me upon my return to Croxbourn on Monday. I wondered Mum did not arrange a picnic outing and hire a coach.

I just wanted to be left alone, but it was not to be. Aunty Mildred left through the front door, accompanied by her married daughters. I had gratefully accepted their heartfelt good wishes and their advice not to stand for any nonsense from 'that immoral woman'. No sooner had the front door closed than Ethel and Angie, with young Mark in tow, tapped at the back door. They had judged that Aunty Mildred must be the last family advice-giver; and as they could sniff a melodrama across the other side of England, let alone the other side of a garden fence, they decided it was time I regaled them with the latest thrilling events in the chronicle of Linda's life.

Ethel and Angie both howled with delight. Their favourite radio serials were not this thrilling. How did I manage to have so much excitement in my life?

CHAPTER SEVENTY EIGHT

O N Monday morning Mum, Mary and Bertha all decided to accompany me to Croxbourn, to provide familial support in the face of Loretta's expected jealous tirade. Ralph would have made his story good, we were all certain of that; and although Walter had promised to tell Loretta the true events of Friday, would he, though, when Loretta faced him with his own duplicity and ungratefulness?

If nothing else, Mum and Bertha presented a large physical front. They shared the same generous build; shoulder to shoulder they represented dominance and power. An army on the march rarely displayed a more terrifying image than Bertha and my Mum.

Mum had insisted Dad come with us but he demurred he was unable to take time off work. Well, that was understandable. Ever since my birth he had been rushing away from repairing the church roof, or whatever, to deal with the next major crisis in Linda's life. I secretly suspected Dad was immensely relieved he was unable to accompany us.

Florrie would have given her right arm to join us. She enjoyed a good scrap and disliked missing really newsworthy family events. Mum made it clear from the very start that Florrie was not invited. Poor Florrie!

I wished I was anywhere else in the world but in that car heading to Croxbourn and a showdown with Loretta.

Loretta, watching from the window, was aware of our arrival outside the front door.

I ensured she was alone. No point in embarrassing her in front of the rich and famous.

We marched through the door like the aforementioned invading army; Mum and Bertha side by side in the vanguard, Mary holding my hand tightly and dragging me in the rear.

Loretta, seated behind her writing desk, drew back involuntarily. She was ready for me, don't you believe otherwise, but she looked positively terrified of the regiment of Bigfords that supported me on the sortie.

Politeness dripping from their tongues like venom from the fangs of angry snakes, Mum and Bertha wished Loretta good morning. Mary and I politely echoed the greeting.

I knew I was in for it, but none the less I felt sorry for Loretta. I could not begin to imagine Ralph's version of the events of Friday night but Loretta would believe his every word, besotted as she was by the hideous old freak.

Loretta's appearance shocked me. There were heavy bags under her eyes; okay, so she had sleepless nights; well, I knew what that felt like. Her usually immaculate hair was haywire, and her cheeks were abnormally flushed.

"Linda, how sweet of you to pop in!" Her eyes were

enormously bright, she had been crying. "And you've brought Mummy and the girls for company, isn't that nice?"

"Miss Thackray, could you please spare us a moment for a private word?" honey again dripping off Mum's tongue.

Loretta feigned surprise. "Concerning what, Mrs Bigford? The only member of your family I wish to speak to is Linda; and I can assure you I really must talk to Linda alone; so if you would care to wait outside, I will be brief. Perhaps you could sit in the car."

When pushed, Mum could be more condescending than Loretta could possibly imagine. Mum had watched Lady Margaret 'condescend' for years, and imitation had turned her into a pass master in the art of patronisation. She drew herself to her full height; that alone was sufficiently intimidating.

"Miss Thackray, you must understand that Linda is just seventeen years old; and whatever you may have heard concerning the events of the weekend, I feel this is a matter to be discussed with me, her mother. Unfair advantage was taken of my daughter by someone she trusted; a person you obviously trusted also. Linda was in no way responsible for what happened. You may have heard a different version. Well now, perhaps it is time you heard the truth."

Loretta sucked in great gobs of air. Unshed tears glittered in her eyes. Her hands shook.

"The truth, Mrs Bigford; well, I hope truth is a concept you can understand; because I assure you Linda cannot."

"When I employed her I knew she had a child; well, I told myself, that can happen to anyone. I even felt a great deal of sympathy for her, as I was aware she had relinquished her daughter for adoption. I considered such a painful lesson would teach her to be sexually continent; obviously I was wrong!"

"She may only be seventeen, but when it comes to the opposite sex she knows it all. Anything in trousers, that's Linda's outlook on men! Any man, so long as he is alive and kicking, he'll do! She was even making eyes at Walter, my trainee manager. As I say, no man is safe from her; oversexed little tart that she is."

"And as for the truth, well, she is a stranger to that in more ways than one! I don't know what she has told you about the weekend, and I don't want to know; but I'll bet she forgot to mention her light-fingered habits in the cottage!"

Four pairs of eyes regarded her in absolute amazement. It was some time before I realised what she was talking about.

She jutted her chin forward in my direction; her eyes blazed, she spat her words with sadistic malice: "You see, Linda, if we had been able to keep this between ourselves, I would certainly never have upset your poor Mum by telling her that you are a thief. You insisted she stay during our little talk, so she knows now, doesn't she? The small matter of fifty-seven pounds from the petty cash!"

"Going to have a super shopping spree at my expense in London, were you? Oh, you stood there, wringing your hands: 'Oh dear, Loretta, what can I do, Loretta, where can the money have gone, Loretta?' My dear girl, I had been watching you for weeks. Did you really think I was that gullible?"

Mum and my sisters had stopped breathing. Amazement and disbelief registered on all three faces. Mum flopped into a chair, her shoulders sagged. My own breath was coming in great gasps. I screamed in my defence: "NO, NO, NO. I did not touch the money. I do not know what happened, but I did not take it! Don't blame me; don't call me a thief."

"Come on Linda, a little girl who plays grown-up games with other people's men and other people's money should be able to accept the consequences of her actions. Running to Mummy when you break the law will not save you, you know."

"However I have decided not to call the police. As long as you have packed your bags and are out of here by noon I shall pretend the whole sorry mess did not happen. I just feel sad that your poor Mother had to hear this, because I intended to keep this little matter private. You are dismissed."

Loretta bent her head to the day's correspondence.

The light of battle showed in Mum's sapphire-coloured eyes; her voice had dropped her broad Hampshire vowels; Lady Margaret spoke through my Mum's mouth

"Miss Thackray, did I hear you call my daughter a thief? I did not know about this; and without even discussing it with Linda, I am telling you here and now, you are mistaken. I know Linda would not steal from you. I insist you apologise to Linda immediately. And I seriously suggest you think twice before you cast such serious aspersions on my daughter's honesty."

Bertha, Mary and I all stared at Mum in amazement. This was Mum addressing a grand jury. Mum who went to the Women's Institute and took her turn at washing up the tea things was a million miles away.

Loretta's cheeks had darkened to a mottled purple; her lips had narrowed to a thin scarlet line in her livid face. "Mrs Bigford, will you and all your daughters leave my property before I change my mind and summon the police? Your youngest daughter is a cheap thief and a whore. The sooner you face up to these harsh truths, the sooner you can help her to mend her ways. Now, if you could leave as quickly and as quietly as possible, I would appreciate it."

I thought Mum would strike her, I really did.

"Am I to understand you are sacking Linda?"

"I would have thought that was entirely clear."

"How dare you attempt to damage her reputation in that manner without even a scrap of evidence?"

"Mrs Bigford, the sooner you face up to the fact that your daughter is immoral and dishonest, the better it will be for everyone. Now, will you please leave? I shall expect Linda to have cleared her room by noon."

But Mum had not finished yet. "Will you provide Linda with a favourable reference, please?"

Loretta stared at her aghast. "Mrs Bigford, under the circumstances I hardly think I am likely to do that! Surely you have more sense than to request such a thing."

Mum's voice sounded light and airy. "Oh, I don't know. She is bound to tell future employers she was working for you; and they will ask for a reference. When she is unable to provide one, they will probably phone you; and you will have to explain why she left."

Loretta may call me a thief and a whore to my face; but

on the phone, to someone who would then deny me a job; with all the implicit suggestion of libel and defamation? To say nothing of the infidelity of her randy lover; she would not wish that to be common knowledge. Oh no; she would keep this little incident as quiet as possible. Mum won her day: through taut lips Loretta promised me a reference would be in the mail by the week's end.

Mum sauntered out of the front door with the style and panache of an empress being followed by an impressive retinue.

CHAPTER SEVENTY NINE

UM TURNED TO me and asked with a frown: "Linda, whatever happened to the darned fifty-seven pounds?"

Oh no, Mum, please don't think that of me! "I don't know. The petty cash journal always balanced to the last penny, then suddenly it did not; and I could not work out why. Fifty-seven pounds was missing, and Loretta was angry; but she had no reason to think I had taken it. What she said about having to watch me was unfair and untrue. I would never have stolen anything."

"No, I know that, love; she was merely looking for a reason to sack you because she believes her fancy man's stories, and she is jealous of you. He probably told Loretta you threw yourself at him; but we'll never know, will we? Anyway, who did you think took the money?"

Well, the missing money was definitely a shock to Loretta; but who else knew the whereabouts of the petty cash?

In my mind I blamed Ralph. He was the most dishonest person I knew, and he spent enough time hanging around the cottage to have spotted the cash box. But there again, in my current mood I was capable of blaming Ralph for everything, including the Roman invasion, ten sixty-six, and every civil war since. If I had been 'nice to him' he would probably have defended me against Loretta's aspersions and as Loretta believed everything he said, I suppose everything would have been okay.

That was the trouble, Loretta did believe everything he said; and what he had told her about the events of Friday evening I would never know.

I shrugged my shoulders. There were other matters to worry about now. Remaining in Loretta's service was not an option after the scene in the office. I urgently needed a job and I did not know how to go about finding one.

Just a week ago I had so much to look forward to; least of all, the trip to London, staying at the hotel and visiting the theatre.

Loretta had promised so much; the training, the knowledge of the racing industry. She had promised me the use of the Volkswagen, my very own car, but the driving lessons from Ralph had not happened; neither had the riding lessons from Walter.

Walter! Would I ever see him again? I considered writing him a bright newsy little note. But then, what could I write about? Oh yes, I could just imagine: I would write and tell him I have a new job; he would read the letter with mild interest, bury it somewhere and completely forget about it, and probably about me, too. Walter was not mine to lose, never had been, and I knew it.

CHAPTER EIGHTY

RIS HAD UNDERSTOOD, advising me to "Live it down. Think of all the experience you gained. And Mary will work on your typing skills with you." I knew her advice was sound, but I did not have anything to live down. I was the innocent party in this matter.

Florrie was more forthright. She offered to go over to Croxbourn and "knock some sense into the daft old bitch's brain box." Everyone demurred politely, half fearing that she would; she was capable of doing far more than that.

"Oh, you'll get a job, no worries." Dad always had faith in me. I dreaded the day he woke up to the fact that his conviction was totally misplaced.

"Give it a month or so, until a fat girl at the factory makes it known she's expecting; then she'll leave and they'll need someone else. At least you don't smell, and old Polly does. It'll be nice not to have her stinking around the place."

Well, thank you, Angie! I had wondered which aspect of my character and ability I could best promote to prospective employers. Not stinking was hardly the first trait that entered my mind.

"You should consider going to university, Linda.

Teaching is indeed a wonderful profession for a woman, but these days there are so many different opportunities to pursue a worthwhile career. Why not considered journalism, or commercial art?"

Iris, I went to Great Silver School, where Mister Taylor considered he had taught effectively if we had mastered long division by the age of fourteen!

"You don't want another job, girl. All that getting up early in the morning and spending all day fiddling about with a typewriter. You need a nice bloke, Linda, and then you won't have to work. In the summer we could go down the river every day and teach Mark to swim."

Yes, Ethel, but I would expect him to marry me before I commenced the production of a tribe of kids.

Thank God for gentle Mary. She bought me a ream of typing paper and a booklet on the correct procedure for composing a job application.

CHAPTER EIGHTY ONE

M Y SCATTERED WITS did not warn me to stay away from home on Saturday afternoon when Ernie Badger delivered the weekend joint. If I had given the matter a little thought, I would have avoided him like the plague, as I had so carefully avoided his brother Ron.

Ernie did not deserve to be ignored by me, and I knew it. I expected his customary ribaldry, but he wore a slight frown, and the amused quirk that always slanted the corners of his mouth was absent.

"What have you done to my brother?"

"Er, I've been very busy. I don't expect you heard, but I lost my job, and I have been desperately looking for work."

"Yea, Ron phoned the stables a couple of times, but Loretta just slammed the phone down on him. Sort-of made us think that all was not well with you."

Ernie carried on: "Ron has been dead miserable because he thinks you dumped him. He's been so down he can't even work properly. The poor chap's nuts about you, don't you know that?"

I hung my head. I did not want Ron to be nuts about me. I wanted Walter to love me.

"You're just stringing Ron along, aren't you? Just until a better offer comes along."

"I, er, have been very unhappy about all that happened, and I have, er, been staying home. I don't want to go out. It's a long story."

"I'll bet it is; you'll have to tell us sometime," how level his eyes were; Ernie, who missed nothing. There was no laughter in his face; Ernie, who never stopped joking.

"Well, you'll just grow into a lonely old maid if you stay in all the time. That's a fate worse than death, Linda. So make your choice: come dancing with us tonight and be especially nice to Ron, or stay home and help Merle with her knitting."

I did not want to go to the dance; neither did I want to upset Ron, whom I had always regarded as a friend and not as a potential lover.

And as for the fate worse than death, I knew a great deal about that and it had nothing to do with Merle's knitting.

But I was still seventeen. There had been a dearth of people of my own age in my life during the previous few weeks. I longed for youthful company, for enjoyment, for pleasure. Actually I longed for Walter; I knew it was pointless, but I could not stop myself, not yet.

I thought of dancing with Ron; and then I remembered just how good he was at it.

Arrangements were made. They would pick me up in Jeff's old banger, seven-thirty that evening; it was a special-occasion dance in Middleford. That was at least a relief; I

278

was not quite ready for another country hop at Croxbourn memorial hall.

It had not occurred to me that Ethel and Angie never danced further afield than Great Silver village hall; that they would be jealous when I told them about it on Sunday morning. They would have been thoroughly delighted to be invited to a dance in Middleford and would not have understood for a moment why I showed the world such a long face.

My long-suffering parents were spared the beauty parade, the chance to admire Linda all dolled up, yet again. I sneaked out the front door like a guilty party. Perhaps I needed Aunt Beat after all. She would have told me in no uncertain terms I was lucky to be going gadding, when I really should have been in the condemned cell.

CHAPTER EIGHTY TWO

RON WAS OFF-HAND, polite. He promised to teach me to jive. We sat like strangers between dances; but then again we had always done that.

Jeff hogged the bar with some of his mates and looked longingly at the couples of girls dancing together, circling the floor in their jewel-coloured dresses.

I had never felt so lonely in my life.

The evening eventually ended, after what seemed a lifetime of strained silences between Ron and me, and we all piled into to Jeff's old banger. The other four sang bawdy songs at the top of their voices and laughed a great deal during the brief journey to Great Silver. I felt like crying, not singing.

Jeff parked at the bus stop outside the post office. Ernie and Elaine were hoping for a little peace and privacy and the back seat to themselves, so Jeff wandered off for a quiet smoke in the cool April evening. A flower scented-breeze whispered in the trees and somewhere out of sight, a nightingale trilled its love song. Above our heads Orion hunted among a myriad of stars, wielding his sword and his club, his faithful dog following him, and all the while he was being watched from worlds away by the closely-cuddling family group of Seven Sisters.

Ron and I began a purposeful walk back to the cottage. We marched side by side, a million miles apart. We did not speak; and all this in spite of the sidelong warning looks I had received from Jeff, and the hinted warning from Ernie: "He's mad about you, remember....."

Ron stopped dead in his tracks before we reached the cottage gate. Obviously we were not going to complete this farce of him 'seeing me to the door,' followed by an impassioned goodnight kiss; the kiss of two lovers who could not bear to be parted.

His voice thickened: "What was he like?"

Dimly I asked: "Who?" Oh, I knew who he meant, what he meant; but I did not know how to answer him.

"The chap who dumped you. What was he like, who was he? Was he anyone I know?"

Long silence from me.

"Pretty keen on him, were you?"

"I, er, we were only friends. I've known him a long time."

"What happened?"

We were standing on opposite sides of the narrow street. I hoped the occupants of the car back-seat or Jeff were not watching. They expected Ron to do all except ravish me, right here on the street; and as this was fairly obviously not happening it would do little for Ron's pride or reputation. Political opponents met at closer quarters than this.

I was not about to avail Ron of the truth; partly because I did not know what that was myself.

"I, er, had to find out where I stand, where we stood. He has got someone else."

"Chucked you for another bird, did he?"

"It wasn't like that. They, er, have been together for a long time. There wasn't anything between .... me and him. I just thought there might be; that's all."

For someone who was not going to tell the truth, that sounded mighty like it!

In the dark I saw him turn away. The breeze had dropped; the nightingale had given up and gone home to bed. Total silence reigned.

"I care for you, Linda, but I'm not prepared to be second-best."

Silence was deafening. I did not know how to reply.

A lifetime later, Ron said: "Ernie has told me, well, about the baby."

Oh, God. Things just got worse. It was obvious Ernie had told Ron about the child; but I could not face Ron or anyone else and talk about that subject.

"Was he the kid's father?"

I silently shook my head, no. An excellent way to answer a question when standing a street apart in pitch dark.

Ron took that as a yes!

"He's a cheap skite, that bloody Paul Townsend."

My voice sounded small, squeaky, like a child's. "It wasn't Paul Townsend. I, er, met this man when I was working at the stables." Not strictly true, but whatever!

Just as Loretta said, just as the village gossips had it, Linda was anybody's. Well, this conversation certainly made it appear so.

Deafening silence; I wished I was a million miles away. None-the-less, I was rooted to the spot.

"There wasn't anything between us." That sounded pretty defensive. "I just thought there might be, that's all."

He came close to me; he put his arms round me: "Can we start again, Linda? We'll just be pals, while you work out what you want to do. Then we just wave each other good bye, great friends for ever; or you become my girl, and we'll go steady. In the meantime we'll go dancing, to the pictures, you'll come to tea at my house, and I'll go to yours. No big snogs, no promises neither of us can keep. Just take it as it comes? And I'll never dump you for someone else; that is one promise I do make, and will keep."

I doubted whether Ron had ever spoken so many words in one breath in the whole of his life.

At the cottage gate we parted with an affectionate peck, and a date to see the latest Victor Mature film on next Saturday afternoon. At least I would be away from the house when Ernie called; I was relieved I would escape the teasing, or censure, when Ernie delivered the weekend joint.

Ethel and Angie had known I was 'in love.' They said they could tell from my moony expression. They expressed surprise that I was 'going steady' with Ron, as both of them thought he was 'a bit ugly' and 'not much of a catch' and definitely not worth the aforesaid moony expression.

Recently they had both discovered Americans, young USAF serviceman at a nearby peacetime air base; smart young men with a touch of the exotic, with plenty of money to spend on a likely girlfriend and randy enough to satisfy even the raunchy demands of those two village nymphettes;

to say nothing of those of their mother, who appeared to be rediscovering her youth.

Ron and I 'walked out'. The news circled the village like a firestorm that Ron was Ernie-the-Butcher's brother, and this made everything alright. Ernie, with his cheeky banter and his mischievous charm, was the favourite caller of many a Great Silver housewife, not the least of them, my mum and her sisters. Any brother of Ernie's was a friend of theirs.

CHAPTER EIGHTY THREE

O VER THE NEXT few weeks I caught up with all the Great Silver news. Having Ethel and Angie as friends rendered printed newspapers unnecessary, with those two gossip columnists able to put the good word on any person or any event in the last ten years. If minute details were left out, these were immediately covered by the extended family of Bigfords and Springbournes.

Iris, from her duties as schoolmarm at Silver Street, and Bertha from her cottage in that village, were able to apprise me of any events from that particular area; while the outposts of Great Silver, for instance Silver Common, were ably covered by Auntie Hilda. Rarely had a national newspaper such an efficient coverage by its roving reporters.

Mum had heard that Lady Margaret planned to turn Great Silver Manor into a home for seriously incapacitated ex-servicemen, in memory of her son who was killed during the war. She planned to build a neat little bungalow, tucked away in the corner of the estate, where she and Sir Francis would live out their days in domestic simplicity, assisted by the occasional hamper from Fortnum and Masons, and regular deliveries from Harrods. Not more than five bedrooms, and only three bathrooms, you understand. Well, she would find that a little different from eleven bedrooms; to say nothing of her own personal sitting room, morning room, drawing room, gun room, nursery and library.

I wondered how many housemaids, parlour maids, maids-of-all-work she intended to employ in this 'tiny' cottage. Or did she intend to wait upon Sir Francis herself, and cook his breakfasts and lunch with her own fair hands, including washing-up afterwards? I did not think so.

It all depended upon your personal definition of simplicity.

Adrian, Lady Margaret's youngest son, considered taking holy orders; and all this in spite of Maudie's advanced tuition on how to live a fairly unholy life. Sometimes you just wondered why that girl put herself out for other people quite the way she did!

The big news in our cottage was that Doctor Webster was retiring, he who had conscientiously watched all Mum's five babies grow up; and of course also delivered Merle's daughter. A new surgery was to be built at Silver Street, with three practitioners and a fancy waiting room where you would be expected to make an appointment to visit a doctor, instead of just turning up at any odd hour and waiting for Doctor Webster, out somewhere on his rounds, to also turn up at the surgery. Those who were too incapacitated to make the journey to the surgery were in the habit of phoning his long-suffering wife and waiting for him to arrive at their cottage, hopefully before the patient died.

Dad amazed me by saying he was exactly the same age as Doctor Webster and would himself be retiring next year.

He would be sixty-five and an old age pensioner. And he was looking forward to it, don't you think otherwise; his old fingers could no longer manipulate the tools the way they used to.

I was dumbfounded; Dad, retiring, it did not bear thinking about. Dad, on the pension! I had never thought of Mum and Dad as old or young, or any age really; but Dad's tall, spare frame was becoming stooped; and Mum's raven curls were giving way to a snowy crown. Her face was lined; and her swollen knuckles and red, roughened palms were those of an old woman who had endured a lifetime of hard work.

Nellie, next door, had suffered a mild heart attack, and Doctor Webster had forbidden her to continue smoking cigarettes. How could Nellie give up a habit she had practiced every day of her life since she was thirteen years old?

CHAPTER EIGHTY FOUR

IT WAS MERLE who solved my unemployment problem for me. Merle had rarely spoken to me since that fateful day when I was thirteen. She offered trite good wishes at Christmas and birthdays, with thanks to me for my gifts and cards. Mind you, I did not take her silence personally; she rarely spoke to any other family members.

The Vicar apparently knew everything that happened in our house; he very often commenced conversation with any member of our family with 'by the way, Merle told me......', so it was evident her silence did not extend to her few friends outside the family. Over the years she found she had nothing to say to us; or perhaps we were unaware of how to draw out our silent sister.

Mum and Bertha were such chatterboxes; and when surrounded by Bigfords and Springbournes, there were always so many people, many of whom considered Merle was daft anyway. She may have found it impossible to get a word in edgeways. So she gave up trying.

Therefore I was somewhat surprised, one Wednesday afternoon as I sat reading the situations-vacant column in the Middleford Observer and hoping there was at least something I could apply for, when Merle arrived home with pink glowing cheeks.

"Our Linda, I know just the job for you."

Nine words! I could not remember Merle saying so much to me for years, unless it was to answer a question. I stared at her.

"Oh, yes, you'll be so good at it." I was astounded that Merle knew, or even cared, what I was good at.

"You know Doctor Webster is retiring and they are opening a big new surgery in Silver Street? Well, they have employed a receptionist who used to work at the hospital in Middleford, and she is really clever. She will be in charge of appointments and all that. Well, she needs an assistant, someone who can do all the filing and typing; and train to be a receptionist for times when she is sick or on holiday."

"I told Doctor Webster I would mention it to you, and he said you're to ask if you want a reference, as you are one of his favourite girls, and he thinks you would do a great job."

"Ooh Linda, you've got to apply, I mean the money would be fabulous; you'd need to know a lot of medical things and you're brainy anyway."

"It's really posh being a doctor's receptionist. You'll be able to wear all your blazers and skirts, and look ever so smart. You might even be able to save up and buy a car, like Iris did. You didn't need that old car that Loretta had for you; not when you can own one that is really yours."

I continued to stare at Merle; I was amazed that she had any perception of the importance of smart blazers and skirts, car ownership, good wages, or basically being posh.

Merle returned my stare with a delighted smile. "There, I knew you would be pleased. We'll ask Mary to come round, and she can help you write your applying letter."

Still two days to go till my eighteenth birthday! I lay in bed listening to the sounds of a Great Silver Sunday morning. Although it was barely seven o'clock someone had started a mechanized lawn mower, and the strident buzzing vied with the last peals of St Edmund's early communion bells. Baby larks in the cowslip meadows could hardly be expected to compete with that.

My thoughts travelled back to my seventeenth birthday; that Sunday morning a lifetime ago when I had awakened in this bed, and suddenly my world caved in.

In the last year I had been to private hell. Okay, so much of it was of my own doing, but not all. I could not blame myself for my innocence, or my ignorance of life, but I knew there were many who did; but there again, many folk in this village were willing to blame me for being born in the first place.

There were aches in my heart that would last a lifetime; but I guessed everyone had those. On this glorious Sunday morning I decided to ignore the gut-wrenching pains of the past and look ahead, to a future that promised happiness and success. I thought again of my job in the posh new surgery at Silver Street, and the car I had promised myself I would save for. I would succeed at work, I had to. Most people are not offered a second start as splendid as this one and I knew it.

CHAPTER EIGHTY FIVE

ON AND I married two months after my twentieth birthday. Marriage was popular that year. In January Maudie had surprised everyone by marrying one of her long-term friends, a young widower called Eddie Barnes. Eddie owned a small terraced house in Middleford. At a time when most people wished to become home owners, but were daunted by the impossible task of saving the deposit, Maudie succeeded in obtaining her wish with consummate ease. Many of the socially upright, decent and moral young women of the village would secretly envy Maudie.

Ethel was not pregnant when she married Arthur Giles in March. On my wedding day in early July she already knew she was expecting twins. Angie was there, looking immaculate in navy with white accessories, and, as usual, completely outshining the bride. She was accompanied by her new American boyfriend from 'the base.'

I wore a light green summer-weight suit (married in green, ashamed to be seen, I could hear Aunt Beat's heckling voice as I walked up the aisle on Dad's arm.) I wore a little brimmed hat trimmed with lemon and white flowers and carried a similar posy. In spite of anguished pleading from my plethora of nieces I had no attendants. Of course Ernie was best man. It was one of the plainest weddings St Edmunds had ever seen – for one of the plainest girls. We had no choir and no organ, no bells.

Ron and Dad both had new suits for the occasion, Dad's old suit had seen four of his children married, and he felt he needed a new suit for this one. Mum looked truly regal in pastel blue.

Florrie wore lemon, with a saucy little brimmed hat in the finest of stiffened lace. Dennis had met his German wife during his two year's national service. They married just a few weeks before my wedding, in a small town near Hanover. Her parents were wealthy.

Florrie had decided not to let the side down. She had eaten barely a morsel for weeks before the big occasion and had managed to lose a deal of weight. Her lemon suit was expensive; her hat was possibly the most costly thing she had ever owned, but she was going to show Dennis's German in-laws that Bigfords were as good as they were. And now, with all these other weddings to attend, it had all proved a good investment, hadn't it? She looked amazing, royal, a huge pale summery bird. The weight would not stay off of course, Florrie was above all else fond of food, but while it was off, she looked like a film star.

The bride looked plain in comparison. I was not built for yards of white tulle and orange blossom. Dad, Mum and Ron kept whispering to me how beautiful I was. When it came to beauty, this was as good as I got.

The reception was a buffet meal held in the village hall, where else? Every Springbourne and Bigford for miles round had turned up for the free grub provided by Mum and Dad, most of which had been prepared by Mum and my sisters, with help from my squadron of aunts. Iris's wedding present to me was a huge three-tiered wedding cake, perfectly iced and decorated in lemon and white, plus the lemon and white table trimmings for the buffet table.

At least Ron and I looked impressive when we stepped out in the bridal waltz.

I was never more relieved than when the long, hot July day was over, and we left from Middleford station on the evening train for a week's honeymoon in Torquay, the farthest either of us had ever been from home: Ron had only travelled as far as Aldershot when he did his national service at eighteen, unlike my nephew Dennis, who had visited France and Germany.

CHAPTER EIGHTY SIX

RON HAD COMMENCED working on Mister Williams' farm at Little Silver; a tied cottage went with the job.

We settled down to married life in the Rickyard Cottage.

We had planned so carefully. Every day I would cycle the three miles to Silver Street, come wind, rain, snow or hail, to my general dogsbody job at the surgery, Ron would work on the farm and we would live in the cottage until we had saved enough to put a deposit on a small terraced house, probably in Middleford. We both agreed that this may take as long as four years.

Then, while I continued to work at the surgery, driving to and fro in the car we were also saving for, Ron would get proper training – for something – that part of our plan had never been at all clear. He had a keen intellect, was good with his hands, and had absolutely no self-confidence. This part of the plan may take up to three years. Then, with Ron in a nice secure full-time job, and me still in my late twenties, I would gracefully hang up my typewriter and become a full-time wife and mother.

Oh, sometimes we sat in the evenings and discussed

how we could not understand Ethel and Arthur, living with Arthur's Mum in her dilapidated hut on Silver Common. They never considered the future, Ethel just thought about a number of cute babies, and the fun of choosing names.

Arthur's Mum could not risk losing Arthur's weekly 'keep'. Her husband had deserted her years ago, and Arthur was her only source of income. Mrs Giles senior was not all keen on housework or cooking, and she fervently hoped that Ethel was. Even if Ethel wasn't, she would be glad of company, she had been on her own far too long. Besides she liked babies, or so she said, and she was glad to call Mark her grandson; she was pretty sure he would be quickly followed by any number of Giles babies.

She liked to drink a bit; well, actually she liked to drink a lot. She figured that those two would be far too busy with other night time pursuits to hinder her alcoholic enjoyment.

These attitudes of mind were beyond the comprehension of correctly-brought-up Linda and Ron. Our future would be planned down to the last minute detail, and would surely lead to Linda the perfect mother being a model of affectionate devotion to one or two miniature Rons. Oh yes! In mid-July 1953, in that tied cottage at Little Silver, plans were made for the next sixty years, enforced to stay in place, ignoring the effect of fire, famine, national uprisings, or the second coming.

CHAPTER EIGHTY SEVEN

THE CONTENTS OF the cottage were a new bed, a fairly battered old wardrobe, a new three-piece suite, a second-hand dining table and some oddly assorted chairs, courtesy of my various generous aunts. The floor was covered by a colourful array of rugs and mats, and in the sitting room we had linoleum square, with an attractive pattern of autumn leaves. I was immensely proud of that.

It was July, and hot. We would discover the endless draughts and the leaks in the ceiling during the winter.

We did not have a personal water supply in the cottage; we shared a garden tap with the occupants of the cottage next door, and there was a deep well full of green tinged water, for bathing and clothes washing. We had a large larder, planned two hundred years ago by a farmer who believed cottagers like to preserve and pickle. Yes, fine; you could have held a hunt ball in my Little Silver larder. Just how much preserving and pickling were you supposed to undertake? Ron drew a couple of buckets of fresh water each morning before he began work; these stood on the larder floor. On the hottest days the flagstones kept the water cool.

There was a huge copper in the shed, which Ron lit for me on Saturday mornings, and I patiently washed everything we had worn during the past week.

Mum had always washed at the Great Silver cottage; I had occasionally given her a hand, but had never completed a whole family wash; in an emergency practical Merle would have taken over without even a qualm. I was quite unprepared for the filthy clothes of a general farm worker.

We had a large tin bath, the Saturday-night use of which involved lighting the copper, filling it from the well, and then carrying buckets of hot water from the shed to the bath, placed in front of the kitchen range. We then pulled all the curtains tightly and sat together, one at each end of the long bath. This would have been considered disgusting and immoral by our Little Silver neighbours, we were married but the idea of bathing together was something our neighbours would have been totally unable to understand or tolerate, apparently there were some things even married people did not do. We always washed each other, and dried each other, even behind the ears, with the utmost gentleness and care.

In Mum's cottage, there were drains, but we had no drains at the farm at Little Silver. A series of holes were dug at the rear of our large garden, and used one by one and then dug over when full.

We had a bucket lav at Mum's cottage, but a weekly visit, each Wednesday, from the 'shit' lorry had removed the contents of the bucket without even a thought from us. Mum had then been immensely generous with the Jeyes Fluid and things were pristine again until the 'shit' lorry's next visit.

At Little Silver, Ron buried the contents of the lav bucket each Saturday, come wind, rain, snow or shine, at the very bottom of the garden, making sure that every hint of ordure or odour was completely covered.

Our lav at Mum's cottage had been just outside the back door, and under-cover in the rain. At Little Silver, it was a long walk on the open Downland, along a cinder path, to relief at the bottom of the garden. The views were magnificent.

The kitchen housed a chipped earthenware sink, with a sinkhole below which one placed a large bucket. This, along with the range, was the total contents of the kitchen until the inhabitants provided all else.

In July 1953 we were only going to live there for a few years. Oh yes, I could put up with it.

CHAPTER EIGHTY EIGHT

LOVED RON. WHY wouldn't I? He was the answer to a maiden's prayer, except that I was hardly a maiden. He was gentle, sensitive and considerate.

We sat in the evening and listened to the radio, avidly following each episode of the Archers; we both knew a number of 'Dans' and 'Dorises' among the local folk. We loved Top of the Form, trying to beat the twelve and thirteen year olds and each other to answer the questions; we hooted with laughter at Dick Bentley and Jimmy Edwards in 'Take it from Here'.

Every morning I free-wheeled the three miles downhill to the surgery at Silver Street, to arrive by eight-thirty. Doctor Zabrieski, the chief of the three practitioners had agreed that married-Linda with all her wifely responsibilities should be allowed to leave work at four-thirty; I pushed my bike most of the three miles of continuous climb and was usually home soon after five.

Ron would arrive home before the Archers at a quarter to seven. In the winter he would arrive at dusk.

On Saturday morning I washed the clothes. Ron worked on Saturday mornings, as did most men at that time, regardless of their jobs. Saturday afternoon we shopped for food and household necessities.

Married life was hardly a fever of exhilaration and ecstasy. Mind you, having plans helped. We would lie in our new bed, beneath our fashionable lemon sheets, listening to the autumn winds' brutal assault on the old cherry tree, and talk excitedly of the house we planned, the holidays, the car, Ron's job, the furniture; and then we would make slow, experimental love and fall asleep in each other's arms.

CHAPTER EIGHTY NINE

ARLY DECEMBER SAW the arrival at Middleford hospital of Ethel's twin daughters, Wendy and Verna. We visited her on Saturday afternoon; she reclined regally, enthroned on a rubber ring "never thought I would have stitches; they are murder, make weeing hell." She wore a pretty floral nightie, and, attractive as ever, her stunning blonde hair provided a perfect frame for her faultless complexion.

After three days she was home, with Granny Giles smoking over the babies, hacking her cough in their beautiful tiny faces. Granny Giles despised dummies, she preferred a few sugar knobs wrapped in a bit of old calico, tied at the end with a sliver of embroidery silk. "All Arthur ever had, and look at him! Give the little'uns something real to suck on. Can't expect a bit of old plastic to keep 'em quiet."

We had a wet Christmas. Granny Giles' advice to Ethel was to hang wet nappies out on the line in the rain. "Saves washing 'em, my girl! Wash the pooey ones, of course."

The babies cried little; which was fortunate for their future health, as when they did, Granny Giles was unable to tolerate the noise. She usually slipped a smidgeon of brandy from her secret cupboard into their bottles when Ethel was not looking.

Ethel and Arthur were certain these were the two most beautiful girls ever born. At least I was no longer living at Mum's cottage and being forced to listen to her lyrical assertions of their infantile charms.

Ethel visited her Gran, in the cottage next door to Mum at Great Silver, on most days. She enjoyed swanking along the village street, in the hope of seeing someone who would listen to her bragging about her perfect babies. She would do anything to escape from the smelly confines of the Giles' cottage.

Mum would fill me on the most mundane details of dear little teeth and all the other minutiae that grandmothers always find more fascinating then world-stopping news.

Robbie, the youngest of Mum's grandchildren, would be leaving school next year; she certainly thought I should look to my laurels in the baby department. I had proved my ability, after all; and Mum had lived in a rented cottage all her life. She thought all this nonsense about owning a house was just so much codswallop.

Ron and I longed to visit Ethel, but Granny Giles did not welcome visitors, who would probably expect tea and biscuits; Granny was notoriously parsimonious; a bottle of brandy a day tends to wreck the domestic budget. Also she had no time for me, who gave babies away, and then refused to produce one, in normal village fashion, in the first year of marriage. She made it known around the village the Ron must be mad 'to take that one on.' I missed Ethel's brightness and good humour, being in low stock of either virtue myself.

CHAPTER NINETY

WET OCTOBER WAS followed by an even wetter November. Each December morning the steep hill was a sheet of glass when I slid down it.

Now that I knew better than to plead help from my family we doubled our saving for a car, but we were getting nowhere fast.

Christmas came and went; I was mostly too busy to notice; all I remember is the daily rush at the surgery, as it appeared the whole of the county of Hampshire went down with coughs and colds; I expected bubonic plague to break out any day.

On New Year's Eve we attended the village hall dance at Great Silver; it was our first evening out, other than to harvest supper, or to the endless number of family gatherings, since we returned from honeymoon. Angie was there with Art Kronfeld, her American boyfriend. She introduced him with great pride. Both Ron and I noticed that he was no dancer. Uncharitable really, not everyone could be a rural Fred Astaire and Ginger Rogers, as we were. By midnight surly Art was very drunk.

Ron and I felt uncomfortable, like members of a

previous generation, watching the antics of the present youth and sneeringly thinking 'how pathetic'. I was still twenty; Ron had just turned twenty four. My niece Thelma, aged seventeen, was there with all her cronies; wearing the latest fashions. One of the young men was wearing yellow socks, for heaven's sake! My clothes seemed formal by comparison, outdated, like stuff that gets passed over at the church jumble sale. Ron was wearing his wedding suit.

Don had borrowed Bertha's car and was waiting outside to pick Thelma up at one a.m. I was middle-aged enough now to feel a pang of pity for my brother-in-law, who probably would have retired about ten o'clock on any night, including New Year's Eve, if he did not have to wait up to protect his daughter's virtue.

CHAPTER NINETY ONE

R ON AND I spent happy evenings together. His hobby was philately, and he had an impressive collection. He knew the history of each stamp, and all the statistics from all the different countries: weather, currency, racial mix. We would plan extravagant holidays – to be taken after we had finally moved into our own house of course. We did jigsaws together, racing each other to get to the final piece and be the one to complete the picture. After it had been admired by all callers, it would be broken up, boxed, and put in the cupboard for the next time.

Then we ended up in the warmth of our bed, in each other's arms, and we would make gentle love while the wind hissed through the sodden leaves of the cherry tree and the call of the little owls echoed over the open Downs.

When we visited Mum at Great Silver we would always pop in next door to pass the time of day with Nellie. We hoped that Angie would be home, but she spent every spare moment with her handsome yank.

"I don't like the bugger," complained Nellie. "He is a cruel bastard under all that false charm; he'll treat her shocking. And anyway, who is going to look after me when she takes off to the other side of the world?"

Nellie was no longer capable of caring for herself. Occasionally Maudie and Eddie would visit on a Saturday afternoon, if they could afford the bus fare. Maudie still wore see-through blouses, and when Eddie wasn't looking, gave any man in sight the glad eye. But that was all she gave them these days. Oh, yes, Maudie had become a very proper married lady. I never heard of her stepping outside her marriage for relaxation and comfort, and let's face it, in Great Silver it would have been the item on everyone's lips, even if the dastardly deed had taken place in her town house four miles away. She also never became pregnant again; Maudie had always known how to 'look after' that. She had only produced the family she wished to have.

Angie's care for her grandmother was erratic and spasmodic. Occasionally Angie would have a cleaning blitz and the battered furniture in the tiny cottage would shine. More likely Nellie's knickers were airing on a chair before the fire and the remains of last Tuesday's tea reposed on the piano top. Nellie ate a lot of stale bread and margarine.

Angie and Art made a handsome couple. They appeared at each village function; Art was usually in his uniform. He was a vain man and he was quite aware that he caused a stir, appearing as a handsome young airman. I believe he worked in the pay office. Angie demonstrated perfect dress sense, and was as slim and graceful as a young sapling tree. Angie attended many functions at the base. The village held its breath; it was only a matter of time.

"No-one ever thinks about me," complained poor

old Nellie, to anyone who would listen. "Five of the little bastards I popped out and not one of them has the time for me these days." Nellie was chronically lonely. She missed Peter, and although she saw Ethel frequently she longed for the girl's cheerful presence in the cottage, and she desperately missed young Mark.

Mum had a hacking cough, and frequently fought for breath. She smoked, that was how it was. Dr Zabrieski had pleaded, threatened, cajoled Mum to give up the dreadful habit, but she could not.

"Been at it all my life, can't give it up now," hack, hack, cough, cough. "Started when I was fourteen, I know it's killing me, but you cannot teach an old dog new tricks," as once again she sat breathless and wheezing after a prolonged session of coughing.

CHAPTER NINETY TWO

ATE JANUARY BROUGHT the inevitable snow. Ron and I gave up the idea of bathing; the ordeal of hoisting the water from the well would be such a nightmare, although soaking in the hot water in front of the roaring range was a delectable thought. We strip-washed, alone.

The garden was frozen solid; Ron found difficulty in cracking the iron-hard earth so that he could dig a hole big enough to dispose of the contents of the toilet bucket. He returned to the kitchen with sweat pouring off him, despite the sub-zero outdoor temperature.

We allowed the range to roar too much. We ran out of coal. So did the coalman. The whole country was blanketed by snow and supplies were not getting through. I allowed myself a mean thought that Lady Margaret Stockbridge-Howe probably had coal; even in nineteen fifty four it still was "Yes, m'lady, no m'lady." I just hoped the coalman's faith was rewarded with a prompt payment, as the upper classes, the nobs, were notorious for not paying bills promptly.

Although the country was thickly wooded, there was none to spare. Every log had been carted away and sawn on cottage sawing horses long before winter began. Trespassing onto farmland was against the law. Cutting live trees was forbidden, and anyway all you got was green wood. Any dead wood had been harvested by the village boys long ago. Country kitchens were heated by coal ranges, except that currently coal was unavailable. Aware of our desperation, Mister Williams charitably gave us a load of wood.

February was a long, bitter, desperate month and it was early March before the thaw set in. The roads were awash, and on higher ground they still had an untidy fringe of grey melting scum-like snow. The skies were still leaden; a sunless thaw. An early dawn would see a black frost on the highways.

As I cycled towards the bottom of the steep hill, I was careful not to dismount; the brackish slimy snowmelt was almost to my wellie tops. Each evening, as I climbed away from Great Silver to the open downland it grew colder with each wheelspin. The elms beside the road dripped merciless shards of ice inside my scarf. Three miles had never seemed longer.

There were lights in the windows as I passed the other cottages belonging to the farm; the chimneys puffed apple woodsmoke with its pungent fragrance of other seasons into the gathering dusk. Rickyard Cottage was lonely, deserted, no thin column of smoke from our chimney. Obviously Ron was not home yet. I just prayed the wood had not burned through, and that the range was still lighted.

The red brick of the cottage was the only colour in the encompassing greyness. The garden resembled a Pathe Newsreel depicting an area of desolation, many shades of grey, none of them totally black. It was as though no-one lived here, a deserted cottage, no signs of habitation.

I remembered longingly my days at the Co-op, when I alighted from the Middleford bus and rushed through the bright, lighted village to the warmth of Mum's cottage, to the cheerful welcome, the fragrance of fresh baking, and the ubiquitous teapot brewing on the corner of the range. I remembered her inconsequential chatter, Merle's quiet presence as she crocheted in the corner, the redolence of Dad's tobacco which always lingered in the kitchen, even when he was hours and miles away. I wanted to go home.

I chucked my bike in the shed, shook myself, gave myself a brief lecture on being pathetic and infantile, unlocked the back door, and prepared to do battle with the range.

Ron's cheeks were purple, his nose scarlet as he charged in through the back door. His eyes sparkled; he was glowing with the exertion of a brisk walk through the still evening air. His affectionate kiss was met with a sulky order to "Take those boots off before you come any further, if you don't mind." His query as to the events of my day was met with "Nothing much," followed by silence more chill than the bitter winter moonlight on the bare Downland.

I think desultory would be the best way to describe my replies to Ron's attempts at cheerful conversation. We sat down to listen to the radio in silence. Ron reckoned it was 'the time of the month.' Actually it wasn't.

We slept in each other's arms as the only way to keep even slightly warm. I had, unromantically, been using a hot water bottle for the last month.

Ron was dead to the world in no time at all; his days

in the fresh air, and the exercise his work involved meant he was asleep within a few moments of our nightly kiss and cuddle. Ron did not snore; he slept like a dead body, fortunately a very warm one. I would lie awake listening to mice tangoing in the cottage roof, the wind buffeting the cherry tree, the hooting of the owls in the elms, trains shunting down at Middleford deep in the river valley, the water dripping from the hole in the ceiling which we had patched unsuccessfully a couple of times, now we always had an enamel bowl at the ready, and I would remember the warmth and luxury of Loretta's cottage; the Aga spreading its all-encompassing warmth to the farthest corners of the house; the plush stair carpet, so soft to bare feet; the independent snugness of my very own bathroom and toilet, and I would feel cheated, hard-done-by; how ever did I end up here? Then Walter would sidle into my memory, Walter who had loved Jeanette, Walter, who had barely been aware of my existence. I would lie next to my patient gentle husband, and I would long for someone who may as well be a million light years away. I longed for his elegance, his handsomeness; I longed just to touch him, to smell him, to hear him breathe. Walter, who had never touched me, never kissed me, never held me, I longed for him to do all those things, forever.

I would fall asleep, cringing with shame. At least Ron was rewarded with a friendly wife when we awoke.

CHAPTER NINETY THREE

I T WAS NOT winter forever, it just seemed that way. March had come in more like a polar bear than a lion, and left gently, truly a lamb. The Downs stretched their cramped knees and opened their arms to the sunshine. April brought children in short sleeves and short socks, seeking violets under the lee of the Downs, primroses on the fringes of the woods. Birds in the elm trees sang me to work each morning, and chorused me back each afternoon. The green spotted woodpecker flaunted his gaudy feathers and hacked away at the bark of the trees. Life in the cottage became pleasant once more; my hyacinths and daffs in the front garden bloomed like jewels; each evening Ron dug the back garden, the soil amazingly fertile from all the well-buried human ordure.

There were lambs in the Downland pastures as I cycled home each evening. At the surgery, the number of coughs and colds dwindled, but were replaced by the diseases of spring, chicken pox, and followed by measles.

Gentle April did not diminish Mum's hacking cough. She had managed to quit smoking, and Dad was strictly forbidden to smoke in the cottage, tolerating his nightly puffs in the garden with a bad grace. Mum's cough still worsened.

Nellie died quietly while Angie was fornicating in Paris with Art. Nellie was alone in the cottage, either alive or dead, for the whole weekend. No-one thought it odd that Nellie had not been seen; she had long ago dispensed with the outside world, rarely leaving the tiny sitting room which also contained her bed and her precious photographs of her absent children. Angie discovered the corpse, surrounded by empty tea cups and mice feasting on half eaten biscuits in the open tin, upon her return late on Sunday evening.

Nellie joined Henry in the damp sod of St Edmunds graveyard on a drizzly late April Tuesday morning. Angie and Ethel were there, weeping buckets; Maudie in her saucy black funeral hat was crying fit to flood the village. Nellie's eldest son, who lived in London, could not get time off work.

"I'll join her soon; I know I will", sobbed Mum, between hacks and hawks into her handkerchief. "The next funeral will be mine." The mere thought caused the hairs on the back of my neck to rise. I could not bear to contemplate Mum's mortality.

Aunt Beat had always told the story – that when she was young she had attended the funeral of a prominent political figure. It was essential that the electorate saw him mourned. His open grave had been completely surrounded by weeping constituents; they had stood shoulder to shoulder, three deep. Aunt Beat said one lady was sobbing into her handkerchief when she dropped the freshly-peeled onion that it contained. Aunt Beat said her father told her

313

that the mourners were paid to cry; some of them made a career of it. The extra cash came in handy to buy coal at the beginning of winter.

Nellie was truly mourned; peeled onions thoroughly unnecessary. She was one of the oldest inhabitants of the Silver Villages, she had been born, married, had five children, and died within the parish boundaries. Hers was our history.

CHAPTER NINETY FOUR

THE VILLAGE WAS duly shocked by Angie's romantic adventure; could you imagine anything more wicked than a dirty weekend in Paris? The subject titillated gossip for many weeks. That family needn't think that just because two of them had become respectable matrons that their true colours were unknown. It was to be expected, Angie was only acting true-to-type, was stated across many a picket fence; hopefully he will marry the girl. Americans were not trusted by some of the villagers to 'do the right thing'. Trans-Atlantic films had destroyed the reputation of many a decent young American man.

But they were not true-to-type. Ethel, now a mature matron with three children, was appalled by her mother-in-law's personal habits. She had become a paragon of hygiene since her marriage, not an easy role to fulfil in a cottage with no bathroom, and all personal ablutions conducted in a leaking earthenware sink, which was also used for dish washing and vegetable preparation.

On the whole, Mrs Giles did not bother with personal hygiene. The amount of time Ethel and Arthur devoted to teeth cleaning caused her merry amusement. She considered that you only ruined clothes by washing them, and she had no wish to do that. She had not purchased a new garment in a decade.

Ethel stuffed a handkerchief into her mouth, and cried a brief tear for the comparative cleanliness of her grandmother's kitchen. She was getting her Arthur and her kids out of this, if it killed her.

She investigated her chances of being allocated a council house.

"Sorry, Mrs Giles, "I'm afraid you don't have enough kids. What with the post-war boom and everything, only larger families are being allocated houses at this time."

Did he think one more child would give her the necessary points to score a council house? He hummed and hahhed a bit, not knowing how to answer her question. He did not want any statement that issued from his mouth to be used by a mother of four, standing before him, desperately clasping her newborn, crying profusely and claiming he had promised.

Ethel suppressed a giggle; He had given her the answer. What was another baby anyway, or another couple if it came to that; after all, she had the prams, and enough matinee jackets and stuffed teddy bears to start her own infant outfitters. She knew what was necessary. If it took six more kids to get her little family out of Ma Giles pernicious hovel, so be it

CHAPTER NINETY FIVE

S A WORKER at the surgery I knew only too well that more of my family were being born each year, and also that a lesser number of them died. The first event caused a rowdy rejoicing that involved every other inhabitant of the Silver Villages, after all, no matter which door you opened in Silver Street, round the village green in Great Silver, on the farms at Little Silver, or in the posh houses with large gardens that edged Silver Common, there was bound to be a close relative somewhere. My aunts would call into the surgery to 'chat to Linda' and look expectantly at my extremely flat abdomen. It remained flat.

The funerals guaranteed St Edmunds was filled to overflowing. At each funeral the pews would be so jam-packed it appeared that Anglicanism had received a huge boost of rustic popularity. Springbournes and Bigfords had seen each other barely a month ago at the last Christening, but there was always a surfeit of newsworthy prattle to be absorbed and taken to the next great family event. Like the whispering game, the end result of the stories often varied greatly to the original telling

CHAPTER NINETY SIX

TURNED TWENTY-ONE IN May. All the great events of my life seemed to have occurred in May, so I dreaded my birthday, but it is impossible to ignore being twenty-one.

Neither Ron nor I enjoyed being in the pub but we held a party at the Silver Bell. To my mind it was a waste of our hard earned savings, as Ron bought round after round of drinks for people we barely knew, and probably did not like. Beer drinkers would always request an expensive short; they would not wish to offend the buyer by requesting a lowly beer. Many of our younger friends came to drink with us, including Angie, and Art, who was already drunk when he arrived; and Ethel and Arthur, who had left their three children in the doubtful care of Arthur's mother. This caused Ethel to worry severely; the poor little brats probably consumed more alcohol that evening than she did.

The army of Springbournes and Bigfords came to a Sunday tea laid on by Mum, whose chest was upset by the thoughtlessness of people who should have had better manners than to smoke over the custard trifle and jam sponge. I received an endless variety of hand crocheted and embroidered doilies, pink glass jam dishes and 'boss and slave' pillowcases.

Upon opening each gift I exclaimed an excited "just what I wanted; Oh, how did you know?" And I was absolutely truthful. This was the freely-given love of the greatest family on earth. I had been down enough rocky roads to know that it was irreplaceable. Yes, I wanted this family affection more than any other gift.

Iris and Len gave me a leather-bound Concise Oxford dictionary: Ron's Mum gave me a home-bottling set: Bertha gave me a silver-framed photo of her handsome family: and Florrie, a bonanza edition of popular love stories.

Dad had spent his retirement days making me a pinewood jewellery box, the lid inlaid with darker woods, and Ron gave me the slimmest silver bracelet, our names engraved on the inside.

CHAPTER NINETY SEVEN

I KNITTED RON A warm jumper, for autumn 'best'.

Ethel announced she was pregnant again; a ribbon of smart new council houses was creeping along the edge of Silver Common; she had timed it right, hadn't she?

Angie and Art seemed joined at the hip; rather like Siamese twins, you never saw one without the other during those harvest days. Angie tolerated her employment at the factory; it was just a means of earning money to be spent on her amazing appearance, to enhance Art's pleasure in her beauty. There would be no factory slog for Angie in her future life in Denver, Colorado.

Our visits to Mum in her cottage became more frequent. Our presence always premeditated floods of tears.

The floods of tears would precipitate another bout of coughing, leaving her speechless, flushed and breathless.

We would cycle the three miles to Little Silver, discussing under our breath whether or not she had deteriorated since or last visit, in quietude, as though our worries were too horrific to share with the cawing rooks. We agreed she was worse each time.

Doctor Zabrieski seemed unable to help her: He

referred her to a specialist in Winchester. This man wore expensive suits and spoke like Prince Philip; Mum was terrified of him, and I am sure he never obtained sensible answers to his questions. Mum was still being 'a good sweet maid,' and would have told him anything he wished to hear. Dad looked perennially puzzled and frightened. He still nipped outside, even in sheeting rain, to have three or four 'puffs' during our visit.

CHAPTER NINETY EIGHT

THEL WAS FINALLY allocated her brand new council house at renamed Honeysuckle Rise, which had previously been called Chapel Lane, on the very edge of Silver Common. A Primitive Methodist chapel had once existed there, the farthest end, away from St Edmunds, but now it was a historic memory. With the renaming of the new council estate demonstrating due deference to the slightly preposterous, even the name would follow the building into history.

She immediately invited all her many friends, and more than a few of her enemies, except that being Ethel, she had never seen them in that light, to visit her for afternoon tea. I had greatly missed her good-natured happy company during the months of her sojourn in the gloomy territory of Granny Giles' old hut.

I don't know what I expected; it certainly was not what I saw. Her furniture was second-hand, but in good condition. There was a lacy cloth on the kitchen table; the saucepans hanging beside the range gleamed coppery as the afternoon sun shone through the spotless windows, throwing long shadows from the plant pots with their promise of early spring hyacinths. A spotless tea cloth hung beside the range. There was not a mote of dust to be seen.

Her twin daughters sat in separate highchairs, gurgling and smiling, and dressed in look-alike pink frocks, stiff with fresh ironing. Mark played in the garden, his shorts and t shirt clean that morning.

She had baked cinnamon scones. Her apron was fresh, her make-up, let's face it she had always been good at that, was immaculate. She resembled a model from the cookery section of the Women's Weekly. And she looked happy.

I don't think I had ever been so glad to see anyone in my life, but my heart wept, I had expected the familiar grotty Ethel, sitting on the broken bench outside her Gran's backdoor at the old cottage, her grubby bare feet kicking up the dust. Unfortunately her sister had not experienced a similar metamorphosis. Angie's grubby feet were still in the dust, in spite of her faultless make-up.

But Ethel had learned a lot, and fast.

She was as enthusiastic as ever about her gorgeous children, about the expected one as she patted her rising stomach.

Her Mum loved living in Middleford, walking down to the shops each day, and to the pub with Eddy most nights. Peter had started at the new secondary school, just outside the town boundary. She reported his academic brilliance, needless to say, even though Miss Landport had always considered him to be the same as the rest of his family; as thick as two short planks.

Ethel queried us knowingly about "when it was our turn?" We shook our heads and reiterated that we had decided to wait until we had a house, and Ron had retrained for a better job. She said 'Oh, yes, well I don't blame you; Mum loves living in her own house.' She looked sad for us.

While 'we two girls' chatted the afternoon away Ron amused the twins by playing cars across the trays of the highchairs. When they became bored with that, he exhausted them by giving them donkey rides round the kitchen on his back while they shouted and crowed with joy. When they both fell into an exhausted nap he played cowboys and Indians with Mark in the garden.

We parted with promises: "I'll write that recipe out for you." "If you can bear to walk all the way to Little Silver, please come to tea one Sunday." "I'll let you know immediately this one's born" again patting her abdomen.

We climbed the steep hill in the dusky glow of late September. Ron had not spoken a word since we left Ethel's house. We had been married long enough for me to be aware he was leading up to an important exclamation.

As we reached the hilltop, and walked along the beech-lined lane to the farm he began to speak, and then swallowed his words, then started again, stammering.

Okay, so he had something important to say. I'm listening Ron, go right ahead, and astound me.

He did just that.

"Linda." He said my name slowly, turning it over with his tongue, as though it was a boiled sweet. He began again.

"Linda, if we had a baby, we could probably get a council house too. We would be okay on the farm until we did; we've got our little home really nice and snug. Yes, I would like us to have a baby, pretty soon, really. Then you wouldn't have to cycle down the hill every day, all winter, and go to that old surgery and work so hard."

I thought: "You have got to be joking. Do you seriously expect me to abandon all my plans and risk living for ever in that leaky-roofed hovel, on the offchance that we may be allocated a council house one day? I am not a breeding machine like Ethel; this is her fourth child and she has only just been given a house. How long do you think it would take for us to arrive at that point? In the meantime I will be washing nappies in green well-water and you will be burying the shit-bucket each weekend." But I said nothing. I seethed in silence.

There was little chance of a baby: any tender advance from Ron was met by a distinct cold shoulder, in fact cold anything else, by me. I finally said to him: "You are just not prepared to try to understand me. You may be delighted by what you see as a rural paradise, but I hate every pitiable inch of it. I will get out of here if it kills me." I hurt him dreadfully; he never spoke to me for two days.

Of course our funk did not last long. We visited the Michaelmas Fair in Middleford, and spent a great deal of hard earned money acquiring a stuffed alligator and a hand mirror decorated with plastic fairies. At least we held hands and cuddled each other tight as we rode on the big wheel. Our sex life returned to normal.

Ron was afraid to raise the eruptive subject of babies again, but it had been said. Ron wanted his dinner in the middle of the day, and Linda washing nappies in the chipped sink in a haze of steam. Linda wanted a neat semi in Middleford.

CHAPTER NINETY NINE

AT THE BEGINNING of November Ernie dropped a bombshell; Elaine, his scatterbrained, artificially-blonde, giggling girlfriend was pregnant and they would 'have to' get married. I had heard the term 'reluctant bridegroom,' but that did not begin to illustrate Ernie's lack of enthusiasm for the urgent nuptials. All his jocularity, his endless sense of the ridiculous had deserted him. He professed undying love for Elaine to anyone who would listen, and Ron and I generously put his reluctance down to the shock of a shot-gun wedding. The ceremony was held in Middleford. Elaine wore a neat blue suit, her bulging stomach barely hidden by the blouson jacket. Ernie wore a neat blue suit and a bemused expression.

Ron's parents had been shocked by the news; they had expected their first grandchild to be the offspring of Ron and Linda. However, they were to become first-time grandparents in just a few months and they were thrilled by the prospect; they soon recovered their equilibrium: "Elaine, welcome to the family, we'll 'settle something' in the baby's name as soon as it is born." The gran-to-be applied herself diligently to the necessary supply of little knitted jackets, and smocked nighties: "I found a pretty pattern in the Woman's Weekly; just look at those cute little field mice."

Ron had been well on the way when they married, over a quarter of a century ago; they had always been happy together and had never regretted the hasty decision for one moment. It just hurried things along a bit, that's all.

Elaine's strictly religious family did not adopt the same liberal attitude. They had been shocked by the assault on their daughter's virtue, and were not prepared to believe that she had willingly taken any part in it. The ceremony and following wedding breakfast were more like a wake than a wedding.

Ron was the best man of course, but he just did not share Ernie's line in amusing homilies and pithy jokes, and try as he may, he sounded stilted and formal. I died a thousand deaths for him during his necessary act as master of ceremonies; some of the guests were bored stiff, obviously wishing they were elsewhere.

My savings account grew by the week, but oh, so slowly. With Len's help we explored the possibility of buying a car on hire purchase, but it was still not a viable proposition; "better put it off until next year" advised my big brother. That made the little house in town seem eons away in the future.

I dreaded the thought of another winter of freezing cold morning cycle rides to the surgery and of course the bitter rides-cum-walks up that steep hill to home.

Ron amazed me. He had lived all his life in the town, surrounded by shops and streets, traffic and lights. Yet Ron adapted to living at Little Silver; in his customary way he accepted everything that happened to him, good or bad, with an easy equanimity, and much cheerful enjoyment. He loved the open air life of a farm worker. He was delighted by the homely little cottage, and considered his endless chores resulting from the cottage's lack of proper facilities to be part of every-day life; he got on with it.

Guiltily, I often wished I was almost anywhere other than at Little Silver. To me going home each night from the surgery was just something I did, because that was life, and basically I had to. Our real home life was out there in the unseeable future. The events of today had to be merely tolerated,

Mum had lost weight, she who had always been 'three axe handles across the behind.' She constantly fought for breath. Mum rose late in the morning, while Merle made breakfast and started the washing; and Mum retired early, long before her favourite radio comedy programmes had been broadcast. She had lost her irrepressible good humour. I think we were all aware that 'there was something she was not telling us.' Dad was permanently worried. He spent long hours sitting beside her, listening to her wheezing.

As I approached Christmas nineteen fifty four, each day seemed pale grey, a washed-out carbon copy of the previous one. There were no sunny days on my horizon.

In my mind I spent many nights in Loretta's well-appointed cottage. Pity about Ralph. I knew he was always there. Trouble was, I knew Walter was always there, too.

CHAPTER ONE HUNDRED

O N A SODDEN Saturday afternoon three weeks before Christmas I saw him. I was in W H Smith and Sons, trying to decide whether a leather-bound stamp album would be the ideal gift for my husband, or just another frivolous waste of hard-earned money.

Ron and Ernie were at the local soccer match; we were to visit Ernie and Elaine's flat for tea afterwards. Elaine was a passable cook, and once you got past the bright yellow hair with the jet black roots, she was pleasant and talkative.

The last bus to the Silver Villages left Middleford at ten. I dreaded the long dark walk up the steep hill, in my best town shoes, carrying my various packages.

Suddenly he was there; his presence hit me like a jack-knife. I could feel him, smell him, taste him; his aura, his ambience engulfed me; he whom I had never been within an arm's distance of in my whole life. He was inside my skin, in my heart, bursting in my brain.

He was buying some rolls of Christmas paper from W. H. Smith's pavement display. He was heavy-laden with expensively wrapped parcels; his clothes were quality, his shoes had cost my man's total week's wages. His dark gypsy-ness glowed amongst the pale Anglo Saxon faces of the shoppers. Suddenly the shops seemed ablaze with brilliance, the wet streets shone radiant beneath the tawdry festive lights.

Walter: I stood and gawped.

He turned; I tried to close my gaping mouth, to adjust my expression to a mild disinterested smile as he caught sight of me.

"Linda!"

I had lived the past three years for this moment. No, I had lived the last twenty one years so I could stand on soaking wet Middleford High Street and gaze into his eyes.

"How are you, girl?" He clasped my sodden-mittened hand in his cold bare one. Oh, the perfectly manicured nails, the softness of the glowing olive skin, which bespoke care and attention. Ron's hands were shapely, but the grunge of his job left a telltale griminess however frequently he scrubbed them.

"I'm fine," my voice squeaked, I sounded flustered; for heaven's sake, I chided myself, this is just a slight acquaintance enquiring as to my health.

"I often wondered what happened to you." I'll wager not nearly as often as I have wondered what happened to you, Walter.

"Look, I've finished my shopping, have you got a moment to have a cuppa, so you can catch me up on all your news? I know you are married, saw it in the Middleford Observer. How does the Lilygarden Café sound?"

The Lilygarden Café sounds expensive, seeing as you asked, Walter. The next thing I knew I was gliding above street level, my feet never touching the pavement, with Walter's hand comfortably holding my elbow.

We had tea. Neither of us ate. We sat for two hours in the warm, pink-light shaded softness of the cushioned wicker chairs. It seemed but a few moments. I did not complete my shopping.

He asked me about Ron, I told him about my cottage at Little Silver, about work at the surgery. He asked about my Mum, I told him her health was poor; he sounded sympathetic, said his Mum had a lot of heart problems too; she had lived a hard life on the road. We talked about my sisters and about his sisters. I acquainted him with all the Silver Villages gossip: Ethel a respectable matron, Angie with an American boyfriend.

He was wearing a thick gold wedding band. I asked him about Jeanette; he hedged my question. He asked me if Ron and I were considering starting a family; I said, no, not yet. He told me they had a son named Adam; I was curious, but again he chose not to answer my query.

I glanced at my watch and realised with horror that I would be late for Elaine's tea. He offered to drive me to their flat.

By the time he dropped me outside Ernie's flat we had agreed to meet for lunch the following Saturday. I spent the next week trying to invent an excuse to present to my unsuspecting husband for my unaccustomed behaviour. I could have told him I was meeting an old schoolfriend; absolutely true, and anyway Ron wouldn't mind at all.

But it wasn't like that was it? No it never was, Walter and I were both fully aware of that.

CHAPTER ONE HUNDRED AND ONE

HERE WAS THIS little, minor detail that Art had forgotten to mention to Angie. One of his pals, catching Angie alone at the bar of their favourite hostelry, fancying the blonde beauty like mad and eager to press his own suit, saw fit to apprise her of this tiny fact Art had neglected to reveal in the last year.

Art was married, to a respectable Denver girl, had been for five years, and they had a small son. The family was deeply religious, and divorce was unheard-of in their community. Not that Art had any intention of divorcing his wife, she was domesticated, obedient and compliant, and suited Art very well, thank you. The so-called pal delivered the pronouncement with relish, fully aware that Angie was unaware of Art's marital state, and would be distraught by this revelation.

Rather than promoting the pal's charms, this disclosure caused Angie to rail on him, hurl abuse at him, blaming him loudly, as a member of the male sex, for the disillusionment and bitterness already whirling inside her brain. The pal was unmoved by the extent and volubility Angie's stridently expressed anger, called her slag, left her presence immediately, and went on with serious drinking at the bar. Dumb broads like her were ten a penny, after all. Art had waxed eloquent regarding the nubility of Angie's charms and her willingness to oblige his every sexual demand, during their barrack room chats. Yeah, you'd have to be desperate; the good pal would press his suit elsewhere.

Angie called a taxi, paid the tariff herself, a new experience for her. She let herself into her grandmother's old home, threw herself down on the bed, on the quilted purple silk cover that felt so voluptuous and luxurious, chucked her handbag and shoes at the dresser mirror, and cried herself to sleep.

CHAPTER ONE HUNDRED AND TWO

A WEEK LATER I visited Mum at the cottage. She was still in bed at eleven o'clock on a Saturday morning. Merle was performing miracles of productivity and hyperactivity in the kitchen. Bruno the dog was sulking in the garden, not permitted to even think of placing a paw on Merle's spotless kitchen floor.

Mum's complexion was the colour of mouldy hay; there were violet shadows beneath her eyes. She gasped for each breath as though it was something unobtainable.

I clasped her broad, practical housewife's hands, now soft and white; gone was the rough redness from all the years of hard domestic work. She no longer wished for the hands of a lady, and now she finally had them.

"Please, Linda, call next door and see Angie. I think she's fallen out with his nibs; and a jolly good thing, if you ask me. But she never went to work until Wednesday, and she has been in every night. She was always out, you know; never home. Then she's home all the time; and her eyes are all red, definitely been crying. She misses her Mum, and her Gran; got no-one to confide in."

A spasm of desperate coughing followed; Mum could

only manage short sentences these days. She settled down against the plumped-up pillows, her eyes closed. Dad came in with a cuppa for me, his eyes hollow from sleeplessness.

The cottage next door was the same, but the passing years made it appear seedier, more decrepit than I recalled. I had last sat on the sagging sofa the day before my wedding; it seemed a lifetime ago. There had been little evidence of domestic efficiency in the intervening months. Angie only did housework when no other more exciting alternative presented itself – and one usually did.

It was midday, and she was dressed, but her face showed traces of the previous day's makeup; her frizzy tumbled golden hair framed for her blotched complexion.

Last night's uneaten egg on toast poised precariously on the edge of the piano top, vying for position with a cornflakes packet and a jumble of soiled lingerie. The odour of cigarette smoke perpetrated every corner of the small room.

"The filthy bastard, he let me think we were engaged, that we were getting married next year, and that I would live in Denver. If he had just told me the truth, he probably could have kept shagging me anyway. I wouldn't have minded; I loved the arsehole. And a fine lot of good it did me! Left me like a pile of junk!"

Unfortunately she continued to say a great deal more along these very lines.

I gathered that Angie may have loved the possibility of an exciting new life in the Mile-High City rather more than its would-be provider, and now she had a mess to clear up. She had grown disinterested in her job at the factory, become slovenly and slack in her work practices, had snarled and snapped at her colleagues who had once been her friends. Her treatment of her mother and sister had been shameful; she showed little interest in their husbands and children. Her life's energy had been devoted entirely to Art and her planned future of unadulterated luxury in Denver, Colorado. His duplicity meant she was stuck in her Gran's cottage, and if she intended to keep eating, she must go to the factory on Monday. She had cried herself out; no more tears would come; now she was just haggard, hard-bitten and resentful. She, who had thought life would be just a long sumptuous weekend-in-Paris.

CHAPTER ONE HUNDRED AND THREE

OST OF MY waking hours I had only one thought in my head – Walter. After the luncheon at an expensive restaurant we had ended up at Walter's friend's flat. This was not a couple of jumbled rooms full of auction-room furniture, over a shop, the toilet shared with the occupants of the opposite flat, as was the one in which Ernie and Elaine lived. Oh no, this was the attic-floor of a large mansion in a nearby village, furnished to the utmost degree of taste and luxury. I don't know how I had ended up at the flat, and far less how Walter and I had ended up naked in the friend's bed. What had happened in that bed was a revelation to me.

The brilliant, soaring sensation of flight, of suns and moons bursting in our heads, of complete abandonment to sensuality, of the feeling that we alone in the world mattered, that we were omnipotent, supreme. The star-shot brilliance of his eyes, the scent of him, the smoothness of his glowing olive skin, his maleness, his beauty: my beauty, for in those moments my beauty was certain. That we could never live alone again, that we could only exist if we could be in each other's arms: that this must go on forever.

We were silent as he drove me through the rainy streets to Middleford, the mundane task of Christmas shopping forgotten. The ecstasy in that bed had been an earthquake, and the earth was still shaking.

We parted without a word. None was necessary. We both knew it would happen again.

And it did. I became a practiced deceiver. My trips to Middleford became more frequent, my stays longer. I lied my way in and out of most of his friend's beds, in and out of hotel rooms in neighbouring towns. I suffered paroxysms of shame when my thinking mind kicked into operation, but mostly I just longed to be held in the agony and rapture of his embrace, my body pulsing in perfect accord with his, to soar to the pinnacle above paradise where only Walter could take me.

Deception of this nature improves with practice. Most of the time I suffered excruciations of guilt, and I promised myself I would end my liaison with Walter. However, a few days of withdrawal from his powerful masculinity and I would have traded every shred of my marital respectability to be in his arms.

I knew Walter did not love me; that my infatuation with him had no future. I was well aware Ron did love me, and I was not worthy of his love. Whether or not I loved my husband was beyond my comprehension, beyond my reasoning. However, most of the time I was prepared to lie my brain off to maintain the outward appearance of our ordinary life as a happily married couple.

Walter and Jeanette had their troubles, most of which had arrived with Adam. Jeanette was convinced the child was delicate; she devoted every spare moment of her life to sycophantic attendance on her son. According to his father, he was a perfectly normal one-year-old, who was slightly affected by asthma, and he also suffered occasional febrile convulsions; Jeanette had been unduly alarmed by his twitching arms and legs, by his drooling mouth. Fortunately the earl's daughter was able to afford consultations with the country's top paediatricians, all of whom told her the boy would grow out of it. Jeanette wanted him to do that right then, on that day, and was just as distressed when the next convulsion occurred. She smothered the child in the proverbial cotton wool, and spent anxious nights worrying herself to a frazzle.

Walter's childhood in the ancient removal van, surrounded by an ever-growing number of siblings, had caused him to regard most childhood ailments with little concern. All his brothers and sisters suffered the usual health problems without long-term damage, and the fuss and bother that Jeanette expended in caring for Adam struck him as ridiculous and affected. Jeanette spent her nights asleep on the day bed in the nursery, frantic with anxiety, while Walter took to their lonely marital bed with the latest thriller and a bottle of bourbon. He would have preferred to have Jeanette, soft and compliant, lying beside him.

Walter had described his childhood to convent-bred Jeanette as dramatic and thrilling, accustomed as she was to being supervised by dogmatic and inflexible nuns. He had recounted the travel, the fairs, the freedom from parental pressure, the lack of formal schooling. Jeanette, who saw herself romantically involved with a gypsy, had been charmed. The reality of the shabby, overcrowded removal van and the grubby clothes would have appalled her.

They had eloped as soon as Jeanette turned twenty-one. Her parents were still recovering from the shock.

"Well, I'd better be getting home, girl; Jeanette can't have guests for dinner this evening, although we were supposed to be treating the Spencer-Frobishers. Little Lord Fauntleroy was sick last night. I'm not surprised, the hooch Jeanette forces down the poor little bugger's throat. He'd be better off playing in the garden in the dirt. Fat chance there is of her allowing him to do that. He might catch something!"

"I'd better go, though; I can probably knock her up some scrambled egg while she is bathing little Lord Fauntleroy."

He dropped me at the end of the lane. My bike was still at the surgery. I would have a long walk in the rain tomorrow morning.

Ron was surprised by my late return. I told him I thought I had a puncture.

Mum summoned a family conference as soon as twelfth night had passed and the decorations were packed away in the old tea chest under the stairs. No-one in the family doubted the reason for the gathering, but hearing the word 'cancer' from Mum's own pallid lips was an overwhelming experience we were ill-prepared to accept. "Doctor Zabrieski says I've got lung cancer."

This was followed by complete silence. Mum wasn't good at silence. She started to waffle on about someone to care for Merle, and not being there for the birth of my children, and how we must all look after Dad, and a great many etceteras, which, in that moment of agony, no-one else gave a damn about. One question hung in air, as sour and acrid as bonfire smoke, even though no-one had voiced it: "how long?"

I looked at the faces of my brothers, all my sisters, their spouses, their grown-up children. Our faces presented a shocked lack of expression, as we saw ahead of us the graveside, a familiar experience for any Springbourne or Bigford, because of their numerousness; but this was Mum's open grave, we would be unable to walk away from it and resume our normal life after a few sandwiches and cakes, and a cuppa in a familiar sitting room, followed by a few kind words uttered to the bereaved, just as if nothing much had happened. This was Mum, whose forceful personality had been the mainstay of our lives.

CHAPTER ONE HUNDRED AND FOUR

THE NEW YEAR brought the inevitable ice and snow. I suffered a distressing bout of bronchitis which prevented me from attending the surgery for more than a fortnight. If anyone had told me this would happen I would probably have uttered whoops of joy and danced round the kitchen; but the reality was far removed from the enticing idea of a few days spent in the warmth while the blizzard raged outside.

After the first few days, in which I had sat beside the range and coughed between long visits to my bed with the hot water bottle, Ron came home at lunchtime to baked beans on toast and the tea already brewing. If Ron had requested a seven course meal I would probably have managed to cook it between coughing bouts, so desperate was I for companionship and for occupation. I was totally unaccustomed to my own company. I had been ordered not to visit Mum, for obvious reasons, and the three miles between Great and Little Silver seemed as if the breadth of oceans separated us.

I was longing to return to the company, the occupation,

the urgency of the surgery, even if the wet cycle journey was necessary to get me there.

Ron was happier with me home all day. His lunchtime visits showed a smiling face, his vivid brown eyes brilliant in his glowing complexion, he ate his repast with a relish which baked beans on toast had never deserved. We chatted contentedly about the goings-on in the Rickyard and about the other workers. Then he returned to help with afternoon milking and I was all alone.

My heart, my soul, every part of my body cried out for Walter. He turned up on the Friday before my return to work. "Just tell the old man it was one of the patients from the surgery;" as he popped a tiny posy of snowdrops under my chin. The sports car was bound to raise comment among the other workers.

We sat either side of the kitchen range; Walter drank tea and ate Mary's cake. We talked about the latest family events, about Mum's cancer, about his youngest sister's imminent appearance in court on a shoplifting charge. Jeanette was never mentioned, neither was Adam.

Just having him there, to be able to look in his face, to feel his presence, made me feel whole. We never even touched; I would quite honestly be able to tell Ron about the visit of an old school friend – this time!

"Er, one of the patients from the surgery paid me a visit today; you probably remember Walter Sikes, he used to live in Great Silver." As far as I knew, Ron and Walter had never met. "Used to sit next to me at in the Little Ones. Fancy him popping in like that; he brought me those snowdrops. He comes into the surgery pretty often." Untrue!

"Yeah, I heard you had a visitor." I was aware of the efficiency of the farm telegraph. "I'll bet all the people down there have missed you something terrible." Ron settled down to read the Daily Express.

CHAPTER ONE HUNDRED AND FIVE

ARCH BROUGHT THE spring thaw; rivulets of ankle-deep water coursing down the steep hill with the power of a bore wave, gales that made cycling impossible; and Ethel's baby Clive.

He weighed almost ten pounds and Ethel was keen to avail anyone who would listen with every detail of each contraction, each bodily miasma, every after-pain. I saw her point; he was a huge child, pushing him out was something I chose not to even consider. Needless to say, he was a beautiful child. Ethel and Arthur were delighted with him, with each other and with life in general.

Nurse Dinningsby treated Ethel with a grudging respect these days, now that she was a married lady and gave birth easily, thereby causing the midwife little inconvenience; much like falling off a log, her Mother said, when she visited my parents to impart the good news.

"Let's go round there on Saturday afternoon, Linda. I'll help you with the shopping, so we can get home on the twenty-to-three and drop it all off before we go and see the new baby."

That would inevitably involve cycling against the storm

down to Silver Common, and pushing the bikes up the steep hill to home through the ankle deep water, in the fading evening dullness. I agreed with a bad grace, which must have made my long-suffering husband wonder what on earth he had said this time.

Trouble was, I had already made plans for Saturday afternoon, and they had nothing to do with visiting Ethel. Oh well, needs must, I suppose.

When I visited Mum I always popped round next door to see Angie. The cottage appeared untidier each time. Angie was unaware of the shambles, even though during those days she spent long hours inside its protective portals; Art's defection to the drinking men's' club had left her fresh out of personal resources. Angie had neglected all her friends and her family during her ardent courtship of a future in a far away city, and when fate had robbed her of those daydreams she had nothing on hand to replace them. She spent most of her evenings alone: all the friends of her girlhood were busy with husbands and babies, not the least of them her sister, now a busy Mum with four small children.

Angie still attended village dances, occasionally even sneaked into the Silver Bell if she could manage a lone visit with diplomatic elegance; above all else Angie was not cheap and common. No, it could be said that Angie was never cheap. The fun of her previous life had departed with Art's attentions. She could probably have spent time at the American base; she had made friends amongst the clique of potential wives who advertised their offerings there; most of the men were reliable and represented excellent husband material, but she made it clear in her conversations with me that she despised Art, and had no wish to commence a relationship with another of his ilk.

As most of Ethel's chat seemed to concern the brilliance of her four children and the wonders of her marvellous husband, the two sisters had little in common.

It must be said that Arthur's amazing charms were evident to Ethel alone; and Angie was, for the first time in her life, very lonely.

Conversation with her became difficult; we had little to say to each other. She had never been interested in my job at the surgery, or in my aspirations to own a semi in Middleford. There was nothing to be said about either family which we had not both known all our lives.

My parents expressed concern; "Such a beautiful young girl, and her with a broken heart over that no-good yank." Angie's heart was actually not broken; more like the floor had been swept from under her feet, leaving her no place to stand. If she caught sight of Dad in the garden she gave him a smile and a wave, but rarely spoke to him. I was of the opinion that she spoke to few people during that time.

I knew from snippets of conversation heard at the surgery, and from the attitude of Florrie and her daughters, that the good people of the Silver Villages considered Angie had got her just desserts.

CHAPTER ONE HUNDRED AND SIX

I T WAS MAY, in a few days I would be twenty two. Outside the surgery, blackbirds sang in the willows. A large jamjar of honey-scented cowslips stood beside me on the desk. I was concentrating on various government forms associated with the National Health Service. Somewhere in the background I heard the formally-mannered middle-aged receptionist, advise a patient that Doctor Zabrieski had been called away in an emergency, and if they didn't mind waiting just a little longer, she was certain one of the other doctors would attend them; and apologies for the unfortunate wait, etcetera.

Besides a mild curiosity over what had occurred this time I never gave it another thought. This was part and parcel of the job; anything could happen next, and it was always bad news for someone.

At four-thirty, as I gathered my handbag and jacket ready to leave, Doctor Zabrieski, who had returned to the surgery about an hour previously, called me into his room.

He asked me to sit down. What was this, the sack? I tried furiously to recall anything stupid I had done in the last few days, but nothing serious enough to warrant this interview sprang to my mind.

"Are you going straight home, Linda, or did you intend to visit your Mum on the way?" I shook my head, straight home and cook Ron's tea. I wondered vaguely why Doctor Zabrieski was interested in my plans; he had certainly never asked such a personal question prior to this afternoon

"Linda, there is something I feel you ought to know." I looked at him, puzzled. "I know you have been friends with Ethel Giles since your schooldays. I feel you should hear this at the surgery, because you will be asked about it as soon as you arrive home, I am sure.

"Arthur Giles was killed in a road accident in the Winchester Road this afternoon. I have told you this because I am aware of the concern you will feel for your friend. Ethel will need all the support she can muster; I suggest you take the rest of the week off so you can help her with her arrangements.

"Poor girl, she is totally devastated, but I believe her mother will take care of the three older children for a few days. Of course Ethel must keep Clive with her because of breast feeding. The absence of her children will probably make her sorrow even harder to bear.

"If there is anything the people at this practice can do to help - just ask.

"I know that your wonderful family will do everything they can to support Ethel at this trying time."

I was out in the street, cycling furiously towards Mum's cottage. I did not remember leaving the surgery. I could not see through my tears. The birds were singing, the sun was shining; how dare they, how dare it!

CHAPTER ONE HUNDRED AND SEVEN

STAYED WITH ETHEL at Honeysuckle Rise. Misery and shock immobilised her features to an ashen mask; to her, the events concerning Arthur's death were totally beyond belief. And Doctor Zabrieski was right, most of the time Ethel just wanted to hold all her children as close to her heart as she could; they were spending the week with their Gran in Middleford, a whole four miles away, but at the moment of greatest emotional need that may as well have been four hundred. Ethel never placed Clive in his cot for the whole of my sojourn in her home. It seemed as though if he was not in her arms he may disappear, as had her darling Arthur, as had, temporarily, Mark, Verna and Wendy. Out of this situation Ethel would get, amongst other things, a seriously spoilt son.

Ethel had cried herself out in the first day. Her anguish was beyond tears. The undertaker came and went and made sympathetic noises, hovering at a professional distance in the background. Wreaths were ordered. The Vicar spent time with Ethel, holding her hand, assuring her that the love of God encompassed us all, and that she may not believe it now, but Arthur was in paradise.

Arthur's mother did not believe in paradise. Arthur was all she had in the whole wide world, and now the wide world had cheated her of the only person she had ever loved. How could she live without Arthur? Her reliance on brandy doubled, as did her neglect of her personal hygiene. Sad and grubby, she tottered round Ethel's home, keening to herself, ignoring Ethel, occasionally threatening the baby if he should cry, generally getting in the way, bitter and hurt in a spiteful world that had taken away the mainstay of her whole existence. A question regarding her requirement as to a wreath was met with demented sobs. Did she know where Arthur's father was? Her replies indicated he was probably already in hell.

She offered no assistance with the funeral arrangements.

Angie visited each evening, bringing provisions: bread, milk, a quarter of tea, attempting to talk to her sister about the good times, the wedding, how she and Arthur had loved each other, but Ethel was alone with Arthur in her private world. She would come back to us, but not yet.

On Monday afternoon Maudie visited with the three older children to collect some clean clothes and some cash from Ethel. Maudie's budget, scrappy at the best of times, could hardly be expected to accommodate the appetites of three hungry children entirely without warning.

When the children entered the house, the twins, still only babies, called "Dad" and looked expectantly around. Ethel swamped all three of them in a broad embrace. They squirmed to escape the stranglehold; it seemed Ethel would never release them.

Mark was looking surprising spruce and clean, allowing

for the fact that Maudie, his gran, had never understood the need for cleanliness in children. Following his grandmother's tuition, he held his Mum's hand tightly in his miniature fist, gave her a little kiss and said "We're sorry, Mummy." Ethel, who hadn't cried in twenty four hours, produced heart-wrenching sobs from the very depths of her being.

Ethel finally allowed her three eldest to leave in time to catch the teatime bus, holding them in a bone-crunching cuddle until the bus driver started up the engine and cried 'all aboard.'

Ron never spared endeavour. I was overwhelmingly proud of all the little errands he ran, never thinking twice about disruptions to his personal life. That was my Ron; he would do anything for anybody and not think twice about it.

The funeral was to be on Wednesday afternoon.

CHAPTER ONE HUNDRED AND EIGHT

IT POURED WITH rain, but that was only to be expected. Ethel had insisted the twins wear their little red and green plaid kilts, their fluffy white jumpers and their black glace leather strap shoes. Her Arthur had been proud of his beautiful daughters, and she insisted they, in turn, did him proud. Mark was in neat shorts and a dazzlingly white shirt; poor little brat was blue with cold. My mind, ever a rogue, travelled back down the years to the clothes Ethel and Angie had worn as children, never washed, and very often not even paid for.

Clive was parted from Ethel's accommodating bosom for the duration of the funeral; he spent the afternoon in the generous confines of Florrie's Mum's arms, in her untidy cat-infested kitchen, receiving more character-wrecking thorough spoiling and his first bottle, to keep him quiet. Mrs Caundle may have had ten of her own, but there could never be too many babies in the world for her maternal embrace. She considered the offspring of Great Silver families she had known all her life to be grandchildren by proxy. At least one of the inhabitants of Great Silver thoroughly enjoyed the afternoon of Arthur's funeral.

Ethel was hysterical with grief; Ron and I stood on each side of her, each firmly holding an arm; her emotional stability was so disorientated we were both terrified she would attempt to throw herself into the sodden grave. Her poor puzzled children stood before her, their smart Sunday shoes clogged with Hampshire clay, their neat spotless clothing sodden, gazing at the coffin which enclosed their Dad. Neither Maudie nor Angie offered her any physical or emotional support; both were too busy howling frantically.

Arthur's Mum was so inebriated it was feared she may topple into the grave anyway, whether this had been her intention or otherwise. My brothers, Len and Ray, held her in a vice-like grip, both with their heads averted from her putrid breath.

The funeral tea was held at the village hall; the whole village turned out to mourn with Ethel. Needless to say my poor pensioner parents had provided many of the eatables; they would never have considered doing otherwise.

CHAPTER ONE HUNDRED AND NINE

RETURNED TO MY cottage at Little Silver on Saturday morning in the haze of early midsummer heat. The antirrhinums glowed scarlet and gold beside the front path, Canterbury bells were blue and mystical beneath the privet hedge.

Inside the door, there was my furniture, the glass ornaments I had received en masse for my twenty first birthday, my cushions, and the dried honesty in the old milk churn before the empty grate.

Ron had swept and spruced, fully aware that his Linda disliked untidiness; I silently observed that if every other job opportunity my husband investigated failed, he could always obtain employment as a housemaid. He had left the teapot, neat below Merle's striped cosy, the milk in my Royal Doulton jug, two cups all ready for the tea. The kettle was singing on the range. Ron would have a cuppa with me.

But it was Saturday and after my welcoming cuppa, it would be a mish-mash of sweaty, dusty shirts and overalls for me; already the copper was lit in the shed, and Ron had drawn the buckets of green water from the well, ready for the washerwoman to start.

Get to it, girl! And some food would be a good idea! I had best get weaving and get all this done if I planned to cycle down to Great Silver and buy some provisions from the village shop, No time for a visit Middleford today, tarted-up and in my best dress.

No time for canoodling with Walter. I could have thrown myself on my bed and wailed with disappointment. The last place I wanted to be was in the woodshed, washing at the old copper, dust motes glistening on the rough ceiling beams, the sharp odour of coal, the springtime fragrance of freshly cut firewood. I thought lovingly of Ethel's bright council house, with the bathroom, the indoor toilet. I steeled myself to be sweet to Ron; it wasn't his fault I was such a restless, disagreeable woman. He deserved a better, loving, faithful wife, and yes, I did know that.

He received a display of passion rather than mild affection with his mid-morning cuppa; he was pleasantly surprised, and totally assured that Linda had missed him terribly.

Ron had even changed the bed for me. That night between the fresh lemon sheets he was provided with further proof that I could not bear to be away from his arms. He was totally, happily, delightedly convinced that my longing had matched his own.

And all the time I was longing to be in Walter's arms.

CHAPTER ONE HUNDRED AND TEN

O N SUNDAY AFTERNOON we visited Ernie and Elaine; Ernie provided a lift there and back in his car. They had exited the grotty shared-bathroom flat with the greasy gas stove, and moved their auction-room belongings into a pleasant two-bedroomed terrace house off Middleford's High Street. Although the front door opened straight onto the street they had a small backyard, complete with clothesline, garden shed and car-parking space. No room was left for even a blade of grass, but in spite of their lack of a pleasant green lawn, Elaine had planted a bed of asters in a corner nook, and pots of geraniums stood in a sunny position by their south-facing kitchen wall.

Elaine had returned to her job at the laundry; "Doing every bit of overtime I can get my hands on. It's a washing machine for yours truly. I don't intend to ruin my hands scrubbing his dirty old meaty aprons," said Elaine, smoothing her soft white hands with their scarlet nails against her flowery, flouncy skirt.

You should try a farm worker's clothes, my dear, especially during the wet weather or during really dusty occupations such as threshing! I made a mental note, a washing machine came after our car, but immediately we moved into my semi. The lack of running water at the farm would render using a washing machine impossible.

Ernie and Elaine were delighted with their new habitat; they had both recovered from the shock of the miscarriage, and having made their marital bed, were delighted to lie upon it. They had plans for the future; like us, babies were part of that plan, but not yet. Unlike us, they seemed to maintain a fairly extensive social life. Both were gregarious people, accustomed to enjoying the company of their many friends, rather than stuck at home listening to the radio. Elaine still bought bright pretty dresses suitable only to be worn at parties, and her defiantly flaxen hair had moderated to a deviant shade of dazzling auburn, less at variance with her inevitable black roots than her artificial blondeness had been.

Ernie had recovered his amiability, and his ribald wittiness had returned. Elaine provided an excellent 'straight woman' for Ernie's endless teasing and jibes. They were happy, adored each other, and seemed ideally suited. It comforted me that someone was obtaining satisfaction from their marriage.

CHAPTER ONE HUNDRED AND ELEVEN

R ON SAID:" LINDA, are you really unhappy here?" I gaped at him, dumbfounded; why did he ask such a pointless question? Of course I was unhappy. I hated the dusty little cottage, the leaky roof, working at the surgery, not having a car, a hiking expedition to reach the toilet. He had to be kidding; what did he expect me to reply?

Then I knew what he expected; me to be as contented as he was, for Ron took his day-to-day existence head-on, as a challenge worth all his energy and endeavour, and he enjoyed every moment of the dirt, the hole-digging, the appalling weather, the temperamental kitchen range; because in his mind he overcame these trials and got on with the next bit of life. All the while he was joyfully anticipating our future family life in a semi in Middleford.

He was genuinely worried about his grumpy taciturn wife, and in that moment I was aware that, although he had no idea why I was such a misery, he blamed himself for my obvious discomposure. Now, just how was I going to explain that although I loved him dearly, even as he spoke I was longing to be in someone else's arms? I could not do that.

I hurled myself into his arms. I kissed his lips, passionately? Well, yes, I hoped so. We went to bed, it seemed the easy answer. Bed at two o'clock on a Saturday afternoon was a luxury enjoyed by many young married couples; well, usually, by both parties.

He helped me shop. We bought a toy each for the twins, because Ron was concerned their pretty noses had been put out-of-joint by His-Nibs, Clive. So we ended up at Ethel's, she was gradually becoming her old optimistic self, her healthy good looks reasserting their obvious appeal.

I was delighted to see her looking so well. We drank tea in her neat, sparsely furnished sitting-room and talked about Angie's heartbreak, about her Mum and Eddy going on holiday to Hayling Island. Maudie had never previously travelled further than Winchester. Ethel asked about my Mum. We discussed old schoolfriends, recipes for winter puddings, where to buy decent clothes cheaply.

Ron galloped round the yard, playing cowboys and Indians with Mark; he crooned till grizzly Clive fell asleep.

"Uncle Ron, can you be Daddy for my teddy?" This from Verna

"No, you promised me you would be Daddy to my doggy." Wendy's doggy.

Ron sorted out the resulting fisticuffs by accommodatingly being a parent to both animals

It was a pleasant afternoon. Trouble was; I had planned to spend it in quite a different fashion.

CHAPTER ONE HUNDED AND TWELVE

I T WAS A scorching Saturday morning in late August; Walter and I sat opposite each other in a pleasant teahouse in a picturesque Thameside village. Uneaten fairy cakes rested on an ornate silver cake dish between us, we were too busy surreptitiously holding hands under the gingham table cloth. We were a lifetime away from the Silver Villages, from Middleford, from prying eyes. We planned a stolen hour in a historic hostelry, the staff of whom must have been well aware that I was 'his bit of spare.' We had used this hotel a number of times, and Walter paid a night's tariff for an hour in their bed. Seemed a pity to change the sheets really, didn't it?

My whole body was aching for the ecstasy of Walter's embrace.

A shadow passed over the table. Suddenly I was aware of someone standing behind my chair.

Angie's voice said: "Well, well; you never know who you'll bump into, do you?"

I spun round so quickly I almost knocked Angie over. I pulled the edge of the cloth with my swift movement;

the silver dish bounced on to the floor, sending pink and orange fairy cakes flying in all directions.

Walter's squeaky voice sounded like that of a teenager part way between a boy and a man: "Angie, what are you doing here? Nice to see you, girl, pull up a chair and join us." At least someone had the sense to behave as though nothing untoward was happening.

"Do you two do this often?"

"No, no; I met Linda in Middleford. She was real upset about her Mum; verge of tears, she was. I thought if I got her away for half an hour; showed her a bit of the countryside, bought her a cuppa, she might feel a bit more cheerful."

I was totally speechless. Angie did not pretend to be convinced by Walter's lies. She had taken part in plenty of forbidden liaisons; she could have written the script for this one.

Walter ordered some more tea. Any physical desire I had been anticipating had flown away with the aerialised fairy cakes.

Angie wore a hot pink low-necked dress. The dress left little to the imagination; her full breasts rose and fell enticingly beneath their brilliant covering, but in spite of the day's heat, Angie was icy cool.

Walter always made me feel beautiful; he was the only person alive who had awoken my sexual confidence. My self-assurance took rapid flight: I felt gauche, the catalyst of flying fairy cakes, of disorientated table cloths. Again I was just large, plain, Linda; clumsy, sweaty, undesirable; as obviously out of place as a hogweed in a rose garden.

I couldn't think of a word to say. Walter produced a

line of inconsequential chatter; about his horses, about his Mum in her bungalow at Bosham. Yes, he still worked for Loretta; had Angie noticed his car? I remained totally silent.

Angie chatted amiably. She also made it obvious she was fully aware of what had been going on.

Angie had applied for a job as a housemaid at the hotel we had been planning to use for our few moments of pleasure. She thought it would be a good idea to quit the factory, to leave Great Silver. She felt uncomfortable in the cottage on her own. No, she did not get the job. She wasn't sorry; she considered the hotel rather tawdry, she said; it had not lived up to its reputation. She still hoped to get into that line of work, but somewhere a bit more classy than that, thank you very much.

She said she must leave immediately, to catch the Reading train, or she would arrive home very late.

Walter immediately offered her a lift home; really what else could he have done. Walter had opened his car passenger door without even a sideways glance at me; Angie strode forward to the proffered passenger seat. I got to tuck my long legs anywhere I could fit them, in the tiny back seat of the sports car. I was massively uncomfortable. Walter and Angie chatted away merrily as we drove through the hot afternoon, through the rose-scented summer glory of the Thames-side villages.

I could not think of a word to utter.

I still had to buy bacon and other etceteras at the International Stores in Middleford. Walter dropped me off in the High Street, with a "See ya again, Linda," after all, we were just casual acquaintances, weren't we? He then continued his journey to drop Angie at Great Silver. She gave me a little wave as they drove away.

For the rest of that week I hated the sight of bacon and tins of condensed milk.

CHAPTER ONE HUNDRED AND THIRTEEN

W HEN I ALIGHTED from the bus at the bottom of the lane I was surprised to find Bertha waiting in her car. "Get in," she commanded. Her appearance shocked me; shabby house clothes, although it was late in the afternoon and she was out visiting. Her curly hair was haywire and her eyes were red with crying.

"Mum's much worse; she's in a dreadful state. They've got her into Middleford; I phoned the ambulance this morning. I thought she'd had it, honestly I did. Mum saw a young African doctor, black as night she was. Says Mum will be okay, but needs a few days off. So do we, if it comes to that.

"We'll drop off your shopping and I'll drive you over to see her."

And I could have been lying flat on my back, screwing in an anonymous hotel room, instead of here at the bottom of the lane, being collected by my sister, going to visit my dying Mum!

Ron was waiting for us, washed and cool in his summer best. I felt hot, sweaty, and generally uncomfortable, but there was no time to change. He held me gently in his arms, and wiped the springing tears from my eyes. In that moment I never wanted to be held by any other person in this world.

Mum died late that night. We had all spent the evening trying to convince ourselves and each other that she would get over it; a few days rest the doctor had said.........

An army of brothers and sisters sobbed with me; Ron held me while my heart broke. Dad sat beside her lifeless body with his head bowed; he had lived a dozen lifetimes of happiness with her. Marriage is never easy, but they had made it seem so. After fifty years, what would he do?

They told me Mum was dead, showed me her lifeless corpse. She will be alright tomorrow, won't she? Then I knew that I would never see her again, and I craved to be cuddled by her, to be in her vibrant, lively presence. I was unable to think, I could not feel. There was no comfort. She was my Mum, no matter who had borne me; she was mine, and I was hers. I would never be whole again; she had taken something of me with her to Heaven when she left us on that hot August evening.

CHAPTER ONE HUNDRD AND FOURTEEN

W HEN I HAD supported Ethel during the time of Arthur's death I had been so helpful, so practical and jolly, organised and capable. Now, when my family could have used some plain level-headed assistance, my common-sense defected.

As I recall those few days after Mum's death I can only see a grey mist, in which my family appeared to be continually occupied with the business of despatching Mum's remains to the cold sod of St Edmund's churchyard. I sat at Mum's kitchen table. Movement was beyond me. I was aware that Ron was continually occupied with assisting the family, aided by capable Merle, by my brothers-in-law, who arranged flowers and cars, by Florrie, who cried loudly and often, but amazingly she cleaned Mum's house from top to bottom and did the washing and the ironing. Bertha cooked enough shepherd's pie to feed an army.

There was a will; those of Mum's generation always wrote a will, even if they had nothing to bequeath other than the power of their personality and their love. I was present at the reading; I do not remember a word of it. I wanted nothing from Mum: what I wanted from her was her presence, her strength. I knew my nieces and nephews came, with their husbands, wives and fiancés, and mourned her, saying sweet words to Dad, each with their own special memory of their Gran. I barely spoke, I ate nothing, I barely breathed. Crying would have been a blessed relief, but I could not cry. Ron held me, pampered me, and whispered to me; at night he cuddled me to sleep.

The funeral was on the hottest day of the year. The apples were turning yellow on the orchard trees. In the glebe at the back of the church a Gloucester Old Spots sow grunted contentedly while her fourteen piglets browsed along her flank. Old man's beard was beginning to whiten the hedgerows. In the churchyard, Mum, who had raised five children and one errant, disagreeable granddaughter, who had set an example of goodness and generosity to a generation, who had never spared herself if others could benefit from her effort, was gently laid to rest amongst her forbears.

I shed not one tear, although Dad, supported by Ron and Dennis was weeping like a baby, and Merle, whose self-possession rarely deserted her, was sobbing uncontrollably into Bertha's ample bosom.

Uncle Charlie came to mourn his eldest sister; he looked eons older; his black curls replaced by a sparse snowy crown. He was shunned by my accumulated aunts. He was alone; I was never to meet Hughie.

Maudie and Ethel were present of course, and outdid the rest of the mourners in the profligy and volume of their mourning.

Lady Margaret stood slightly apart from the family,

not wishing to intrude, the gulf between her and the other villagers being to immense to overcome, in spite of her obvious grief at the death of a servant who had been a true friend for over half a century. This was the rightness of things, Mum would have understood.

Doctor Webster came to say goodbye to a woman he had known and truly admired since her youth.

CHAPTER ONE HUNDRED AND FIFTEEN

WENT BACK TO my work at the surgery. Life returned to normal. Merle cared for Dad; doing his washing, his ironing, making him hearty stews, not talking to him, because Merle rarely spoke to anyone.

My brothers and their wives went about their lives as they always had. My sisters dealt with sons set on marrying, and daughters ready to explore the world. Don was as quiet as non-existence, the way he always had been. Alf was his usual charmless self.

Life without the robust good humour of my mother was unbearable. I was still the little girl who rushes to her mother's arms every time life deals her a backhander. In my mind, I told Mum every event of my life, far more information than I had ever given her during her living days. I asked her opinion on everything, but there was no answer. I told her about Walter, asking her forgiveness, when I should have asked for Ron's. I knew her disapproval would project beyond the grave.

The grave was a cold place; just a patch of green amongst many others, in the shade of the elm trees. The chilly clay had nothing to do with my loving vibrant mother, with her vivacious personality, her strong physical presence. Mum was not there; her bones may be, but her soul would be forever in my heart.

Dad had ordered a stone, and the family spent many agonised hours deciding upon a suitable epitaph.

"I think we should consider MIZPAH, from Genesis 31:49. The Lord watch between me and thee when we are absent from one another." Len had obviously been schooled by Iris to make this suggestion. Iris was only a daughter-in-law when it came to matters of such significant family consequence, and was for that reason, voiceless.

"Love conquers all," suggested Florrie, behind a massive slice of her own date and almond cake. Yes, well this family had needed some conquering over the years.

Other inane suggestions were made, none of them pertinent.

There were not enough words in the English language to speak adequately of the substance of my mother's life, of the love she had given us, of the adoration the whole family felt for her. Her name, the dates of her birth and her death were deemed by all to be sufficient. When Dad joined her an expressive epitaph could inform the parish of the esteem we all felt for both of them.

I performed my duties like a robot. I knew what life demanded of me and I fulfilled the requirement. I smiled at people across the desk in my office at the surgery; I answered all Doctor Zabrieski's kind inquiries regarding the ongoing life of the Bigford family. At home I washed and ironed, cooked casseroles and roasts, dealt with the copper and the range, loved Ron, and felt nothing at all.

If I thought of Walter, it was with slight shame, more like puzzlement as to why I no longer felt the passionate hunger for him that had permeated the whole of my existence. Longing to be within sight, sound and smell of my mother was all that suffused my life during those dark days when I was gradually coming to terms with her death.

I longed to sleep; most nights I dreamed about her. She was there, in her flowery crossover apron, good natured, always happy. The frail waif of the last six months no longer existed; in my dreams Mum was the staunch, generously proportioned maternal figure of my youth. Her whitened cap of thinning hair had become the jetted curly crown I remembered all my life. She was strong, firm, able to deal with every misfortune. The alarm clock would wake me and Mum would shrink from my view, never quite whole in my wakeful imagination. The dead soon become faceless, I learned that.

September became October and Merle arranged chrysanthemums with their sharp spicy fragrance in Mum's bowl on the kitchen table.

We invited Dad and Merle to Sunday lunch, and Ron talked about the successful harvest. Dad had spent a day with Bertha's offspring, the grandchildren he had always adored.

Ron and I managed to restore our loving existence, without me bursting into tears at the most inappropriate moments, and love between the lemon sheets blossomed again with a refreshing frequency. My husband's tenderness towards me at that time was absolute.

CHAPTER ONE HUNDRED AND SIXTEEN

WE VISITED ETHEL at least once a week. Slowly she recovered from the awfulness of Arthur's death. She was plump, beautiful, a superb mother to her little family, and desperately lonely. She truly mourned Arthur, but I was certain it was only a matter of time until a replacement came courting, and I wished her joy. Ethel's optimistic, joyful disposition, which she had inherited from Maudie, never intended her to bury herself in grief, although the deep love she had felt for Arthur would never be cheapened by her new commitment.

She had cooked ginger biscuits; admittedly they were a little burnt at the edges, but she said she was new to the recipe. My memory, ever unkind, remembered the seventeen-year-old mother of Mark, who would have experienced difficulty cooking hot water.

We talked about her Mum, about my Mum, about the old days, about clothes, furniture, and her amazingly beautiful and talented kids. The afternoons flew.

Normal life also meant the frustrations of life in the cottage, the difficulties experienced by a working wife. Autumn was making its presence felt; when I woke in the morning it was either pouring with rain or the lawn was frosty. Ron would have been up and gone an hour now that he gave a hand with early morning milking. I had not been aware of his rising, even though I awoke to a cold space in the bed.

I dragged myself downstairs for a strip wash in the warm kitchen. At least Ron would have put a match to the range, which he had carefully laid before he retired to bed the previous evening.

A breakfast of porridge, made overnight and cooked slowly on the rear of the cooling hob, then down the hill to start again. Nothing ever changed, including my frustration. At least the bank account was increasing. I would have a car before Christmas.

My life depended on being a good wife to Ron, on getting on with the deal fate had presented me with. Let's face it, it wasn't so bad. I had a marvellous husband, a good job, a loving family. My ambition to own a car was to be realised as our Christmas present to each other. We were incredibly excited; we talked about it each night before we slept.

And all I could think about was lying beside Walter in a stranger's bed.

CHAPTER ONE HUNDRED AND SEVENTEEN

LINDA THE GREAT deceiver had learned to cover every trace.

Walter's voice answered. I was so excited I dropped the phone and the sheaf of accounts scattered on the floor. For someone who did not wish to draw attention to myself this was probably the wrong way to go about things.

"Walter, it's Linda," I was shouting; I sounded like a giddy schoolgirl.

"I know this call is against the rules we made, but I just have to see you. Please, plee-ase come and rescue me. I need you so much. If we can be together for just a few moments, oh Walter, please, I cannot go on without you." If only I could communicate to him some part of the ecstasy I felt in his arms. I was aware I was pleading. My demands were not an invitation, more a command; one I had no right to make.

Silence followed my outburst; a silence that was a fraction too long.

Then he said: "Look, I have to be at a racetrack tomorrow. I will be busy all afternoon."

"I could come with you."

"And how do we explain you to Jeanette?"

"Say you just happened to bump into me; old pals, and all that."

"Linda, my wife may be a lot of things, but plain stupid she isn't."

"Oh Walter, please," I was almost sobbing, I was haranguing him. He acknowledged no right to me, and he expected me to act in the same manner. If we were together, all well and good, and pretty unforgettable at that, but our respective spouses always came first. These are, I believe the base rules for most clandestine affairs.

"You'd hate it. It's not all glamour, it's standing around in the freezing cold. Unless you know about the horses, or understand gambling, racing's a mug's game."

"You don't want me!" I was aware that I was crying; a peevish child denied her own way.

The smallest sigh of impatience: "Look, Linda, I know you've had a tough time. Let's get together in about a fortnight, eh? We can go somewhere quiet, and you can tell me all about it."

Not exactly desperate for my caresses, was he?

In the end Jeanette would win every time. I had always known that.

CHAPTER ONE HUNDRED AND EIGHTEEN

THIS TIME I really did have a puncture. I climbed the steep hill in a light drizzle, wheeling the bike beside me, feeling unloved and hard-done-by. I had given myself to Walter, body and soul, and in that instant it occurred to me that he had given very little.

I had perceived him as a glamorous lover and we had spent aeons furtively cuddling in someone else's bed, which at the time had seemed romantic, passionate, and now seemed cheap and superficial. He had cheated me! His commitment had been for the moment, mine had been more absolute. I could not imagine a lifetime without him. He was Jeanette's, not mine: never had been, never would be. I had always known that, and I still managed to delude myself that what we had was not just transient, for an instant in time and no more.

My tears fell; I had not worn my wellies, in my haste to get away and be alone I had undertaken the walk up the steep hill in my best high heeled shoes. They were ruined.

I hurled my bag on the kitchen table, my shoes at the range, and tore up the stairs and threw myself on the bed in paroxysms of sobbing. I screamed and hollered; I swore, rent my hair, and threw the ornaments from my dressing table at the window. Dad's carefully crafted jewellery box broke the mirror.

I was alternating between hollering and swearing when Ron found me an hour later.

He rushed to my side, and gathered me into his arms, his face full of distress and concern.

"Linda darling, whatever is wrong?" For his trouble I rolled away from him, kicking out at him with my damp-stockinged feet.

"Go away, clear off. I don't want you!"

"Linda, calm down; whatever has happened to you?"

I shrieked each word at the top of my lungs. "Go away! I – do – not – want – you. I don't want anybody. Just fuck off and leave me alone."

He tried to gather me into his embrace; my husband, my Ron, the gentlest of men. I punched him in the chest.

He jumped back, amazed at my foul language as much as my violence. I continued to scream abuse at him.

"Just tell me what has happened." He was keeping his distance. My nails had already drawn blood on his cheek.

"Nothing that has sodding anything to do with sodding you! Why don't you go down stairs and do a jigsaw or something."

He stood up, walked to the window; his back was to me.

"Am I to take it you have quarrelled with lover boy?"

That quieted me. I gaped at him. How long had he known, how much did he know?

He came and sat beside me on the bed. Tears streaked the workday grime on his face. "Oh, Linda, I didn't know what to do. I love you, and only you. If he was the father of your kid, well, we can talk about that. But please, I really love you. I'll make it up to you, you'll see. If you don't like living here, that's fine, we can move to Middleford."

I gaped at him. Ron the martyr was someone I had never considered. My voice, so strident just a moment ago, was barely above a whisper: "How long have you known?"

He sounded incredibly weary: "Oh Linda, I could smell him on you."

Well, Florrie had warned me of the danger to personal hygiene from a thoroughly active sex life.

He was sitting on the edge of my bed, forgiving me. Who the hell was he, Christ Almighty? At that moment I was capable of blasphemy as well as profanity. I had returned to him smelling of another man's body, and he said he would make it up to me! Come on!

I pushed him onto the bed but he was too close to the edge. He fell, banging his head against wall.

I leapt up, viciously kicked his side, and stormed through the door. As I rushed downstairs I could hear him sobbing.

CHAPTER ONE HUNDRED AND NINETEEN

MERLE AND DAD had been shocked to find tear-stained Linda on the front door step, complete with overnight case. Anyone who knew me, even slightly, could not be blamed for thinking I made a habit of this.

For five minutes I sobbed incomprehensibly to Dad. He was no wiser at the end of my prolonged outburst than he was at its commencement. Only one issue was clear, I was staying there, I was never going back to Ron.

Dad imagined we had quarrelled: I don't think my kicking my husband while he lay on the floor and scratching his face until he bled could truthfully be described as quarrelling. In Dad's mind he was blaming Ron for the as yet-undisclosed events; after all, it could not be his precious little Linda who was at fault.

Merle watched from the corner; she said nothing.

I ran up the stairs, threw myself onto my old bed and howled, I could probably be heard bawling from the street.

Eventually I recovered my equilibrium. I checked my face in the mirror. I looked as old as history. Tears streaked my cheeks, my hair hung in rattails

Dad deserved an explanation for my presence. I had

better get down those stairs, maintain my choler, and tell Dad that Ron and I had fallen out. Without belabouring the point that it seemed unlikely we would ever fall back in again.

Bertha sat in the arm chair beside the fire, looking mulish. She had been following her usual motherly evening-pattern of preparing clothes for the next day, all the while listening to Geoffrey drone through yet another chapter of Piers Plowman in a sonorous voice, reading the written material with less feeling or comprehension than he probably would have read a doctor's prescription.

Bertha had been anticipating the rest of her evening with pleasure; a bar of chocolate, followed by a small sherry enjoyed with Alf while they listened to their favourite radio quiz; she certainly had not planned to spend her time dealing yet again with her inept younger sister's life problems. She glowered at me as I drew towards the fire.

Merle had rushed out to the phonebox, as neither she nor Dad had any skill in dealing with life's little unpleasantries, which in the Bigford family usually involved Linda.

"What happened?"

"We – um – we're not together anymore."

Irritation brightened my sister's sapphire tinted eyes. "Two years' married, and she says 'We're not together anymore.'" She spat the words, like removing grape pips from her tongue.

"Got a bit hard, did it? What did you think marriage was? A glorious love story? What does Ron think of all this? Did you bother to ask him, or did you just run home and cry on Daddy's shoulder the first time there was a tiny difficulty?"

My dear sister, believe me, I know things about your husband which would leave you in no position to pass judgement on my actions. I said nothing, just hung my head. I felt fourteen, and caught out.

"So, are we to assume you'll spend the night here? Does Ron know where you are? If it comes to that, is Ron at the cottage, or has he run home to Daddy too?"

"Um, we've got things to talk over. I will go home, but not tonight."

"You bet you'll go home my girl, if I have to skelp your backside all the way to Little Silver. Your load's been picked up for you too many times. Is about time you started to behave like a grown-up and not a sulky spoiled kid."

Yes, dear Bertha, I am sure that is exactly what I have done, but it doesn't change the fact that I have ruined my marriage as a consequence. Eventually, even the righteous Bigford family would have to come to terms with my broken marriage. I broke it all myself.

I went down stairs and apologised to Dad and Merle for upsetting them, promising I would talk to Ron tomorrow. I did not elaborate further on the state of our marriage.

Both regarded me as if I was a creature from outer space. Dad clearly thought this was the result of a lack of babies to keep me busy. It wasn't.

I sat taciturn and disagreeable, not acknowledging their presence. I drank the Christmas brandy – all of it. Clumsy and sozzled, I once more climbed the stairs to my bed.

I slithered between Merle's freshly ironed sheets. I cried

a little, but the brandy started to do its work. I was just dropping off into an alcoholic coma when I could have sworn I heard a high-powered sports car stop outside the house. Wakefulness and common-sense asserted themselves long enough to persuade me that no, Walter had not come to join me in my lonely bed, much as I wished it. No, I had been dreaming.

CHAPTER ONE HUNDRED AND TWENTY

AWOKE TO THE brilliance of an early autumn morning, golden dust motes glittering like sequins against the grubby cottage window.

Someone was using an electric drill in my head; every muscle of my body was aching, my throat felt like sand paper. I needed fresh air, the tiny room was stuffy. I had not dreamed it; it was there! There was Walter's Aston Martin, parked outside our garden hedge. Okay, so where the hell was Walter. Had he really come for me last evening? Had Ron phoned him, had anybody phoned him? How did he know to come and save me? Oh shame upon shame, I had been too sozzled for him to be able to wake me. Was he in this house? I did not think so; I may have an understanding father but I this might just be too much to expect.

I spent a moment gathering my scattered wits, all the while watching the car, my chariot to freedom. I desperately needed a bath; well, not in this house, there wasn't one. The only clothes I had were my crumpled business suit and blouse, looking grubby and unkempt.

While I attempted to think logically I gazed longingly at the Aston Martin.

Walter trotted along Pyle's front path, looking spruce and businesslike, in Bedford cords and a tweed jacket. He had spent the night next door. Of course, that was the answer, Angie was the one person who would understand, and she had beds to spare.

He unlocked the car, and tossed odds and ends onto the tiny rear seat.

He turned to glance back at Pyle's cottage, giving a small wave. Angie raced along the path and threw her arms round Walter's neck. She was wearing a flimsy nylon nightdress; modesty had never been Angie's strong point. Her greatest assets, her large firm breasts, pointed the way to her world. The nipples were prominent in the cool of the morning and Walter's sexual magnetism.

Their two bodies seemed welded together; the kiss seemed to last forever. They drew apart unwillingly. He gently touched her face; she lightly kissed the touching fingers.

I slumped on the floor. Hypocrite that I was, I pitied Jeanette. All I could think was that we had both been betrayed, Jeanette and me.

Not surprising that he had seemed reluctant when I phoned him yesterday. Just think: no hiding from husbands, no borrowing your friend's beds; oh no, Angie was free, and she had her own cottage. What more could a two-timer want?

I washed my face in the kitchen sink, refusing the fried breakfast that Merle had cooked for me.

I sat upright as a stone statue on Mum's uncut moquette, and I did some serious thinking.

CHAPTER ONE HUNDRED AND TWENTY ONE

ERTHA HAD BEEN persuaded she would give me a lift home, in spite of her planned busy-family Saturday. Her sanguinity recovered, she offered me sisterly advice all the way to the farm.

"Everyone falls out. Gawd knows, Alf and me have had a fight or two in our time. But, you get over it, you have to. And that is called give-and-take; no marriage ever worked without it.

Oh yes, dear sister, I will do everything you say, dear sister, thank you so much for steering me in the right direction. I sat, looking penitent, not replying to her ongoing tirade. Every word she uttered was absolutely true of course.

She dropped me at the garden gate, "go for it, girl." With a blown kiss she had commenced her return journey.

I expected Ron to be as contrite as I felt, even though I had been the one who did the kicking; that was not Ron's style.

Why didn't he rush to open the front door, why was he not standing there with his arms wide in a welcoming embrace? I could not wait to be in his arms. I had not given our marriage a chance to succeed, I had been too greedy, too ambitious over trivialities which did not matter, and I had been unable to accept his true love, which did. I was ashamed of my foolish infatuation for a trickster of the type experience should have taught me to recognise, and also of my disloyalty and unfaithfulness.

I opened the front door; I could not wait to tell him, to assure him; I knew we had a wonderful future together, we would always be sweethearts. We would begin again, and, against all odds, I would make our marriage work.

Where was he? The cottage seemed deserted, although he had finished his farm work two hours ago. He wasn't in the garden.

In the sitting room I noticed the photos of his Mum and Dad were missing, and also Ernie's and Elaine's wedding photo. Our wedding photo, showing a radiantly happy Linda and Ron, was laid face down.

Alarm bells rang in my head.

Upstairs the wardrobe door stood open, and Ron's clothes had been removed; the drawers of the chest also stood open and empty. Even his musky masculine fragrance seemed absent, as though he had never been here. His hairbrush was gone from beside the broken mirror.

On my pillow was a note addressed to Linda.

It said: "We are through. I have not gone to Mum and Dad's, so don't go bothering them. Not that you are the slightest bit likely to care where I am. We made a bad mistake, you and me, so let's forget it."

The note was unsigned. Was this all I had left of my marriage, celebrated in church, consummated with love and passion in this bed?

And where was he? In a flash it came to me, like a bolt of lightning. This morning I had lost my lover to Angie. This afternoon, I had lost my husband to Ethel.

The children, her orderly little house, her endless optimism, her need to be loved and cared for; just being Ethel.

Well, I might as well stay here the weekend, no point in informing my loving extended family of this major calamity a moment before it could not be avoided.

I buried my head in Ron's pillow, absorbing the scent of his hair into my memory for ever. How could he leave me, he who told he would never leave me for someone else; he who had promised me at the cottage gate on a spring evening full of the song of a nightingale. Ron's promises were not like mine; piecrust, meant to be broken; but at the end of our time of deceit and duplicity, even Ron could not keep his promise.

CHAPTER ONE HUNDRED AND TWENTY TWO

T HAT WAS FIVE years ago. I am sitting here in London Airport, waiting to board a plane to New York. Oh, yes, it's a new life for Linda. No longer a Silver Village maiden; I shall become truly cosmopolitan.

I have spent the last fortnight rushing round, saying goodbye to most of the population of Southern England, or so it seemed; however did I manage to be related to so many people? Not one of them was sorry to see me go.

The only one I care about is Dad; lonely, his mind starting to wander back to his childhood, missing Mum every moment of his days.

Merle looks after him with the utmost care, and dusts Mum's endless photographs and irons her crocheted doilies. Before I left I asked her, she who was my mother: "Who was my father?" She turned her broad back to me, it was like a ramrod. She did not answer. She considered that to be her business, hers alone. It was also mine, but she must have had her reasons. I agonised to the ramrod back, anguish breaking my voice: "Did you love him." She did not turn round to face me. She spoke very clearly, loudly: "Yes." Only one word; but it spoke volumes from my silent sister.

Did Merle love passionately, wrongly, the way I once loved Walter, for all the wrong reasons? That is her secret; in her life she has very little that is entirely hers. I never was.

My sisters and brothers, the endless children and grandchildren; they will be content without me; will not even notice my absence.

Ron and Ethel are married; they live in Ethel's council house, although Ron still works on the farm at Little Silver. They have a daughter, Louise.

Jeanette eventually got tired of Walter's tomcatting and is in the process of divorcing him. His parents are dead. He and Angie live in the bungalow on Chichester Harbour. In my mind's eye I see Walter growing the largest onions in the street while Angie embroiders endless piles of tablecloths.

Ernie and Elaine live in a semi in Middleford. They have two children and a happy marriage.

Minnie Weston never married, and her son Ernest, not altogether surprisingly, escaped from the hotbed of gossip and joined boy's service in the navy as soon as he was able.

Loretta and Ralph still maintain their clandestine liaison, undoubtedly still under the title of Mister and Mrs Smith. Loretta has become rather fat, and Ralph, well, he is hideously obese.

I have lived the last five years here in London. Not for one moment of those one thousand eight hundred and twenty six days was I happy.

Before I left England I had one more connection to sever. I rarely think of my daughter, other than I'm aware she exists. I was denied all contact by the authorities, who protect her adopted status. I knew that I must see her face once before I left England. With persistence it was easy enough to find her.

Her adoptive parents live in North London; he is a public servant. She attends an expensive private school; the redbrick detached villa suggests that they are comfortably off. One afternoon I watched the little girls leave the school, all clones of each other in their dull navy uniforms. One girl stood apart from the rest; she was tall, skinny, with a thatch of jet black hair. Her face was unduly serious for a ten-year-old; she had a hunted, haunted look, as though she was always looking sideways at life. The other girls, laughing, joking, teasing amongst themselves, ignored her. She walked alone, like a great dark rook.

They had christened her Tina.

I felt absolutely nothing.

I am a first-rate secretary. Those skills are in great demand in the United States. My broad Hampshire vowels have been replaced by a nasal estuarine English, acceptable to all classes. Apparently the Americans love an English accent; it is as saleable as level-headedness and high speed typing.

I have no idea where I will live in America. I am not short of money; saving was a skill learnt during my years at the Rickyard Cottage. I may stay in New York; but my final destination depends on the availability of employment.

I may go to the Mile-High city and while I am there, look up Art Kronfeld. "Hello Art, remember me, friend of Angie's. Of course you remember Angie, beautiful country girl with a taste for self-important men who think they are irresistible.

"Oh, is this your wife – well, hullo Mrs Kronfeld, nice to meet you. I have heard absolutely nothing about you."

Perhaps I will meet someone to love. I like to think that is not impossible. Some little bit of me must be lovable.

THE END